"What the hell do you think you're doing?"

It didn't surprise Meg that Sam was waiting for her at the airport. His attitude was no surprise, either.

"Whatever happened to hello? Or I'm sorry I stole your map and left you in the middle of the murder case?" Meg gave him a frosty stare, trying to ignore the realization that this was probably the best-looking man in Costa Rica.

"Out with it, Meg. What are you doing here?"

"I decided to take a vacation," she said curtly. She knew she was right not to trust him. Looking over his shoulder, she signaled a skycap and pointed to her luggage. "It's been charming running into you again, Mr. Livingston, but I'm exhausted and I need to find a hotel, so if you'll excuse me..."

"Didn't you hear anything I told you? Costa Rica is the last place you should visit."

"A challenge like that is hard to ignore. I can't help being curious to know why you think I shouldn't be here."

"Don't you get it? There was a dead body in your apartment. If you'd been there, it would have been *your* body. If you stay here much longer, it *will* be. Satisfied?"

ABOUT THE AUTHOR

Margaret St. George has been satisfying a creative urge to write since she was sixteen years old. She has written nearly two dozen novels, many of them historical romances. A full-time writer, Margaret enjoys gardening, traveling and armchair adventure (as evidenced in this book!). She lives with her husband and family in the mountains of Colorado.

Books by Margaret St. George

Cache Poor

Margaret St. George

Harlequin Books

TORONTO • NEW YORK • LONDON
AMSTERDAM • PARIS • SYDNEY • HAMBURG
STOCKHOLM • ATHENS • TOKYO • MILAN
MADRID • WARSAW • BUDAPEST • AUCKLAND

Harlequin Intrigue edition published June 1993

ISBN 0-373-22230-0

CACHE POOR

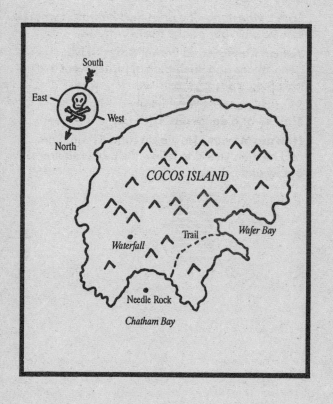

CAST OF CHARACTERS

Meg Mayfair Wolff—Her family history made her a prime target for fortune hunters.

Sam Livingston—She presumed he wasn't what he said he was, but was he trustworthy?

Joseph Mayfair and *Walter Bates*—Five generations ago, their plan of piracy went awry—now Meg's paying the price.

Martin Chango—Was he truly a relative of Meg's—or a dangerous criminal?

Howard Westin—He was in cahoots with Sam, and he didn't need to follow the usual requirements of law and order.

Chapter One

"What the ...?" Meg stared at the man bursting through her office door. Karen, her secretary, followed two steps behind, pink-faced with irritation.

"I'm sorry, Miss Wolff, I told him you were not to be disturbed, but..."

Embarrassingly aware that her eyes were still red and puffy from a recent deluge of furious tears, Meg stood behind her desk and leveled a cold glance at the man striding toward her desk. He was tall, wore faded jeans and a brown leather jacket over an open-collared shirt. The brim of a battered Panama hat was pulled down almost to the rim of his dark glasses.

Meg's immediate impression was one of size. This was a big man, powerfully built with broad shoulders tapering to a narrow waist and hips. Her second impression, following hard on the first, was an awareness of the tension generated by his physical charisma.

"I'm Sam Livingston and I need to talk to you," he said by way of introduction. His voice rumbled up from deep in his chest, low-pitched and tense.

Meg ignored his outstretched hand. "I don't care who you are," she said between clenched teeth, her patience in shreds. Today was one of the worst days of her life and she was in no mood to deal with some arrogant jerk who thought he could bully his way into her office. "You have no appointment and you are not welcome. Leave at once or I'll phone security and have you thrown out. It's your choice."

"My choice is to talk. You and I have urgent business to discuss."

"I don't think so." Meg dismissed him with a glance as she reached for the telephone on her desk, already calculating that it was going to require several guards to eject this powerful-looking man from the building. "Give me security," she said into the receiver.

He leaned across the front of her desk and so close to her face that she noticed the cherrywood edge dented his thighs. She didn't look up.

"We've each got something the other wants, Miss Wolff," he said softly, watching her. "Cocos Island. My great-great-grandfather, Walter Bates. Your great-great-grandfather, Joseph Mayfair. Does that get your attention?"

Her head snapped up. Holding the phone receiver away from her mouth but against her ear, Meg commanded, "Talk fast, Mr. Livingston."

With an insolence that set her teeth on edge, he seated himself, leaned backward, crossed his booted ankles on the edge of her desk, and thumbed back his hat. He removed his sunglasses and folded them into his jacket pocket. Then he gazed at her with deep-lashed turquoise eyes and a lazy, confident grin.

"I have half of a certain map. I believe you have the other half. Hang up the phone, Miss Wolff. We have a lot to discuss."

A long breath collapsed Meg's chest. Family legend had prophesied this moment and warned against it. It was said that one day the Bates and Mayfairs would end their feud and reunite to finish certain business begun well over a hundred years ago. That it should happen now, when her life was collapsing around her, impressed Meg as a crazy joke. Suppressing a sigh, she lowered the receiver and replaced it in its cradle, then slowly sat down.

"Take your feet off my desk," she ordered in an icy tone. After today it would no longer be her desk, but right now it still was.

Smiling, Livingston lowered his boots, crossing an ankle over one knee. A long, lazy glance scanned her elegant blond chignon and cool, dark eyes, moved to the apple green wool suit that softly draped a curvaceous figure. It seemed to Meg that his speculation lingered overlong at the open collar of her lemon-colored silk blouse.

Irritation stiffened her backbone. Surprisingly, she welcomed the feeling. Thirty minutes ago she had surrendered to a tide of self-pity and had broken down in a flood of tears, the first she had shed since Mark Gerard stole her company out from under her.

"You've got three minutes, Mr. Livingston," she said sharply, frowning at the diamond face of the slim gold watch circling her wrist. "What do you want?"

Lifting her head, she examined Livingston coolly and thoroughly, making no effort to disguise her inspection or her distaste. The white-hunter hat wasn't for show; sweat stains ringed the brim and there was a ragged nick on the side edge. The jacket had also seen some hard wear. His boots hadn't boasted a coat of polish since they were new, and from the look of them, that had not been within recent memory.

Finally she examined the man. She supposed most women would describe Livingston as stunningly handsome. But he didn't possess the pretty-boy type of good looks. He was more the type who radiated a powerful ambience of danger and recklessness. When women spoke of men who exuded raw macho appeal, they were referring to men like Sam Livingston. He wore an aura of fearless confidence as evident as his sunburn.

As for features, he had a square face, the angles sharp and crisp. A single, deep vertical line split each cheek, a fine tracing of lines webbed his brow. His mouth was wide and well-defined, surprisingly sensuous for such a strong face. Thick, dark brows slashed across his forehead, a shade darker than the hair that tumbled forward when he removed his hat and dropped it beside his chair.

Finally, Meg met his eyes. Laugh lines fanned from the corners, and the lashes were long and soot-colored. Right now those eyes gazed back at her with a bland expression, but she suspected his expression could flash from warm to icy in the span of a heartbeat. She could almost visualize a giant spring coiled inside Sam Livingston. At present the spring was tamped down tight. She didn't want to be around when it released.

"Do I pass inspection?" he asked bluntly, a smile twitching his lips.

Meg felt a rush of heat beneath her skin. She frowned and made a point of glaring at her wristwatch. "You have two minutes . . ."

He leaned forward, elbows resting on his knees. His eyes fixed on her face. "The captain and crew of the schooner, *Mary Dear,* including our great-great-grandfathers, were hired by the church and aristocrats of Lima, Peru, to transport their valuables—a considerable treasure—to a safe place. They did this because Simón Bolívar's revolutionaries were fighting in the mountains and would soon reach the city. The Peruvians feared Bolívar's men would loot the city when they arrived."

"I know the story from family legend, Mr. Livingston."

"Instead of protecting the treasure, the captain and crew of the *Mary Dear* hijacked it and hid the booty on Cocos Island. Naturally the Peruvians were outraged. They sent a gunboat after the pirates. Walter Bates and Joseph Mayfair were the only survivors after the *Mary Dear* was sunk by the Peruvian frigate, the *Espeigle*. Bates and Mayfair were eventually rescued by an American whaler and afterward spent about two years cruising for whales. This happened in 1820 or 1821."

Meg shrugged, indicating indifference. "Most accounts claim the captain and his mate also survived."

"Possibly. But you and I know for certain that Bates and Mayfair did. And we know Bates and Mayfair drew a map and each took half of it. They swore to raise enough money to mount a return expedition to Cocos Island, but something happened, a falling out of some sort, and their friendship ceased."

"That's putting it mildly. The way I heard it, your great-great-grandfather betrayed mine and tried to recover all the treasure for himself." Meg's eyes, dark as a winter night, narrowed. "The last three generations of my family never met a member of the Bates family. But one of the first things we were all taught was to never trust a descendant of Walter Bates. I learned that lesson in the cradle."

"The way I heard it was that *your* great-great-grandfather betrayed *mine*. Frankly, what difference does it make? A feud that extends to generations who haven't even met becomes blind prejudice and illogical. Ridiculous, wouldn't you agree? It's time the Bates/Mayfair feud ended."

Leaning backward in her desk chair, Meg raised her fingertips to her temples. The last thing she needed today was this kind of fairy-tale nonsense. All she wanted was to finish packing her personal items, get the hell out of here, go home, close the drapes and nurse her wounds.

"Cut to the bottom line, Mr. Livingston. Why are you here and what do you want from me?"

"I think that should be obvious," he replied in a dry tone.

"You want my half of the map." Dropping her hands to her lap, Meg examined his sunburned face. She wondered where he had gotten a sunburn in January.

"You and I are the last of the Bates and Mayfairs. If we're ever going to put the map together and recover the treasure, now is the time."

"You've got to be kidding." Meg stared at him. "The last thing I'm interested in is a wild-goose chase searching for a treasure that almost certainly does not exist. If you ask me, this entire tale is highly exaggerated." When he would have protested, she raised a slim hand. "No sale, Mr. Livingston. I'm not interested. Now, if you'll excuse me..."

A frown pleated his forehead. "I haven't spent a couple of years looking for you just to settle for a brush-off after a five-minute chat. If you're not interested in a treasure hunt, fine. But I am. And I need your half of the map."

The barest hint of a threat sounded a top note above his voice, causing Meg's gaze to chill. "I couldn't care less what you need, Mr. Livingston."

"I'm not seeking a handout. I'm suggesting an equitable split of whatever I turn up as a result of our reunited map."

She dropped her hand to the telephone. "Your three minutes are more than up."

Sam Livingston unfolded from the chair and stood, his expression stubborn and determined. "Look, I apologize for pushing in here. I took you by surprise, and I jumped immediately into a subject most people don't take seriously. I'm sorry for that. I'm not good at small talk.'' A wave of his large, bronze hand indicated the packing boxes, which he seemed to notice for the first time. ''It appears you're in the middle of something. My timing was lousy.''

She gave him an incredulous stare, then a bitter smile touched her lips. ''Obviously you don't read the newspaper's financial pages. If you did, you'd know that someone I made the fatal error of trusting organized a boardroom coup and I've been voted out of my own damned company!'' She spread her hands and gazed helplessly around her office. To Meg's embarrassment, fresh furious tears sprang to her eyes. ''So, yes, Mr. Livingston, you could say I'm in the middle of something here.''

For the first time Livingston seemed to grasp the significance of the packing boxes and the partially dismantled office. ''I'm sorry,'' he said softly. To Meg's surprise, his sincerity sounded genuine.

''So am I.'' For one insane moment she longed to step forward and collapse against him, wanted to bury her face against his broad, solid shoulder. She wanted strong arms around her, wanted someone to tell her that somehow, some way everything was going to work out all right.

That she was fantasizing about finding comfort in a stranger's arms, a descendant of Joseph Bates no less, told Meg how close to the edge she was. ''I really would prefer to be alone,'' she said stiffly, moving past him to the door. Meg placed a hand on the latch and watched Livingston settle his hat atop a tangle of dark curls and walk toward her.

She was so surprised when he lifted his fingertips to her cheek that she didn't immediately step back and freeze him with a glance. His unexpected touch offered more sympathy and understanding than words could have.

"I've been selfish and tactless." To her amazement, his deep voice was gentle. "Let me make it up to you by taking you to dinner. I have an idea you could use some company tonight."

Meg stepped away from his fingertips and the scent of leather and a spiced after-shave. "I don't think I'd be good company. Thanks, anyway." She pressed the door latch, wondering how the conversation had suddenly shifted from irritation to cordiality.

Livingston leaned against the jamb, ignoring the opened door. "So what are you planning to do? Spend the evening alone feeling sorry for yourself?"

"Mark Gerard stole my company, damn it! I think I'm entitled to a few days of shock, outrage and self-pity!" Meg drew a breath, no longer feeling congenial. "Mr. Livingston, I don't know you. Now if you don't mind..."

When he smiled, the left side of his mouth lifted higher than the right. "We're practically cousins. I consider it my duty to prove that all the Bates aren't scoundrels. Your duty is to overcome your prejudice and meet me halfway. You can do this by letting me buy you dinner and attempt to cheer you up."

"I don't think..."

He extended a finger and raised her chin until she was forced to meet those incredible turquoise eyes. "Do you really want to be alone tonight?"

Suddenly Meg foresaw an endless evening of pacing, feeling the condominium walls closing in to smother her. She foresaw a silent interior rehashing of that last fatal board meeting, of the errors, large and small that had led to it.

"No," she whispered, staring into his eyes. For all she knew, Sam Livingston's compassion was as phony as a three dollar bill. In fact, she would bet on it. But she saw sympathy in his gaze and right now she was vulnerable, fragile, and desperately in need of that sympathy.

"I'll pick you up at seven," Livingston said, dropping his hand now that everything was settled. Meg could still feel the warmth of his fingertips on her skin.

"Wait a second," she said. "I didn't agree to—"

"I'll get your address from your secretary."

Right this minute Meg lacked the emotional strength to resist a steamroller approach. She shrugged and gave up. "Make it someplace casual, I don't feel like dressing."

Before Sam stepped through the door, he hesitated. "Keep your eyes open, okay? Don't talk to strangers."

Meg blinked. "What on earth are you talking about?"

His smile didn't reach his eyes. "I'm not the only person looking for the Bates/Mayfair map. If I found you, others can, too. I don't think I was followed, but it's possible."

She had forgotten about the map. "You're joking!"

"Do I look like I'm joking?"

Meg stared into his eyes and a prickle rose along the back of her neck. Right now Livingston looked like a man who couldn't crack a joke if he tried. There wasn't a trace of humor or his former compassion in his expression; his gaze was ice-cold and deadly serious.

"The Peruvian treasure may or may not exist, but the map does. When the news gets out that the last of the Mayfairs is alive and well, you're going to be deluged with adventurers seeking your half of the map. One in particular is very, very unpleasant. He wouldn't hesitate to wring your elegant neck to get your half of that map. We'll talk about it at dinner."

He closed the door behind him and left Meg staring at the polished wood. She had a feeling she had been suckered. A moment of vulnerability and self-pity had allowed her to forget that Sam Livingston had arrived with his own agenda, and comforting Meg Wolff wasn't part of it. But the pretense of comforting her had provided a method of getting his agenda back on the table.

"IT'S BEEN A LONG TIME since I've been in a penthouse," Sam Livingston commented, carrying his drink out onto the balcony that overlooked Denver's twinkling skyline.

It always surprised Meg when someone referred to her condominium as a penthouse. Denver wasn't really a penthouse town. She had paid a few thousand more for her top-floor condo because of the view it offered, not because it was marketed as a penthouse.

Sam returned inside and scanned the living room. "No offense, but this looks like a photo in a magazine, like a room intended to be admired but not actually lived in." He gave her a look of curiosity. "Do you really like this? Can you relax here?"

Feeling defensive, and ignoring the blinking light on her answering machine, Meg sat on the edge of a puffy, ivory-colored sofa. After a moment she decided to swallow her irritation. They would have dinner, then Sam would leave and she'd never see him again.

"I bought this place three years ago," she mentioned in a determinedly pleasant voice. "That's when I knew Treasure Trove was going to be a mega success and take the video game market by storm."

She noticed that Sam had found time to get a haircut. His dark curls were still springy and tousled but noticeably shorter. The shadow on his cheeks had vanished and the scent of an intoxicating after-shave was stronger. Tonight he wore dark slacks topped by a bone-colored shirt and maroon sweater vest. He kept touching his tie as if he wasn't accustomed to wearing one.

As for Meg, she wore designer jeans tucked into navy boots and topped by a red cable-knit sweater. After showering, she had twisted her hair into a ponytail and secured it with a plain rubber band. Since she couldn't summon enough energy to apply a full makeup, she had dashed on some mascara and red lipstick and called it good.

The telephone had been ringing every few minutes since she'd walked in the door and it rang again now. Meg waited until the machine picked up the call, then she glanced at Sam.

"So. Where are you from?"

He smiled and finished his drink. "I live in Costa Rica."

"Costa Rica?" He might as well have announced that he lived on the far side of the moon. "Wait a minute," she said when she recovered from her surprise. "Did you travel from Costa Rica to Denver . . . just to find me?"

"The instant I learned the private detective had located you, I caught the next plane to the States."

"A private detective." Meg dropped her head against the sofa cushion. "This is sounding more and more like a novel. I don't think I'm in the right mood to cope with this sort of thing."

"After your parents died, your trail vanished. I wasted a year trying to find you in the Chicago area before someone mentioned you had married and possibly moved west. Unfortunately no one seemed to know who you married or what your married name might be."

"Charles Wolff. A nice man, but the wrong man," Meg supplied, frowning into her wineglass. "But, then, you must have discovered that. I'm beginning to suspect you know a whole lot about me. Frankly, I'm not sure I like it."

Sam nodded pleasantly. "As I understand it, your marriage ended about the time I learned about it. Short, but not so sweet."

"Charles was a race-car driver whose hobby was skydiving. His profession and his hobby scared me. It was as if he had a death wish or something." Meg turned her head to gaze out the glass balcony doors. She had a feeling she wasn't telling Livingston anything he didn't already know. "I'm not the adventurous type."

The telephone rang again. She placed her wineglass on the coffee table and shook her head. Suddenly Meg was glad she had agreed to have dinner out. She needed to get away from here. Each ring of the telephone jangled her nerves.

Sam leaned against the mantelpiece, watching her grimace. "Some of those calls are bound to be friendly, aren't they?"

Meg shrugged. "The media, my friends... they're all going to ask how I let myself get outfoxed. And they'll want to know the financial details."

"Were you hurt financially?"

"Good God, no." Her laugh was bitter. "By the time the dust settles and the attorneys and accountants have cashed out my shares of Wolff Games, Inc., I'll net in the neighborhood of six or seven million."

Livingston released a low whistle. "That's real money."

"I suppose it is," she said with another shrug. "But the money never mattered, not really. What mattered was the work, the challenge. What mattered was taking an idea, embellishing it, making it work, then marketing that idea to the public and seeing it become wildly successful." Her expression changed, became animated and alive. "Then, after Treasure Trove was successfully launched and sweeping the country, there was the incredible high of taking the company public, followed by plans for expansion. It was exhilarating."

Sam stared at her. "You are very beautiful," he said softly. Excitement sparkled in her brown eyes, their color reminded him of rich, warm earth. Her face transfixed him. He had noticed her beauty at once, of course, but in her office she wore a mask of cool aloofness, her professional image polished to untouchable perfection. Here, relaxed in her own home and speaking on a subject that challenged and excited her, an inner loveliness pushed aside the mask and warmed her features with an unguarded radiance that made his stomach tighten.

Meg didn't hear his compliment. Excitement fading, she stared at a point in space until he called her name. She stared at him, coming back to reality. "Now it's all gone. Tomorrow morning I'm going to wake up primed to go to my office and give the world a shake. Except I don't have an office anymore." Depression nibbled the edges of her mind and she stood abruptly. "Let's get out of here. The telephone is driving me crazy."

As they rode down in the elevator, Sam touched his tie, then broke an awkward silence. "I can't help wondering... are you engaged or seeing someone on a steady basis, anything like that?"

Meg frowned as he took her elbow and guided her through the black-and-white lobby to a waiting taxi. His question was framed in a tone that suggested it was anything but casual.

"I was seeing Mark Gerard," Meg admitted reluctantly. "Obviously the relationship didn't work out." Bitterness soured her voice. "His way of getting back at me was to steal my company."

Sam nodded as she preceded him into the taxi. Just as he was about to get in, he snapped his fingers. "My wallet. I left it in my jacket upstairs in your penthouse." An embarrassed grin apologized for his oversight. "I'm not accustomed to keeping track of heavy coats."

Meg swung her feet toward the taxi door, prepared to return upstairs, but Sam lifted a hand. "There's no need for both of us to be inconvenienced by my carelessness. If you'll give me your key, I'll dash up and be back in a flash."

Leaning to the door, Meg stared up at him. "Did you forget your wallet on purpose? Is this some half-baked scheme to get inside my home and ransack the place for the treasure map?"

She hated to admit it, but he had a wonderful laugh; deep, booming, and filled with delight.

"Sorry to disappoint you, but this isn't a ploy to go through your drawers. Just an example of my forgetfulness," he said, grinning at her. "But I do need my wallet if I'm going to pay for the taxi and buy your dinner." He extended his hand for the key.

It was one of those embarrassing dilemmas. Aside from being a member of the Bates family, Livingston had given her no reason to distrust him, but she wasn't comfortable with the idea of a stranger being alone inside her home. After a brief hesitation, Meg frowned in resignation, then opened her purse and silently handed him the key to her condo. "Don't take too long."

"I'll be back before you know I'm gone."

In fact, it seemed as if he was gone a very long time. Meg reminded herself that minutes spent waiting seemed longer and slower than minutes spent doing anything else. She had just decided to go after him when Sam pushed through the building's door and slid into the taxi beside her.

"Sorry to be so long," he said, waving his wallet to demonstrate his errand had been successful, "you have the slowest elevators in town."

"Really?" Meg stared at his jacket. She hadn't noticed the elevators ran slowly.

"Where would you like to go? Since you said casual, I didn't make reservations."

After a moment's thought, Meg asked, "When was the last time you had a really fabulous pizza?"

"A pizza?" His laugh boomed through the cab. "It's been so long I don't remember."

"I know a terrific place." Leaning forward, she gave the address to the taxi driver, then dropped back on the seat and turned her face away from him. Within the confined area of the taxi, Sam's after-shave was especially sexy. It was a spicy, exotic scent that Meg did not recognize.

Drawing a breath, she edged her thigh away from Sam's and spent the remainder of the cab ride wondering why she always felt drawn to the wrong men. And this one was a Bates, for heaven's sake. While part of Meg's mind fantasized about his wide mouth, another part of her wanted to frisk him and see if he'd made off with her silverware. She was very glad when they finally arrived at Tony's Place.

The air inside the restaurant felt overly warm after the frigid breeze outside. The atmosphere was spiced with the fragrance of garlic and onion, rich sauces and imported cheeses. Italian opera flowed from the speakers overhead.

Meg ordered a pitcher of beer and Tony's specialty pizza, then she met Sam's blue, blue eyes. "There's something you should know upfront. Generations of Mayfairs have been obsessed by the Cocos Island treasure, but the obsession stops here. I'm the only one who ever made a dime out of Cocos Island and I did it without setting foot on the place."

Sam frowned. "Did I miss something?"

"You did if you haven't played Treasure Trove, the video game I developed."

Understanding dawned in his eyes. "Treasure Trove uses Cocos Island as the basis for the game."

"I transferred the family fantasy to software. Now I'm finished with it. I'm not the obsessive type."

"Good for you." He leaned back in his chair as a waiter served their pizza. "If you're not interested in the real thing, that's your prerogative. So sell me your half of the map and I'll be on my way."

Sell her half of the map to a Bates? Meg imagined she could hear her great-great-grandfather rolling over in his grave.

Intellectually, she conceded that Sam was right; a feud that extended into a fifth generation who didn't even know what the original feud had been about was ridiculous in the extreme. But emotionally, well, that was a different thing altogether. Even though Meg considered the map worthless, family loyalty demanded that she hang on to it rather than release it to a Bates.

After wolfing down three slices of pizza, Sam poured more beer. "You *do* have your half of the map, don't you? It hasn't been lost or destroyed, has it?"

"I have it."

"Excellent," he said with obvious relief. "Now we're getting somewhere." The hard look returned to his gaze. "We need to reach an agreement, Meg. I'm not leaving without your half of the map."

Meg answered in her boardroom voice, quiet but unmistakably authoritative. "Is that a threat?"

"It doesn't have to be," he said smoothly, avoiding a direct answer. "I'm willing to accept any arrangement you want to offer. As long as I leave Denver with the complete map."

Tilting her head and tossing the end of her ponytail over her shoulder, Meg studied him across the table. "It occurs to me that you know a lot about me, but I know next to nothing about you."

Sam leaned back in his chair. "There's not much to tell. I was born in Tulsa, Oklahoma, and lived there until I was about five. At that time my father left the oil business, bought a coffee plantation in Costa Rica, and we moved to Puntarenas. My father died of cancer while I was at Yale. My mother lives with a married sister in San José."

"You grow coffee for a living?"

"I'm presently developing a parcel of land just north of Puntarenas. Building greenhouses. By this time next year I'll be shipping commercial orchids."

Meg's eyebrows rose. It was difficult to believe this rugged aggressive man was poetic enough to raise orchids.

Her thoughts must have reflected on her expression because he shrugged and said somewhat defensively. "My degree is in botany."

"A man who owns a coffee plantation and development property doesn't sound exactly poverty stricken. So why are you so hot to find the Cocos Island treasure?"

"Someone is eventually going to unlock Cocos Island's secrets—why not me? Or us, if you're interested."

Meg frowned. "Are you suggesting that I return with you to Cocos Island?"

His answer was prompt. "Absolutely not. I was hoping you had a personal attachment that would keep you here and prevent you from being anything more than a silent partner."

So that's why he had asked if she was seeing anyone. Meg felt an odd stab of disappointment. "You want my map, but not me."

He smiled. "No offense, but the best solution would be for me to buy your half of the map outright. It's clean, it's final, we go our separate ways."

"Treasure Trove is based on fact. I researched everything I could find about Cocos Island and there's no dearth of material. For a century and a half newspapers have been reporting the myriad treasure-seeking expeditions that regularly scour Cocos Island. Sam, hundreds, maybe thousands of people have dug up that island and none have found more than a handful of gold coins. More money has been spent trying to find the Cocos Island treasures than the treasures are worth."

"I doubt it. At current rates, the Peruvian treasure alone is worth in the neighborhood of sixty to one hundred million dollars." A thin smile touched his lips. "Not that I'm willing to pay anywhere near that figure for your half of the map."

"Okay, it's time to put the agenda on the table. My guess is you came here with a proposal. Let's hear it."

Leaning forward, he met her eyes above the candlelight flickering within a hurricane lamp. "If you won't agree to an outright sale . . . then I propose we combine forces on a sixty/forty basis. That's after Costa Rica takes a third of the treasure, their royalty for granting us concession to search the island. You stay in Denver while I go home and put the expedition together. I pay all expenses out of my sixty percent of whatever we find. Does that sound fair?"

"Let me think about it." Standing, Meg glanced at her watch, surprised by how quickly the evening had passed.

"What's to think about?" Sam asked as he helped her on with her coat. "Your half of the map could be earning you forty percent of a fabulous fortune."

"This morning I woke up believing that anyone who claimed Joseph Bates as an ancestor had to be a blight on humanity. Now...well, let's just say I need a little time to make the transition, okay? I agree it's stupid to continue an ancient feud and I'm sure we can work something out. But I need a little time to adjust my thinking."

The warmth of his hands on her shoulders and the stirring of his breath on her cheek sent a wave of weakness jolting through Meg's body. Either she had been much too long without a man's attention or she was more tired than she thought. Probably a little of both, she decided.

Still, as they drove back to her condominium, watching snowflakes pelt the taxi's windshield, Meg wondered how things might have developed if she and Sam had lived in the same area. If they'd had time to get to know one another, would they have discovered that the Mayfairs and the Bates could get along very well indeed? Would a relationship have ripened? One thing was certain. The sexual chemistry was bubbling.

When Sam looked at her, it was as if the rest of the world melted away. Her peripheral vision vanished and there was nothing but his eyes, his face, his wide, sensuous mouth. She wet her lips and asked how long he would be in Denver.

"Until we reach an arrangement regarding your map," he said, stretching his arm across the back of the seat. His fingers grazed her shoulder like tiny shocks of electricity.

This was a persistent man. He wasn't going to allow Meg a moment's peace until he got his way. Before she could deal with picking up the pieces of her life, she would have to deal with Sam Livingston. Under different circumstances, she might have relished the challenge.

"Look," she said as the taxi drew up in front of her building. "You're right. This old feud is idiotic in today's day and age. It's ridiculous to feel like I'm betraying the family if we join forces." Even so, she couldn't bring herself to sell him her half of the map outright. "I'm confident we can reach some kind of an agreement. If you'll leave a phone number, I'll get back to you in a couple of days."

"Why the delay?"

"I need time to contact my attorney." Immediately Meg sensed a new tension leap between them.

After Sam paid the cabdriver, they entered Meg's building and stepped into the elevator, brushing snow from their shoulders and hair.

"Do you really think an attorney is necessary?" Sam asked. "They have a way of complicating everything. We're bright people. I think we can compose a simple contract."

His abruptness of tone and the question itself reminded Meg that despite the links of family history, they were actually strangers. Twelve hours ago she hadn't known Sam Livingston existed.

"I don't sign anything my attorney hasn't read first," she explained coolly, pushing the elevator button for the top floor.

During the silence that filled the rest of the upward ride, Meg wondered if she should invite him inside for a nightcap or send him on his way. There were pluses and minuses to either choice. She was still undecided when they arrived at her door.

"That's odd," Sam said, staring over her shoulder. "I'm positive I closed the door behind me. I double-checked."

Turning, Meg peered at the door. It wasn't pulled shut. Extending a fingertip, she pressed the latch and the door swung silently inward.

"Hold it," Sam ordered. "I'll go in. You wait here." His hand moved to his jacket and slipped inside, then he swore under his breath and stepped forward into the foyer.

Meg stared. The motion with his hand struck her as odd. She had seen that gesture in a thousand television shows. Did Sam usually carry a gun?

One thing was certain. She wasn't going to wait around in the hallway. After drawing a quick breath, she followed him inside.

"Good God!" Halting abruptly, Meg stared into the living room in shock and dismay.

For an instant her mind couldn't assimilate the destruction. When she finally registered what she was seeing, she sagged against the wall and passed a hand over her eyes, then looked again. Someone had systematically destroyed everything Meg owned.

All the paintings had been torn off the walls. Lamps were overturned, drawers pulled out, emptied, and tossed aside. The furniture was tipped up and the bottoms slashed. Cushions were thrown around the room, torn open, leaking stuffing. Books littered the floor. Even her aquarium had been smashed. Water, broken glass, and dead tropical fish splattered the carpet.

Dazed, Meg moved into her den, which served as her office at home. The same scene of wanton destruction repeated here. Furniture had been overturned and slashed, even the drapes were ripped from the windows. Her eyes flicked to the open wall safe, then returned to her desk, which had been thoroughly rifled.

After a moment she stepped to the opened wall safe and removed a velvet-lined box. After she lifted the lid, Meg stared in amazement at the flash of gems inside. She would have bet whatever she still owned that her jewelry would be missing.

"I don't understand this," she said when Sam appeared in the doorway. "Whoever did this managed to break into the safe, but he didn't steal my jewelry. These gems are easily worth fifty or sixty thousand dollars." Suddenly she noticed Sam's grim expression and her blood chilled. "What is it?"

"Don't go into the kitchen."

"The kitchen? What happened in the kitchen?"

"Meg—"

"I'm not a child, Sam. Whatever happened, it happened in my home. I have a right to know." Ducking past him, she hurried toward the kitchen, pushed open the door, then gasped and stumbled backward against Sam's solid chest.

A Hispanic man sat at her kitchen table, slumped forward over a plate. A glass of overturned soda lay next to his hand. When Meg forced herself to look again, she saw a small puddle of blood near his slack mouth, dark and shiny in the glare of the bright overhead lights.

The man had been garroted. There was no question that he was dead.

Chapter Two

They waited for the police in the living room. Sam stood at the balcony doors, smoking a thin, dark cigar and staring out at the snowy darkness. The fragrant smoke drifted to where Meg sat on the arm of the sofa, blinking at the wreckage that had been her living room.

There was a dead man in her kitchen.

Much as she wished it otherwise, Meg continued to see the dead man as if she were still staring at him, continued to see the blood pooled beside his mouth on the tabletop. Even so, it was hard to believe. She'd read about things like this in the newspapers, but she had never imagined such horrors happened to ordinary people. Ordinary people like Meg Mayfair Wolff didn't stumble over dead strangers in their kitchens.

She pressed the heels of her hands against her eyelids.

"What happened? Did that man vandalize everything then calmly enter the kitchen and make himself a sandwich and pour a soda?"

Behind her, she heard Sam draw on his cigar and exhale, but he didn't say anything.

"No, wait," she continued, speaking to herself. "There must have been at least two intruders. That man didn't garrote himself." Frowning, she tugged hard on the end of her ponytail and stared at the ceiling, trying to figure it out. "Okay, at least two men ransacked the place. Then they had a falling out and one killed the other. Afterward, the killer panicked and left without stealing anything." Her reconstruction didn't hang together.

If the intruders had time to make a sandwich, they had time to steal whatever they wanted. It only required a minute to open her jewelry case and spill the gems into a pocket.

"However you want to handle this, Meg, I'll back you," Sam said from behind her. "But I don't think it's a good idea to mention the map or Cocos Island. We'll have to explain eventually, but it would be better not to do it right now."

She swung around in surprise. "It never entered my mind to mention the map or Cocos Island, not for a second. Why on earth would I?"

"Doesn't it strike you as odd that nothing seems to have been stolen?" Sam asked quietly, giving her a long look. "Might that suggest that whoever did this—" he waved at the destruction "—was searching for something specific?"

She stared at him, struggling to see the situation from his perspective. "And the man in the kitchen is possibly Costa Rican? You're suggesting this whole horrible incident is somehow related to the treasure on Cocos Island?"

Sam narrowed his eyes against a curl of smoke. "I don't think we can dismiss the possibility, do you?" He studied her. "Was the map stolen? Have you checked?"

The map was the least of Meg's worries and she waved Sam's concern aside with an impatient gesture. "Forget the damned map, for God's sake. There's a *dead* man in the kitchen!"

At the reminder, Sam's eyes darkened. At once Meg was reminded of the coiled-spring image and she comprehended that he was not as indifferent to the murder as she had supposed. His body was stiff and his expression icy. His generous lips had thinned, and the hand not holding his cigar was clenched into a fist so tight that his knuckles turned pale. An involuntary shiver skittered down Meg's spine.

"What's really going on here?" she whispered, staring at him. Immediately she regretted the blurted words. The hint of rage in Sam's hard expression seemed inexplicable.

"What does that mean?"

"I'm not sure," Meg admitted slowly, noticing he hadn't really given an answer. At this moment Sam Livingston looked capable of inflicting the damage she saw all around her. Making herself sit still, Meg rubbed her fingertips over her temple and the headache building behind her hairline. "Intuition tells me you know more about this than you're letting on. I don't know how that could be possible, but that's how it feels."

"I think the police have arrived." There was absolutely no expression in his voice. The look in his eyes unnerved her.

The rise and fall of police sirens drifted upward from the street below. Minutes later Meg's condo was swarming with lab men, detectives, technicians, and medical examiners. Near midnight, a detective named Mike Johnson sat beside Meg and took her statement.

Yes, she was the Meg Wolff who had been in the newspapers recently in connection with a corporate takeover at Wolff Games, Inc. No, she didn't believe tonight's incident was in any way connected. No, she didn't recognize the dead man in the kitchen, and no, nothing seemed to have been stolen.

"There are no signs of forcible entry, Ms. Wolff. So who has a key?"

Meg thought a moment. "My cleaning lady has a key. I think Karen, my secretary at Wolff Games, may still have a key. The doorman. The super." She glanced at Sam who was watching her, and felt a rush of pink heat her cheeks. "Mark Gerard has a key. We were...involved."

Sam lifted an eyebrow, then turned to the detective. "Is it possible someone could have dropped onto one of the balconies from the roof?"

"We're checking it out. And you are...?"

"Sam Livingston, an old friend of the family."

Meg's head lifted and her eyebrows shot upward. He was deliberately imparting a false impression.

"I'm in Denver for a few days on a business matter that concerns Miss Wolff. We discussed it over dinner."

Detective Johnson asked where they went, what time they arrived at Tony's Place and what time they left. The questions were routine and the detective appeared only marginally interested in Sam's answers. "Where are you from, Mr. Livingston?"

"Tulsa, Oklahoma."

Meg choked. Strictly speaking, Sam wasn't lying. He was from Tulsa originally. But Sam knew as well as she did that the detective was asking where he lived now.

"When did you arrive in Denver and how long do you plan to stay?"

Sam glanced at the end of his cigar, then stubbed it out. "I arrived late last night and hope to finish my business by tomorrow or the day after."

The detective consulted his notes. "This seems pretty straightforward. The two of you left about seven-thirty, went directly to Tony's, then returned here a few minutes after ten. You were never out of each other's sight. As for the scene, nothing appears to have been stolen. And neither of you recognize the man in the kitchen. Is that correct?''

Meg looked pointedly at Sam, waiting for him to mention that they hadn't been together every minute. That he had returned upstairs to retrieve his wallet.

"That's correct," he said.

"No, it isn't," Meg objected, staring at him. She was attracted to him but that didn't mean she was willing to lie for him. "Before we left for Tony's, you returned upstairs alone to get your wallet."

"Oh, yes. I'd forgotten," Sam said, giving her a lazy smile.

Like hell, he had forgotten. For the life of her Meg couldn't figure out why he would lie about something so simple and harmless, but she felt certain he had deliberately chosen not to mention returning for his wallet and jacket.

Maybe the lie wasn't so harmless. Exactly what had Sam done while he was alone in her condo? Her mind raced, trying to recall how long he had been gone. It had seemed forever, but in reality had probably been only a few minutes.

The detective flipped through his notes. "I thought that rang a bell. Yes, the doorman mentioned you returned inside while Miss Wolff waited in the taxi." He looked up at Sam. "Did you notice anyone in the elevator? In the hallway outside Miss Wolff's door?"

"No."

Meg leaned forward, chewing her bottom lip. "Detective, what do you think happened here tonight?"

The detective gazed around the vandalized living room, then shot a glance toward the men clustered in the short hallway leading to the kitchen.

"It's too soon to speculate." He closed his notebook and rose to his feet. "Do you have someone you could stay with for a while? We'll want to preserve the scene for a few days."

"I'll take Miss Wolff back to my hotel," Sam said firmly. "I'm staying at the downtown Hilton."

For a long moment Meg stared up at him, teetering on the edge of refusal. She didn't like him jumping in and making decisions for her. But finally, she nodded. Sam Livingston had some explaining to do. Before she left to pack a suitcase, Sam pushed his hands into his pockets and spoke to the detective in a casual voice. That particular tone of innocent indifference was starting to wave signal flags in Meg's mind.

"Is there any reason why I need to remain available to your department?"

"Are you inquiring if you're a suspect?" the detective asked. A tired smile twitched his lips. "The medical examiner estimates the time of death at about eight-thirty, give or take. That's a ballpark figure, but the ME doesn't miss very often."

"Tony and a dozen other witnesses will verify we were eating pizza at that time," Meg reminded him.

"Unless you can be in two places at once, then I'd say neither of you are suspects."

"I'm sure Miss Wolff will want to remain in close contact with your department, but unless you have an objection, I'll be leaving Denver after I complete my business."

"I'll check with the captain, but as far as I'm concerned, I don't see any reason why you can't leave," the detective said. "We'd appreciate it if you'd give us a number where you can be reached."

"Sure."

"I assume I'm also free to leave town if I need to?" Meg asked, frowning at Sam.

The detective shrugged. "I don't see why not."

Sam's eyes narrowed slightly. "If you'll throw some things in a bag, we'll get out of here. Don't forget to bring the map you were telling me about."

Meg opened her mouth to object, then shut it. Instead of saying anything in front of the detective, she shot Sam a long, hard look that warned he had better have some damned good explanations for all this, then she headed for her bedroom to throw some clothing into a suitcase. After a moment's thought, she stopped in the den and asked the detectives if it was all right to copy some papers she needed.

Fifteen minutes later, they walked out the door, leaving Meg's condominium crowded with policemen. In the lobby, they watched two grim-faced men push a coroner's gurney toward the service elevator.

Meg didn't speak until they were settled in the back seat of a cab, on their way to the downtown Hilton.

"If I were the type of person to punch someone," she said between her teeth, staring at him, "you would be the someone and this would be the moment. You lied."

"Yes, I did."

His answer surprised her and she shifted on the seat, peering at him through the darkness. She had expected a denial or at least an attempt to soften the accusation. Sam Livingston was the most disconcerting man Meg had ever met. Just when she thought she was beginning to get a fix on him, he did something or said something that threw her off balance.

Reaching, he took her hand, squeezed it, then turned his face to the cab window. It had stopped snowing, but a thin layer of white coated the tree limbs and side streets, sparkling beneath the hazy glow of the street lamps.

Meg jerked her hand out of his and struggled to remain calm. "I'm as confused and upset as I can remember being. I need some answers, Sam, and I need them fast. Right now."

"What was that business about you leaving town?" His eyes went flat. "You aren't thinking of going to Costa Rica, are you? Because that isn't the deal I'm proposing. Treasure hunting is no place for a woman who self-admittedly is not adventurous."

"Answers, Sam. Why did you lie to the police?"

"Did you bring the map?"

"All right, if that's the way you want it." Leaning forward, Meg called to the cabbie. "Stop here. I'm getting out."

Immediately Sam turned to her and gripped her shoulders, speaking between his teeth. "Don't be an idiot! Haven't you figured it out? As long as you have the map, you're in danger." He faced the cabbie and growled, "Keep going. The Hilton."

Meg stared into his intense turquoise eyes, feeling her questions coalesce into anger. "I knew you were trouble the minute you bullied your way into my office. I've known you—what?—about twelve hours. And in that time my home has been vandalized and destroyed, a man gets murdered in my kitchen. Now you tell me I'm in danger!" Her chin jutted. "Either you explain all this, or I'm getting out of this taxi and I'm going straight to the police and I'm going to tell them you didn't tell the whole truth! Do I make myself clear?"

To her amazement, Sam stared into her stubborn expression and flashing brown eyes, then his face dissolved in a grin. "You know something? You're an okay broad."

Meg bristled. "In my whole life, no one has ever called me a broad!"

"At least not to your face." Sam smiled at her. If she played poker, she couldn't be too successful at it because her body language betrayed every nuance of emotion. Right now those velvety brown eyes had darkened almost to black. Crimson flared along the sculpted ridges of her cheekbones. Her chin and her magnificent chest thrust forward, and even her ponytail seemed to stiffen with indignation. "Usually I don't think of women as broads, but right now that's the expression that seems to fit."

"I mean it, Sam. Quit stalling."

"We can't talk here," he said, nodding toward the cabbie. "Let's get settled in first."

SAM MANAGED to obtain the room adjoining his for Meg, then ordered sandwiches and a bottle of brandy from room service.

While he paid room service and poured the brandy, Meg stepped into the bathroom and examined herself in the mirror. She looked like hell. Her lipstick had disappeared long ago. Shadows of mascara lay like crescent bruises beneath her eyes. Her skin was pale and colorless. She looked like one of those dazed people on TV who had witnessed a catastrophe.

"I was standing there minding my own business, Officer," she muttered to the mirror. "The first time I knew something was wrong was when this guy came along. His name is Sam." A long sigh dropped her shoulders.

"Did you say something?" Sam called from the other room. "I've got sandwiches and brandy. Coffee if you want it."

Silently Meg took the chair facing him across a tiny table positioned beneath the hotel room window. She started to reach for a sandwich, remembered the dead man, and drew her hand back. Instead she poured a cup of coffee. She doubted she would get much sleep tonight, anyway.

"Okay, let's begin," she said. "Why didn't you tell the detective that you live in Costa Rica?"

"That should be obvious."

"Because the murdered man was Costa Rican?"

"I didn't want the detective to jump to any conclusions or speculate that I might have known the victim."

Meg met his eyes and released a slow breath. "Well—did you know the man in my kitchen?"

"Yes."

She choked on her coffee, hastily set it down, then wiped her lips and stared at him. "I don't believe what I'm hearing! *You knew him?*"

"His name was Enrico Riale."

"Damn it, Livingston! You're poison! I knew it the minute I laid eyes on you!" Jumping to her feet, Meg paced the limited confines of the room. She smacked a fist on top of the TV as she passed. "You are in real trouble, mister, do you know that? You lied to the police. You're impeding a murder investigation. Now you've dragged me into it and I'm in trouble, too! I can't believe this." She threw up her hands. "I don't cheat on my taxes, I don't tell lies, I don't even jaywalk. Now I'm an accomplice to withholding information in a murder case!"

If she had a grain of sense, she would walk out of here right now. Fuming, Meg paced and told herself that was what she would do the instant he answered all her ques-

tions and satisfied her curiosity. She told herself that staying a little longer had nothing to do with her growing
fascination with Sam Livingston. He might be charming
and gorgeous, but he was dangerous. And besides, she had
nowhere to go.

"Do you imagine for a single minute that the police
would permit me to leave town if they knew Enrico worked
for me?" Sam poured a snifter of brandy and handed it to
her as she paced past him. Meg drained the snifter in one
gulp and held it out for a refill when she paced past him
again.

"What do you mean, he worked for you?" she demanded. "Did you instruct him to break into my condominium?"

"Enrico didn't break in. I let him in."

"I knew it!" Meg groaned. Furious, she leveled a kick
at the bed frame, swearing under her breath. "I *knew* you
left your wallet upstairs on purpose! You used it as an excuse to let Enrico inside to ransack my place and search for
the damned map. That's what happened, isn't it?"
Spreading her hands wide, she gazed up at the ceiling.
"Why am I still here? I should be running away from you
as fast as I can! You're crazy!"

Sam gave her a steady look. "I let Enrico inside to guard
your home so no one else would break in and steal the
map. That's the truth, Meg."

"Do you really expect me to believe that? Someone *did*
break in and someone got murdered!"

Sam clenched his teeth so hard that knots appeared
along his jawline. "Enrico was a friend."

Meg's knees collapsed and she sat hard on the end of the
bed. "Can you prove any of this?"

He stared at her. "Not right now, no. You'll have to
trust me."

"Trust a Bates? You're joking! You come along with your crazy stories about treasure and maps and bad guys, and suddenly my home is vandalized, a dead man turns up in my kitchen, and you're lying to the police. You've turned my whole life upside down. And believe me, things weren't too swell even before you showed up. I'm having trouble coping with everything that's happened. I'm about as confused as I've ever been. I'd love to believe you're one of the good guys, Sam, but I don't know what the hell to think."

He started to stand, as if he intended to approach her, but Meg raised a warning hand. "Stay put. I'm not buying this 'trust me' business. And I'm not sure I'm buying the story that you let a stranger into my home for my own good."

Sam's eyes turned the color of glacier ice. "You better believe it, Meg. I didn't have to tell you I knew Enrico. The only reason I did is to impress upon you that you're in danger. Maybe the Bates/Mayfair map is not important to you, but it's damned important to others."

Warily Meg leaned forward and picked up her brandy snifter, holding it up to be filled. "Let's fill in a few details. How did Enrico get into the building? Strangers have to sign in with the doorman."

"It was easier to manage than you might think. Enrico arrived dressed as a delivery man at about five-thirty. He signed in with the doorman, then delivered a bouquet of roses to a random unit on the third floor. Afterward, he went up to the roof and waited there until I came for him."

"He must have been cold up there."

"When I arrived to pick you up, I flipped back a page in the doorman's book and wrote in a sign-out time for Enrico. With luck, it will be a while before the detectives connect the flower delivery to Enrico."

Meg narrowed her eyes. "Assuming you're telling the truth, this whole concept makes me furious. Who gave you permission to let a stranger into my home, damn it? That takes a hell of a lot of nerve!"

His eyes met her angry gaze. "What do you suppose might have happened if you hadn't agreed to have dinner with me? You would have been home alone when the killer arrived."

Meg felt the blood drain from her face. "Oh, God," she murmured, her voice a low moan. Slowly she collapsed backward on the bed and stared up at the ceiling, holding the brandy snifter tightly against her stomach.

"Enrico was a damned good bodyguard. Ex-military. Yet he didn't hear a thing. He was eating a sandwich, for God's sake. He never knew what hit him until it was too late. If the killer could take a pro like Enrico by surprise, what chance do you think you would have had?"

"Okay. I'm paying attention. And I'm starting to get frightened." Meg rolled her head to one side to look at him. "Who killed Enrico?" she asked in a faint voice.

Sam ran a slow speculative glance over her prone body, then stood and frowned out the window, looking down at the cars passing in the icy slush far below. "I don't know."

"Don't lie to me, Sam."

"I can make a guess but there's no way to know for sure."

"Guess."

"I think it's a good bet that one of Martin Chango's men killed Enrico." He turned to examine her expression. "Does that name mean anything to you?"

"Should it? Who is Martin Chango?" Sitting up, Meg moved to the side of the bed, set down the brandy snifter and stroked her temples. Suddenly she felt exhausted.

"Chango is an arms dealer. One of the black hats. The United States Justice Department has been trying for years to get Costa Rica to agree to extradite Chango. England would like to catch him, too. Chango has ignored every law, every regulation, every international agreement regarding the sale of military weapons. He's sold weapons to such swell guys as Idi Amin and Mu'ammar Qaddafi. There isn't a single Latin American country that doesn't owe Martin Chango money. He's sold arms to them all."

Meg's head was swimming. "Okay, I give up. Why on earth would a thug like Chango possibly be interested in tearing apart my home and killing your employee? What possible connection is there? How could a guy like that have heard of me?"

"You must be tired."

"Tired?" She glared up at him. "I'm exhausted! I'm upset and confused. I feel like hell. I want to go to bed and wake up to discover this was all just a bad dream."

"Whatever you say." Sam strode toward the door that connected his room to hers.

"Wait a minute." Dorothy must have felt this way when the tornado snatched her up and spun her off to Oz. In this case, Sam Livingston was cast as the tornado. He was wreaking havoc in Meg's life and driving her crazy. "Chango, remember? Why is an arms dealer interested in tearing apart my home? Why on earth would one of his men show up at my door?"

"Isn't it obvious? Money. One hundred million dollars."

Meg blinked, not sure she had heard him correctly. "The treasure? Sam, that's crazy! Tell me you aren't serious!"

"People don't joke about that kind of money."

Standing, she threw out her hands. "The treasure is a fantasy. It's pie in the sky. There is no proof whatsoever that the Peruvian treasure is still on Cocos Island, assuming it was ever there in the first place."

"Wrong. There's compelling evidence that the treasure is indeed on Cocos Island. I've read the old documents in Lima and all the Peruvian material. It's a good guess Chango has, too. The Peruvians entrusted their gold and jewels to the captain and crew of the *Mary Dear*. That is a documented fact. The treasure left Lima and has never been seen again. Also fact. Your great-great-grandfather and my great-great-grandfather were on the *Mary Dear*. The crew manifest still exists in the Lima archives. It's a fact that our ancestors were aboard that ship. Our great-great-grandfathers admitted to stealing the treasure and claimed it was hidden on Cocos Island. These are all documented facts. If someone had found the Peruvian treasure, believe me, we would have heard about it. There's no way a discovery that sensational could be kept secret. The treasure is still there, Meg, waiting to be found."

"This is crazy. I keep telling you, hundreds of people, maybe thousands, have searched for that treasure. They've dug pits, they have blown up cliff sides, they've moved tons of jungle, and *no one* has been successful! Why do you and this thug Chango think you can sail into Chatham Bay and pick up the treasure when no one else has been able to?"

He met her eyes, looking at her through a sweep of sooty lashes. "Because no one else has had the Bates/Mayfair map. For over a century, serious treasure hunters have shared rumors about the existence of the Bates/Mayfair map. You're surely aware a half-dozen forgeries exist. But history lost track of the Bates and Mayfair families and the real map never turned up."

"Until now."

"Correct." She was pacing again and he watched her storm past him. "Are you all right?"

"No, I'm not all right," she snapped, pushing back the hair that had fallen from her ponytail. "I'm caught up in something that doesn't make sense to me. You're like Alice's Cheshire cat, smiling and grinning and telling me to trust you while you're babbling about pirates and treasure. Somewhere out there is the Red Queen disguised as a criminal named Martin Chango, who is ordering people killed. And right smack in the middle of this mess is a very confused Meg Wolff who doesn't want to be here. I want to be home feeling sorry for myself about my stolen company. But of course, I can't go home because the police have taped off my home as a murder scene. You remember that part, don't you? You should. It looks to me like you led the murderer right to my door."

Sam winced and ground his teeth. "Unfortunately that's probably what happened. And I'll regret it for the rest of my life. But I also know that sooner or later Chango or one of the others would have found you."

"One of the others?" A wild look appeared in her dark eyes. "Oh, great. I can't wait to hear about *them*."

"Why is this so difficult for you to accept? The story about our ancestors is famous. There isn't a treasure hunter alive who doesn't know about Walter Bates and Joseph Mayfair. Every time the media reports a new expedition to Cocos Island, the Bates/Mayfair tale is repeated along with rumors about the map. People have been searching for Bates and Mayfair descendants for over a century." He spread his hands. "It just happens that I— and Martin Chango—are more persistent than most. I stayed with the search and found you." His frown deepened. "Unfortunately, I probably led Chango here, too."

"Thanks a lot."

Stepping forward, Sam gripped her shoulders and gave her a gentle shake. "What do you want me to say, Meg? That I'm sorry I involved you in this mess? I'm sorry you're involved, but I'm not to blame...this chain of events began a hundred and eighty years ago. Like it or not, you're going to be involved as long as you own half of the Bates/Mayfair map. But there *is* a solution. Give me the map."

"Look," she said, stepping back from the big hands tingling on her shoulders. "It's been a long, very bad day..."

"Do you want sympathy that you've had a bad day? That you'll have to endure the inconvenience of calling in an interior decorator to redo your place? That you don't have an office to go to tomorrow? Okay, I'm sorry about your bad day." His gaze was hard. "It hasn't been a terrific day for me, either. A good friend of mine died tonight. In my mind, Enrico's death takes precedence over your bad day."

Shame filled Meg's eyes. His words made her feel about two inches high. "I'm sorry," she murmured. "Nothing like this has happened to me before and maybe I'm not handling it well."

His blue eyes burned down at her. "There's another thing. It's time to get smart. Make a very public announcement that you've sold your half of the map. Or tell the newspapers that someone stole it. Whichever you prefer. But use the media to inform Chango and any other treasure hunters that you don't have the Mayfair map anymore."

"Oh, come on. Why would the newspapers be interested in printing such a story?"

He stared at her. "You have to be kidding. Cocos Island has always generated huge interest. Robert Louis

Stevenson brought the island to public attention by using Cocos Island as the basis for *Treasure Island*. The media has been in love with it ever since. Besides, the media loves stories of treasure. And they love Cocos Island in particular. You're acting as if no one ever heard of the Bates/Mayfair map, and you couldn't be more wrong. In certain circles, Cocos Island and the Bates/Mayfair map are as famous as the United States Constitution!"

Meg stared up at him, listening, refusing to comment.

"As long as you have that map, Meg, you're in danger. A lot of people—like Chango—want that map and will stop at nothing to get it. Get rid of the map and you're out of the loop and safe."

"Why now?" Meg asked finally. "How come you could find me, but hordes of treasure hunters haven't been able to find any of the previous Mayfairs?"

"That's obvious. A video game using Cocos Island as the setting turns up copyrighted under the name of Meg Mayfair Wolff. Coincidence? More like a neon arrow saying, Here I am." Sam pushed a hand through his hair. "Stop looking at me like I'm to blame for every bad thing that's happened to you since childhood. The only thing I've done is locate you and make you a legitimate offer for your half of the map. That, and try to protect you."

Meg pushed back a wave of hair. "Has it occurred to you that before you appeared in my life I didn't need protection?"

After opening the door that connected his room to hers, Sam looked back at her, his deeply tanned face expressionless. "Earlier this evening you said you'd think about selling me your map. The way I see it, you no longer have a choice. As long as you have it, you're a target. The sensible course is to get rid of it."

"Hand it over to a Bates, you mean."

Meg sat on the side of the bed again and stared at him as ugly thoughts tiptoed through her mind. She had only Sam's word about what had happened when he'd returned upstairs to get his wallet. Maybe he had killed Enrico and had done something to make it appear that the murder had occurred later. Maybe Enrico's murder was intended to scare her into selling her half of the map to him. She rubbed her arms as a tremor rippled down her body.

"Sam?" He turned at the door with a look of impatience. "There's something I need to know. Did you tell me the whole truth? You lied to the police . . . have you lied to me?"

For a moment she thought he wouldn't answer. Indecision flickered across his expression.

"Yes," he said finally and with obvious reluctance.

Meg sat bolt upright and narrowed her eyes. "Yes, what? Yes, I know the whole truth? Or yes, you've lied to me, too?"

"This is a complicated situation. More complicated than you know."

"Tell me the truth! Right now, Sam."

"I can't do that. Other people are involved. I've already said more than I should have. Good night, Meg."

The door closed behind him with a final sound.

When it was evident that he wasn't coming back, Meg swore, then let her shoulders slump. She smoothed her palm across the bedspread and cast a longing glance toward the pillows. There was virtually no chance that she was going to sleep a wink. There was too much to think about.

She spent the remainder of the night lying in the darkness, surrendering to a crazy mishmash of disconnected thoughts. She reviewed the last disastrous board meeting of Wolff Games, Inc. She remembered every detail of discovering Enrico Riale's body. She tried to decide if there was anything she could have done to save Wolff Games. She remembered Sam bursting into her office, tall, handsome, and bringing a horrendous package of troubles. She wondered what he had lied to her about and when and if he would confess the whole truth. She tried to recall if she had picked up her favorite suit from the dry cleaners. She asked herself what she was going to do next.

Near dawn Meg heard a noise at the connecting door and immediately closed her eyes and went limp against the pillows. Part of her had expected Sam would attempt to steal her half of the map. He was a Bates, after all, and no Bates was to be trusted. But it still disappointed her to discover that she was right.

Holding her breath, she opened her lashes enough to watch as Sam carefully, quietly, and very thoroughly searched her purse and her luggage. Eventually, of course, he located the paper Meg had copied on her home copier before leaving with him for the Hilton.

After he found the map he silently moved to stand beside the bed, looking down at her. It required every ounce of Meg's willpower to keep her eyes closed and lie still. After a moment she felt him move away, then she heard a tiny click at the door as he returned to his own room.

Releasing a long, low breath, Meg waited another minute, then swung her legs over the side of the bed and approached the room service tray still on the table beneath the window. She poured half a glass of brandy and stood at the window, sipping the brandy and watching the clouds gradually turn a pearly shade of pink. Once again she reviewed everything that had happened since Sam Livingston stormed into her life.

At eight o'clock, showered and dressed, she knocked on the connecting door. As expected, there was no response. When Meg opened the door and entered Sam's room, he was gone.

She stood beside his rumpled bed inhaling the echo of his after-shave and noticing how thoroughly he had removed all traces of his presence.

A grim smile brushed her lips as she thought about scoring a few points for the Mayfairs. She wondered if Sam would get as far as Cocos Island before he realized he had stolen a copy of a fake map.

Chapter Three

Sam handed his tray to the flight attendant, fastened his seat belt, and leaned toward the window as the captain announced the flight would be landing in five minutes at Juan Santa Maria International, the airport northwest of San José.

Hours ago Meg would have discovered that he had gone and her map was missing. By now she would have contacted the press or the police and told them the whole story as she knew it. As soon as the newspapers printed that Meg no longer had the map, she would be safe and out of Sam's life. That was the best thing for both of them.

So why couldn't he stop thinking about her?

In a way Meg Wolff had been exactly as he had expected, and in another way she hadn't been at all what he'd expected. From the beginning, since he knew she had single-handedly created Wolff Games, Inc., he had realized Meg was a smart and clever businesswoman. He'd expected a brisk, no-nonsense attitude and that's what he had found. He'd also anticipated that she would not be interested in personally participating in a treasure hunt. But he had not expected her to be so resistant about parting with her half of the map. He hadn't counted on the Bates/Mayfair feud still being a valid item in her mind.

The biggest surprise had been the discovery that her photograph didn't do her justice. Her beauty had knocked his socks off, that intriguing combination of fire and ice. He hadn't expected a feisty flash in melting dark eyes, or guessed she would have gorgeous legs a mile long, or hair the color of wild honey. Not for one moment had Sam expected to like or admire her so much. Certainly he had not foreseen an instant and intoxicating sexual attraction.

He continued to think about Meg Wolff as the plane landed and as he passed through the customs lines. It wasn't until he emerged into the terminal that he put her out of his mind and cast a careful glance over the people waiting at the gate.

Almost immediately he spotted Howard Westin. Howard's distinctive gray hair was concealed beneath a sky-cap's hat and he wore thick, distorting glasses but Sam knew he wasn't mistaken. For an instant their eyes met and acknowledged complications, then Sam beckoned Howard forward and stood aside as Howard stacked his luggage on a dolly. They walked through the terminal.

"You know about Enrico," Sam said quietly as they stepped outside into the hot, humid air.

"We're taking care of it," Howard said as he bumped the baggage dolly off the curb and started across the street toward the parking lot. "Did you get Wolff's map?"

"You don't know?" For the first time Sam looked at Howard directly. "By now Meg should have told the Denver police that the map was stolen."

"The police haven't heard from her."

Sam swore under his breath as they approached a silver Mercedes gleaming beneath the late afternoon sun. "Then as far as Chango's concerned, nothing has changed. She still has her half. Damn it!"

"Are you sure she doesn't?" Howard asked in a low voice as Sam bent to unlock the trunk of the Mercedes. "That would explain why she didn't contact the police. I cautioned you not to underestimate her."

Sam inserted his key into the trunk lock, his mind racing, swiftly settling on an odd moment. After he had stolen Meg's half of the map he had stood over her bed saying a silent goodbye. He had suspected she only feigned sleep but that hadn't made sense. Why would she pretend to be asleep and allow him to steal her half of the map? At that moment, he had decided he was mistaken.

"She suckered me." He saw it now. If the map he'd stolen had been genuine, she would have gone directly to the police and told them everything she knew. He leaned against the car, scowling as Howard stacked his luggage into the trunk. "I screwed up. I'll bet the farm the map I've got is a phony." He swore and made a sound of disgust. "We're back to square one."

"Not quite," Howard murmured, taking his time with Sam's bags. When he straightened, he glanced at his watch and his expression tightened. "Thirty minutes ago she boarded a plane for Costa Rica. She'll be landing here about eight o'clock tonight."

"*What?* That little idiot! When Chango learns she's turned up in his backyard, he'll think he's died and gone to heaven! Meg is as good as dead!"

"I haven't had time to fully analyze this development, but it may work to our advantage."

"Not if she ends up dead." Sam dug in his pocket for a tip, knowing their time together was running short. "Howard, I've got to tell her everything."

"If you do, we'll have to pick her up. We can't have a loose cannon running around out there. We've worked too hard to set this up. Give me twenty-four hours to get in touch with my people and see how this plays."

Sam ground his teeth and cursed. "I'll meet you tomorrow at the greenhouses. Tell your people if one hair on Meg's head gets hurt, I'm out."

"Sorry, friend. You know it's too late for that," Howard said before he turned away. "If you want to protect Ms. Wolff, then get her out of Costa Rica. I'd say you have forty-eight hours tops before Chango learns she's turned up on his turf."

A nasty headache pounded behind Sam's eyes.

HE WAS WAITING when Meg came off the plane and passed through customs.

Some blondes had a pale, washed-out look, but Meg Wolff wasn't one of them. Her hair was a rich honey color, swept into a smooth chignon. Her eyes were an intelligent earthy brown. Thick, smoky lashes cast a shadow over the top of high-fashion cheekbones. For the flight she had chosen a jewel-toned emerald suit made of a silky material that suggested more than it revealed. But it suggested enough to turn a man's palms hot and moist. There was nothing whatsoever inconspicuous about her; she drew every eye in the terminal. Sam sighed and shook his head.

Meg spotted him at once, leaning against the wall outside customs, his ankles crossed, his arms folded over his chest. He didn't take his eyes off of her and he didn't look happy.

So much for sneaking into Costa Rica. There went her plan to do a little spying and discover exactly who Sam Livingston was and why he had lied to the police.

As soon as the custom's official waved her inside the terminal, Sam pushed from the wall and stalked forward.

"What the hell do you think you're doing? Why are you here?"

"Whatever happened to hello? Or, I'm sorry I stole your map and left you in the middle of a murder case?" Meg gave him a frosty stare, trying to ignore the realization that this was probably the best-looking man in Costa Rica. She wished he wasn't a Bates, wished she could trust him, wished they had met under vastly different circumstances.

"Outraged innocence won't play, Meg. It took a while, but I've figured out that you gave me a phony map."

"Gave you? The way I remember it, you *stole* what you thought was my half of the map." Which proved that she was correct not to trust him. After lifting on her tiptoes, she spied a skycap, signaled to him, and pointed at her luggage.

Sam waved the skycap away. "Then I'm right. What I've got is a phony." He swore under his breath. If looks could kill, Meg would have fallen to the floor.

She signaled another skycap. "It's been charming running into you again, Mr. Livingston, but I'm exhausted and I need to find a hotel. So if you'll excuse me..."

Sam's scowl ran off the second skycap. "Out with it, Meg. What the hell are you doing here?"

Clearly she was not going anywhere until she dealt with Livingston. Meg stared into his deep-lashed turquoise eyes then shrugged. "I can't go home because of the police cordon. I no longer have an office to go to. Since I don't have anything else to do, I decided to take a vacation."

"Didn't you hear anything I told you? Costa Rica is the last place you should visit."

"A challenge like that is hard to ignore. I can't help being curious to know why you think I shouldn't be here." A frown tugged the delicate skin between her eyes. "By the way, how did you know I was coming? Or that I'd be on this plane?''

Sam bent for her luggage. ''I have a friend who makes it his business to know who enters or leaves Costa Rica. If you'll take the makeup case, we can manage this luggage ourselves.'' He gave her a glance that began at her stockings and ended at her mouth. ''You'll be staying with me in Puntarenas.''

''I'll be staying at a hotel, thank you,'' Meg said stiffly, picking up her makeup case. She liked Sam too much to actually believe he had murdered Enrico, still…she didn't know anything for sure except that he was a liar and a thief. Trust her to be attracted to a Bates, absolutely the wrong type of man. She suppressed a sigh. ''There's another thing. I'm tired of your high-handed manner, so back off. I'll make my own decisions.''

''Not this time you won't. I'm calling the shots here.'' He drew an exasperated breath, then softened his tone. ''Look, Meg. Martin Chango wants your map so badly that one of his men killed Enrico.''

''So you say. I don't recall any proof.''

''If you'd been home, it would have been you who ended up dead. Chango wouldn't care, as long as he got what he wanted.'' Sam met her eyes. ''Now you turn up in Chango's backyard. What kind of proof do you want? A bullet in the forehead?''

A pinpoint of alarm appeared in Meg's dark eyes. She swept a glance across the terminal. ''Is Chango your friend who knows who enters and who leaves Costa Rica?''

''Of course not. But Chango's information network is almost as good. Believe me, the instant you check into a hotel, Chango will know it.'' Heavy brows descended over his eyes. ''So here's the plan and I'm in no mood to argue. I'll take you home with me. Tomorrow evening I'll put you on a plane back to Denver. With luck, we'll get you out of Costa Rica before Chango knows you ever arrived. I don't want an argument, Meg. I've already made your return reservations under an assumed name.''

This was not going as Meg had planned.

''Oh, for God's sake. Stop looking at me like that,'' Sam said with a grimace. ''I'm one of the good guys. Honest.''

''So. We're back to 'trust me'. I hate that.'' She studied his rugged features with cool eyes. ''I make it a practice never to trust liars and thieves. Generally speaking, they aren't trustworthy.''

''In this case you'll have to make an exception,'' Sam said shortly. Carrying her luggage, he walked toward the terminal doors.

Meg pressed her lips together, then reluctantly followed her bags toward the parking lot. Sam Livingston was about the most arrogant man she had ever met. Who did he think he was? This was practically kidnapping. And that business about making plane reservations for her and ordering her out of the country! He had a lot of nerve for a man who had done nothing but lie to her.

''Suppose I don't want to return to Denver?'' Meg asked, gazing around the parking lot at sprays of palm trees and tropical growth. The evening heat pressed in on her. It was hard to believe that a few hours ago she had left Denver in a snowstorm. ''What if I've decided I want to join you for a little treasure hunting?''

Sam dropped her luggage beside a silver Mercedes and gave her a furious look. ''Forget it,'' he said flatly. ''Aside from the fact that you aren't interested in treasure hunting, it should be obvious that you've walked into something very, very dangerous. If you're as smart as I think you are, you'll give me your half of the map then get the hell out of here while you still can!''

Meg tilted her head back and looked him straight in the eye. "You lied to the police and to me. You're involved in a murder. You made me an accomplice in a cover-up attempt, and you tried to steal my map. You owe me an explanation, Sam. I'm not going anywhere until I hear it.''

"You came all this way just to demand an explanation?''

"Partly. Or maybe I'm an adventurous type, after all. Or maybe I figure you're lying about the danger, too.''

He stared down at her. "The danger is real. As for the rest, I'd love to explain, but that's not my decision to make.''

"Who's decision is it?''

"I can't tell you that.''

"Just trust you, right?'' Meg made a face.

Sam tossed her bags on top of his in the trunk and slammed the lid. "Right.''

"Sorry, that's not good enough. I can't think of any reason why I should trust you about anything.''

"If you don't think any danger is involved, think about Enrico!''

"If I'm in so much danger, then let's sell Chango both halves of the map and be done with it. You're going treasure hunting just for the hell of it. I don't believe there's any treasure on Cocos Island, anyway. Neither one of us has any stake in this, not really. So why not just give Chango the map?''

"We can't do that,'' Sam said, opening the passenger door for her. He watched her slide her long legs inside.

Meg strove for patience. "Why not?''

"There are good reasons why not, which I can't explain right now.'' He closed the door on Meg's exclamation of exasperation and walked around the car to the driver's side.

"Let me ask you something," Meg said after he slid behind the wheel and shifted to face her. "Are you really going treasure hunting? Or is that a lie, too?"

"I'm really going to Cocos Island. That's the plan."

"And you need my half of the map to do it?"

Sam hesitated, then his gaze narrowed. "I'd have a better chance for success with the united map."

"Fine. I'll give it to you."

He looked at her in surprise. "You will?"

"Absolutely," she said sweetly. "As soon as you've told me everything. I have a right to know why someone was murdered in my house, Sam. That's the deal, take it or leave it."

"You just don't get it, do you? We aren't playing a video fantasy here. What's happening is very real and very dangerous. You can believe this or not, but I like you and I'm sorry you're involved. My job right now is to get you uninvolved before something nasty happens to you. That means you are going to be on that plane tomorrow if I have to carry you on board."

After shrugging out of his jacket and tossing it and his tie onto the back seat, he reached for the ignition and switched on the air-conditioning. Even at this late hour, the tropical air was hot and sticky.

"Just tell me the truth and I'll go willingly." Meg had never been one to fight battles that she knew in advance she couldn't win. Whether or not she departed Costa Rica tomorrow was a battle yet to be waged. But there was no point fighting the outcome tonight. For the moment she was stuck with Sam and therefore she might as well make the best of it. She drew a breath. "Will we be driving through San José?"

"We'll skirt the city and leave immediately for Punta-renas. Make yourself comfortable, it's a long drive."

Meg waved a hand at the heat trapped inside the car, then pulled off her suit jacket. Beneath it she wore a cream-colored silk camisole that hugged small, perfectly rounded breasts.

Scowling, Sam concentrated on backing out of the parking space and pointing the Mercedes toward Punta-renas. It had been a long time since he had seen skin as milky white and smooth as Meg's. Trying to keep his thoughts focused on safer areas, he made a mental note to pick up some sunscreen for her. He suspected by this time tomorrow, she would need it.

"What's wrong?" she asked, frowning. "You have a peculiar look on your face."

After rolling down his window, he lit one of his thin ci-gars. "I was trying to picture you on a treasure-hunting expedition." He smiled. "It occurs to me that you're about the last person a sane man would take to Cocos Island."

Her eyebrows lifted. "Oh?" A glacier surfaced in that one word. "I think I'd manage as well as anyone else, thank you."

"In most cases I imagine you would," he said, easing the Mercedes out of the parking lot. "But not in this in-stance. You'd sizzle in the tropical sun like butter in a skillet." He glanced at her pale, creamy shoulders. "I'll bet you're one of those people who don't tan—you burn."

When she didn't answer, he knew he'd guessed cor-rectly. He cast a quick glance toward her high-heeled pumps.

"When was the last time you hiked through a jungle? Or did anything more physically strenuous than dictate a memo?"

"I work out," she said defensively. She dismissed his questions with a wave. It was moot, anyway. She didn't intend to join Sam on a treasure-hunting expedition. She had merely been testing his reaction to the suggestion.

Her throat arched toward the air-conditioning vents and she turned her face, letting the cool air bathe her skin. The ends of her collarbones met above a deep moist cleft. Sam swallowed and forced his attention back to the road.

"Sam?" Meg folded her hands in her lap and looked out the windshield, speaking in a quiet voice. "I don't think you killed Enrico...but you could have, you had opportunity, and that's scary. Maybe being here is a little scary, too. Suddenly I can't remember why I came or what I'm doing in a car with you, going God knows where."

"If you're looking for reassurance, you won't find it here. All I can tell you is that I didn't kill Enrico. Enrico was my friend."

"There's more going on here than just a treasure hunt, isn't there? Surely you can tell me that much."

"I wish I could explain, but I can't."

"Or won't?"

"Look, Meg. Let's declare a truce, okay? I know you're frustrated because you sense something beneath the surface and don't understand it. I'm frustrated because I'd like to explain but I can't. Can we agree to put this mess on hold for a while?"

A long sigh collapsed her breast and she leaned back against the leather seat. "How long is a while?"

"I don't know. A while."

"Maybe forever, right?"

"Possibly."

Meg rolled her head across the top of the seat and looked at him. "Tell me something. Does every woman you meet want to smash you over the head with the nearest heavy object? Do you always have this frustrating whirlwind effect on people?''

Her question surprised him and he laughed. ''Hardly. I'm a simple man with simple tastes. Dull, really.''

Meg smiled in the light from the dashboard. ''Now why don't I believe that?''

''It's true. I prefer the company of plants to that of most people. The activities I enjoy are largely solitary. Reading, diving, riding, sailing. I detest parties and party chat. The minute the conversation strays toward standard small talk, my tongue rolls up in a ball and I can't think of anything to say. Far from having a whirlwind effect, I usually bore women, put them to sleep.''

''We're making small talk now and you're holding your own just fine. I'm still awake.''

''Good God.'' He gave her a look of mock horror, then laughed when she did. ''I don't know, you're different,'' he said after a minute. ''You're easy to talk to.''

He felt her shift on the car seat to glance at him. ''You seem that way to me, too,'' she admitted in a low voice. Then hastily added, ''It's probably because we know our situation is temporary. There's nothing personal at stake.''

He hesitated, then said, ''Probably.''

The headlights swept the curving two-lane road, illuminating glimpses of craggy hills, encroaching ferns, and the cedar forest that nudged the highway on both sides. A crescent moon hung suspended in the sky like a paper cutout pasted on dark velvet, dipping in and out of view as the Mercedes curved through a series of descending turns.

Warm air rushed in Sam's opened window, pushing at the cooler air inside the car and circulating the sensuous fragrance of Meg's perfume. He knew every time she glanced at him, was acutely conscious of the shared intimacy of the darkness and the close quarters within the automobile. A taut air of subtle expectancy shortened the distance from his thigh to hers, exerting a gentle magnetic tug. He couldn't remember ever wanting to touch a woman this much.

He found his concentration drifting to wonder if her milky skin was as soft and smooth as it looked, if her hair was as fine and silky as he guessed. It was all he could manage not to continually glance at the long expanse of crossed legs. The dim interior lights seemed to gather along her tinted nylons, gleaming at the corner of his eyes like a homing beacon.

As for Meg, she found the scent of his cigar oddly erotic. Usually she didn't care for the smell of cigar smoke. But the thin, dark brand that Sam favored evoked thoughts of leather and tobacco and earth and rain and wood shavings and sunlight. Good masculine scents.

And Sam Livingston was definitely masculine. Upon entering the car he had opened his collar to reveal crisp, dark curls feathering his chest. Already a hint of shadow had appeared on his cheeks and jaw.

And he was big. There wasn't an ounce of superfluous fat on his body. He was lean and tight, but he was a big-boned man. Watching his large, square hands firm and sure on the wheel, Meg realized that part of the reason she was having difficulty accepting the danger he kept mentioning was because she felt safe in his presence.

This thought struck her as idiotic. Sam Livingston was a liar and a thief and was involved somehow in a murder.

His size also impressed her as sexy, and that thought erased everything else. When he glanced at her with those all-knowing, turquoise eyes, she swallowed hard and looked aside as if he could read her thoughts.

"Tell me about orchids," she said when their silent awareness of each other had reached a level of tension that demanded something be said or done.

"Orchid is the popular name applied to perennial epiphytes from the *Orchidaceae* family." He smiled at the road. "Is this a test?"

She returned his smile. "Maybe. I'm having trouble picturing you as a plant lover. I'll say this, orchid is a more romantic name than epiphytes."

"Did you know that commercial vanilla flavoring comes from an orchid? The *Vanilla* genus."

"I didn't know that. Are you planning to grow vanilla?"

"Probably not. Artificial vanilla has reduced the cost-effectiveness of growing real vanilla. I intend to cultivate cattleya, which you've probably worn as a corsage at some time, and *Paphiopedilum,* which will be more familiar as lady's slipper. The roots of the North American version were once dried and used by folk doctors as an antispasmodic."

Meg turned to face him, fascinated. The journey to Puntarenas passed in the blink of an eye as she listened to Sam explain the difficulties of growing commercial orchids. He told her about the almost countless varieties, including the delicate variations that lived solely on nutrients in the air, and he spoke of the challenges involved in exporting. The difficulties in shipping such delicate short-lived flowers were enormous.

"Each orchid must be shipped in its own tiny vial of water." Self-conscious at having monopolized the conversation, Sam broke off his discussion and nodded at the countryside. "I wish it were daylight and you could see the countryside. Costa Rica has some of the most fertile soil in the world. In recent years the government as well as private individuals have been successfully experimenting with dryland rice farming. We've passed several farms worth seeing. Now we're in the coffee fincas."

Meg peered out the window, amazed. While Sam had been talking, the rocky hills and dense cedar and mahogany forests had given way to moonlit farmland and coffee shrubs. Directly ahead, the horizon flattened into the Pacific Ocean. Starlit waves rolled toward the dark silhouette of Puntarenas, which appeared to be a small town of approximately forty thousand or so. Gazing down at the town, Meg noticed a glow of lights ringing the plaza and the fat rounded spires of a palatial church.

Sam cast her a sheepish glance. "I've been talking nonstop. I probably bored the hell out of you. I apologize."

"I wasn't bored at all," Meg insisted truthfully. Plus, for the first time since she had met him, he seemed relaxed. The tension on his inner spring had eased as he spoke about his new business. "You make botany—orchids—sound fascinating."

What was fascinating was Sam Livingston. All the while he was speaking, Meg had been trying to imagine those big hands cupped around a blossom as fragile as an orchid. By the time he was midway into explaining his passion, she could imagine it easily. This was a man who loved growing things, a man with a hidden gentle streak. He understood plants the way a doctor understood the human body. Sam understood an orchid's needs and preferences, what made it flourish or decline, how to tend or mend it.

Moreover, there was something wildly appealing about a man who loved his work, who could become passionate about it. Meg understood that kind of intensity and passion; she responded to it at a visceral level. In the same way as she was beginning to respond to Sam Livingston the man.

A deep sigh lifted her bosom and she crossed her arms over her chest. The last thing she needed was this deepening attraction to a man who had turned her world upside down. Who, based on hints and innuendos, was involved in some kind of dangerous derring-do right up to his gorgeous eyeballs. Meg's ex-husband had enjoyed flirting with danger. One such man was enough for a lifetime. She didn't want it to happen again.

Yet here she sat, shivering in the tropics, flushing hot and then cold with a growing attraction she seemed unable to halt. To her dismay, she discovered herself wondering if those big hands would be gentle or rough on a woman's body, wondering how his kiss would feel and taste. She was fantasizing about a man who had involved her in lies and murder. It was insane.

"Are you cold?" he inquired. He noticed her slight shiver and reached toward the air-conditioner switch.

"A little," she lied. A flash of heat lightning traveled up her arm when his fingers accidentally brushed the back of her wrist. "Are we almost there?"

"Almost."

He slowed and turned the Mercedes onto a graveled road that skirted the land side of Puntarenas, heading north through hilly fields of coffee shrubs and cattle ranchos. They passed through a wrought-iron gate, then drove down a lane bordered by rosewood and palm trees.

At the end of the lane was a sprawling house fashioned of stucco and terra-cotta, roofed with red tiles. Banana palms shaded a corral behind the house and to the right. To the left was a kidney-shaped pool that appeared to hang suspended on the very lip of a sheer rocky drop-off. With a tiny gasp of pleasure, Meg realized the pool and the house offered a magnificent view of the Golfo de Nicoya and the Pacific.

She turned wide eyes to Sam as he eased the Mercedes to a halt before a spacious veranda that sheltered tall, carved wooden doors. Immediately lights switched on inside the house.

"This is your home? And you pretended to be impressed by my penthouse, as you called it?"

He came around the car to open her door. "I liked your place." A grin deepened the lines splitting his cheeks. "I wouldn't want to live there, but I liked it."

It seemed to Meg that a dozen people poured out of the door to welcome Sam home. Someone whisked their luggage away, someone dropped a sweater around Meg's shoulders, a woman wearing a bathrobe and a long braid down her back beckoned them inside and asked in Spanish if they wanted something to eat.

Sam introduced the Costa Rican family that tended his house, then looked at Meg and lifted an eyebrow. "Did you eat on the plane? Are you hungry?"

"Nothing for me, thanks. I don't want to put anyone to any trouble. What I really want is a good night's sleep. I can hardly keep my eyes open." Suddenly Meg felt the effects of too much excitement and not enough sleep.

All she could manage was to glance around and murmur polite comments about Sam's house. The tour would have to wait for tomorrow. But she already knew she would love it. The instant she stepped inside Sam's home, Meg was conquered by its warmth and charm. She couldn't have said what she expected, but she hadn't expected such a relaxed cheerful ambience.

There were plants everywhere, of course. Hanging plants, trailing ivies, tall trees growing in massive planters, potted plants. And there were books. It seemed every room had at least one crowded bookcase. Vivid paintings, wool blankets, and flowers pressed within frames decorated the white walls. The furniture in the living and dining rooms was light and upholstered in bright patterns, inviting in a way that reminded Meg how exhausted she was and how relaxing it would be to sink into one of those puffy deep chairs, slip off her heels, and press her feet against the coolness of the floor tiles.

"Melda will show you to your room," Sam said, touching her elbow. Before Meg understood his intentions, he drew her into his arms, gazed into her widening eyes a moment, then brushed his lips across hers.

Sam's kiss gave Meg an electrical jump start. Her body didn't know this was a Bates, a liar and a thief, an absolutely unsuitable man. Her body reacted as if this was a chemical bonding it had sought from the moment of birth.

A thrill of surprise swept the tiredness from her limbs, a tremor of heat shot toward the big hands cupping her hips. She felt each of Sam's fingertips as if they touched her bare skin instead of silk. Her blood heated and fizzed, racing through her body at dizzying speed as Sam's wide mouth lingered on hers and his hands slid to her waist.

It was the damnedest thing. One minute Meg was so tired she could hardly stand. The next minute her nerves had charged into overdrive and her skin felt as if it were on fire. Expectancy quivered in the pit of her stomach. A fiercely urgent heat began where his lips met hers, melted through her body and flared where his large hands circled her waist.

For an instant Sam's hands tightened, molding her firmly against his rock-hard body. Then, as if he suddenly remembered that others were watching, Sam released her and stepped backward. Desire intensified his gaze and deepened his voice.

"Welcome to my home."

Speechless, Meg could only stare at him. Never, not ever in her life, had she responded so totally or so helplessly to a simple kiss. Her body was still on full alert, her pulse pounded in her ears. The knowledge staggered her. What was it about this man anyway? His deeply sunburned good looks? That sexy lopsided smile? The warm male scent of his skin and hair? Or was it some karmic recognition deep in the cells that lay beyond her understanding?

"Good night, Meg. Sleep well."

She gave her head a hard shake, trying to clear the feverish thoughts from her brain. "Good night," she murmured, still breathless. She tried desperately to think of something else to say but her brain would not cooperate.

"If you'll follow me...." Melda suggested. Melda was the woman with the glossy black braid swinging down the back of her bathrobe. Smiling, she led Meg to a suite of rooms that included a luxurious black marble bath, a bedroom, and a sitting room that opened onto a patio facing the lush hillside. Moonlight revealed neat rows of coffee bushes and a feathery fringe of palms.

After Melda had unpacked her suitcases and hung her clothing in a cedar closet, Meg thanked her in rusty Spanish remembered from high school, then entered the lavish bathroom. She scanned the black marble and shining brass fixtures, shook her head, then washed her face and brushed out her hair. After cleaning her teeth, she slipped into a gold silk nightgown the color of her hair and gratefully slipped between cool starched sheets covering an oversize feather bed.

Moments later she was sound asleep. One of her last thoughts before going out like a light was to wonder why a man this obviously wealthy would waste two minutes on a wild-goose chase like a treasure hunt. And why was he involved in something he continually referred to as dangerous?

Her very last thought was the memory of Sam's kiss. Before her brain whirled into another feverish spin, she told herself firmly that it could not happen again.

MEG WOKE to the sound of squawking parrots and quarreling guinea hens. It took her a moment to recall where she was. The large spacious room and the hot sunshine pouring through the floor-to-ceiling windows were totally unfamiliar.

As if by magic the household staff seemed to know she was awake. Melda rapped at her door, then bustled inside carrying a tray that she placed across Meg's lap. Hot, buttery croissants steamed beneath a snowy napkin next to a pot of blackberry jam. Melda smiled at Meg's expression and poured frothy hot chocolate from a heavy silver carafe. She placed the thin china cup back on the tray in front of Meg. The aroma drifted upward, eliciting a sigh of anticipation.

"Señor Livingston extends his apologies that he is not here to welcome you properly," Melda said. She opened the draperies wider to emit a stream of dappled sunshine. "It was necessary for *señor* to attend to business in town. He says you should go for a ride—the stable is behind the house—or a swim. He says his house is your house and he prays you will be comfortable. He will return in time to drive you to the airport."

Meg smiled, wondering if Sam had really said all that. It seemed more likely that he had instructed Melda to simply tell her he would be gone most of the day.

Meg had slept late enough that not much morning remained, but she used it to explore the house and grounds. José took her on a tour of the stable and corral, but she declined his offer of a horseback ride through the fragrant hillsides. Inside the house, she wandered about admiring the many rooms and she inspected the titles in Sam's ubiquitous bookshelves. It appeared Sam was an eclectic reader; he read everything. She discovered volumes of history, biography, bestselling novels, travel accounts, and even collections of poetry. If Sam had a preference, it was probably for spy novels and science fiction, which made her smile.

After a light luncheon served on a shaded patio offering a magnificent view of the Pacific, Meg yawned, then decided to have a swim before she surrendered to a brief siesta during the heat of the afternoon. She changed into a neon pink, two-piece swimsuit, then walked to the pool area where she found towels laid out for her and a sweating pitcher of freshly squeezed lemonade waiting on a silver tray. Although she didn't see anyone, she called a grateful thank-you in the direction of the house.

The pool truly was a marvel. It perched on the very lip of a rocky drop-off, designed to appear as if suspended in space. Had it not been for the gentle rattle of palm fronds behind her and an inconspicuous railing, Meg could have believed she floated on the inflated chaise longue high above the waters of the Pacific. It was a stunning illusion.

Relaxing, she found it difficult to remember that twenty-four hours ago she had been in cold Colorado dodging ice patches and wiping snow from her shoulders and eyelashes. Now hot sun gleamed on her bare skin and ocean breezes plucked at her hair. The tropical heat sapped her energy.

Closing her eyes, Meg drifted lazily on the chaise longue, occasionally dribbling water across her chest and thighs. And she realized how badly she had needed a vacation. Even before Sam Livingston had whirled into her life, she had been so completely consumed by problems that she had forgotten places such as this existed. Places where time appeared to move slowly and problems lost their urgency.

Today, bathed in lazy sunlight and feeling relaxed for the first time in months, it didn't seem such a life-and-death matter that Mark Gerard had stolen her company away from her. Today, she could believe that she might survive the blow.

As for Mark himself, his marriage proposal had stunned her. And she had stunned him with her refusal. After that, things happened very fast. Too late, she had seen the wisdom of not mixing business and personal relationships; Mark had known exactly how to exact revenge, had known exactly what would hurt her most.

Well, that was behind her now. History. Now she had...Sam Livingston. Despite Sam's protests, he was an enormously interesting man, a man of intriguing contrasts. A big, dangerous-looking man who wanted to grow one of the most delicate flowers in the world. Meg smiled and shook her damp hair. A man chasing childlike dreams of treasure, who lived in luxury surrounded by people eager to please. A man whose beautiful blue eyes spoke truth while his wide sensuous lips spoke lies. A man who frightened her just a little, while at the same time he awakened long-dormant stirrings of desire.

Finally, like a treat saved for last, she let herself remember his kiss and permitted herself to wonder where it might lead.

Meg would never know where this line of speculation might have taken her. She heard an explosion of noise and her eyes blinked open and she jerked upright on the chaise.

Frightened screams erupted from the house behind her.

Before she could move or comprehend what she was hearing, half a dozen men appeared as if by sorcery and surrounded the pool. One minute there was nothing but silence and solitude, the ocean and the palms, the next minute armed men were pointing Uzis at her naked stomach.

They stood silent and menacing, staring at her through slitted eyes. The barrels of the Uzis looked like cannon mouths. Meg's glass of lemonade dropped from her boneless fingers and plunged toward the bottom of the pool; her mouth dried and tasted like dust. Her eyes widened on the Uzis until they ached.

"You will come with us."

A fat man with a missing front tooth and a scar jagging across his nose and cheek gestured with the barrel of his gun, ordering her out of the pool.

"Me?" Meg whispered through dry lips. Disbelief warred with heart-stopping fear. She couldn't believe this was happening. She stared hard at the Uzis and a deepening sense of unreality made her feel dizzy and light-headed. "There must be a mistake, I—"

It was like strolling through paradise then suddenly falling into a viper pit. Her mind struggled to make the abrupt transition, helped along by the ugly snub noses of the Uzis. They impressed her as deadly ludicrous against the backdrop of shining sun, glistening sea and feathery palms.

The fat man gestured sharply with his Uzi and snarled at her. His dark eyes were flat and expressionless.

"Now, *señorita.* You come *now!*"

The rough menace in his tone announced there would be no explanations, no negotiations, no further discussion. Shaking and suddenly chilled to the bone, afraid to look at the guns and afraid to look away from them, Meg hastily slipped from the chaise and waded toward the pool steps.

"What do you want with me?" she asked in a shaky voice, wetting her lips. The tiny pink bikini made her feel naked and agonizingly vulnerable.

One of the men laughed.

The blood drained from Meg's face and black dots of fear speckled her vision as the fat man gripped her arm and his fingers bruised into her skin.

Chapter Four

An illusion of unreality overwhelmed Meg and continued throughout the kidnapping. The Uzis and the men who aimed them were very real, very menacing, and exactly what one would associate with an abduction.

Nothing else was.

While Meg stood trembling and terrified at the edge of the pool, staring into a gunbarrel, one of the men entered the house and returned with a bathrobe and her luggage.

The fat man sporting the missing tooth waited until she donned the robe, then he relaxed somewhat and invited Meg to accompany him to the front of the house. As if she had a choice. She stumbled along beside him, acutely conscious of the Uzi pointed at her stomach.

A battered truck waited in front of the house, which wasn't surprising, but the long white limousine was. Several of the Uzi-waving men piled into the back of the truck while the fat man opened the limo door for Meg.

"Inside, *señorita.*"

"Who are you and where are you taking me?"

"You go inside. Now!" The Uzi gestured.

Meg slid into upholstered luxury and pulled the collar of her robe to her throat as cooled air enveloped her. Behind a glass partition, the driver turned to look at her and touched two fingers to the bill of his chauffeur's cap.

"There is a bar in the compartment in front of you, *señorita*," he said into a speaker. "If there is anything you wish which is not stocked in the bar, please inform me and I'll get it for you."

"I'd like some coffee," Meg blurted, staring at him, challenging him. She was chilled through and through, as if she had dropped into a glacial dream. The limo and the driver—the entire abduction—impressed her as absurdly bizarre.

"As you wish."

The limo swept away from Sam's rancho and turned toward Puntarenas. Meg's shock didn't thaw until the limo glided to a stop before a small outdoor café and the driver stepped outside. Then, quick as a flash, she slid to the far door and scrabbled for the handle.

The interior door handles had been removed.

She stared in disbelief, then pounded on the windows and shouted for help. But the windows were tinted; no one could see inside. She had no idea if the limo was sound-proofed, as well, but it seemed likely as none of the people sitting at the outside tables even glanced toward her cries.

When the driver returned, he lowered the glass parti-tion and handed her a cup of steaming coffee. While Meg was trying to decide whether to hurl the hot coffee in his face, the glass partition slid up again and the limo glided out of Puntarenas.

"He who hesitates is lost," Meg murmured with a sigh of regret and resignation. She sipped the coffee, taking its warmth inside. There was simply nothing in her back-ground or nature that permitted her to throw scalding coffee in someone's face. At the moment she considered this a character flaw.

Eventually she realized no one had covered her eyes. Although this impressed Meg as ominous for her future, she began paying attention to their route. Another minute passed before she conceded the futility of trying to memorize where they were heading. Nothing was familiar. All she could have said with any certainty was that the limo sped out of the city and into the mountains, eventually leaving the paved road for a series of graveled roads that wound through a dense cedar forest.

She gave up trying to memorize the twists and turns long before the limousine drew up in front of a sprawling villa perched on a rocky promontory overlooking the Pacific. When the driver helped Meg out of the limo, she had a moment to gasp at the beauty of the villa, the sea, the towering cedars. Then a man dressed in crisp butler's livery hurried across the villa's veranda and down curving steps. He all but bowed to Meg, ignoring her bare feet, bathrobe, and tangled wet hair.

"Welcome to Villa Estes, Señorita Wolff." A snap of his fingers brought two young men hurrying forward to collect her luggage. "You will come with me, *por favor.*"

"Are you the person responsible for my abduction?" Meg demanded. She had no idea where she found the courage to confront him, except this man was armed with nothing more dangerous than a carnation in his lapel.

"My name is Estoban, *señorita.* Should you require anything during your stay, it will be my pleasure to serve you." He waved a hand toward the interior of the house. "Permit me to show you to your suite." He consulted a gold watch. "Cocktails will be served on the west terrace in an hour." A quick glance flicked across her bathrobe. "I understand your luggage was assembled hastily. If suitable attire was damaged or left behind, you'll find a wardrobe has been provided for you."

"Estoban, I've been kidnapped. You know that, don't you? I'm here against my will. I demand that you release me at once."

Estoban gave her a pleasant smile, as if he spoke English but didn't comprehend when he heard it addressed to himself. He gave her a little bow and performed a flourish with his hand. "This way, *por favor.*"

Meg had no idea where she was except that Puntarenas was a long distance away. The villa was splendid in its isolation; there was no place to run except over a cliff. At the moment she had no choice but to do as Estoban asked. She sighed and wondered if all Costa Rican abductions were conducted in this manner. Uzis followed by cocktails in an hour? A wardrobe provided for the victim's pleasure?

Meg pressed her lips together, then nodded shortly and followed Estoban into a palatial dwelling fit for a Mediterranean prince.

By the time Estoban led her into a luxurious suite of rooms, a maid had arrived and was unpacking Meg's luggage, setting aside items in need of pressing. Meg studied her suitcases, contemplating the ripped lining.

"It appears you require new luggage, *señorita*," Estoban said blandly. He gestured to the maid. "Lena cannot speak, but she understands simply stated English..."

"Did your thugs do this?"

Estoban looked shocked. "*Señorita,* you are our guest!"

"You're suggesting my luggage was savaged before your people stole it? And then kidnapped me?"

That wasn't entirely impossible, she thought suddenly. Sam or one of Sam's people might have ripped the lining in her bags while searching for her half of the map. She didn't want to believe that.

Right now, she wanted to believe there was a way out of this. Despite Estoban's efforts to make Meg's arrival seem ordinary, it wasn't. Trying to look casual, she stepped onto the balcony, seeking an escape route. No such luck. She was in a third-floor suite and the balcony off her sitting room extended over a cliff. Meg peered down at a sheer dizzying drop before she stepped inside again, biting her lower lip.

"You have time for a bath and a brief siesta, *señorita*," Estoban suggested, moving toward the door. "I shall return for you in an hour."

After Estoban departed, Meg studied the maid, who avoided any eye contact, then she tried the door. It was locked. Resigned, she entered the bathroom. A fragrant tub had been filled for her, and thick, fluffy towels laid out. An expensive line of hair and cosmetic products were arranged on a marble countertop.

It was the damnedest kidnapping Meg had ever heard of.

ALTHOUGH THE DESIGNER ensembles in the cedar armoire put Meg's wardrobe to shame, she chose one of her own outfits for the cocktail hour on the terrace. The peculiar sense of unreality returned as she slipped into a blue silk pantsuit, wound her hair into a French twist, then spritzed on one of the expensive perfumes provided by her host.

"Pearl earrings, I think," she said aloud, stepping back from the mirror to examine her image. Her grandmother had always insisted that when in doubt, wear pearls. Pearls were proper for any occasion. Meg thought about choosing proper jewelry in which to meet her abductor and decided it was distinctly possible she was losing her mind.

Estoban arrived punctually on the hour and led her through a labyrinth of corridors and lavishly appointed rooms, finally bowing her onto a stone terrace that afforded a breathtaking view of the Pacific. There was no chance of escape here, either. Sheer cliffs soared upward on three sides. The drop from the terrace to the boulders below was a good forty feet.

"Would you prefer wine or champagne, *señorita?*"

"I would prefer to leave," Meg snapped. When Estoban did not acknowledge her reply, she said, "If I have to have one or the other, I'll take white wine, please."

A deep voice spoke behind her. "Forgive me for not being present to welcome you in person."

Meg turned to watch a tall, handsome man striding toward her with a smile. His hair was thick and dark, beautifully styled and wonderfully right for his smooth olive-toned skin. He was dressed entirely in crisply tailored white. White linen trousers and jacket, white tie and white shirt with diamond studs running down the front and glittering at his cuffs.

He took her hand and pressed her fingertips to his lips. "You are stunning, even more lovely than I was informed."

"You must be Martin Chango." Who else could he be? When he straightened from kissing her hand, she gazed into intense dark eyes fringed by thick black lashes. The scent of a lime-based cologne reached her nostrils and lingered on her fingertips. "You kidnapped me!"

"I profusely apologize for the circumstances of your arrival, but I'm delighted to have you as my guest. If there is anything we can do to make your stay more pleasurable, you have only to mention your wish to Estoban."

"I wish to leave at once!"

"Please call me Martin, and may I call you Meg?"

"You may call me a cab."

He laughed and accepted a glass of champagne from Estoban, who bowed and then withdrew. "Had I believed Livingston would permit a meeting between us, I would gladly have issued a more orthodox invitation. But I think we both know Livingston has a stake in keeping us apart." Touching her elbow, he directed her to the stone balustrade that ran the length of the terrace. "It's a breathtaking view, is it not? Familiarity diminishes none of the awe-inspiring qualities."

Meg ignored the view. "Mr. Chango—"

"Martin."

"Are you saying I'm under no restraint? That I'm free to leave if I wish?" Her stare challenged him.

"Certainly." A charming smile curved his lips. "I'll summon a driver this minute if you prefer. But I hope you'll consent to remain and enjoy my hospitality. I think we have much to discuss."

"We have nothing to discuss. Call your driver," Meg demanded. Fury darkened her eyes. "How dare you suggest that I'm your guest! I'm a prisoner! And I demand to be released at once!"

"My dear, an hour from now twenty people will arrive for a dinner arranged in your honor. One of my guests is a former government official, another is an internationally known author, one is a banker, another a sheik. Would a kidnapper parade his 'prisoner' before such a distinguished assembly?"

"You've arranged a dinner party in my honor?" This astonishing information stopped her cold. It didn't make sense. "That's crazy." The whole thing was nuts. Being kidnapped in a limo. Standing here sharing a civilized glass of wine with her abductor. The dinner in her honor. It was something out of Fellini. A puzzled frown shadowed

Meg's brow. "Would you mind telling me what the hell is going on?"

"If I may inquire, what did Livingston tell you about me?"

"That you are a ruthless, unscrupulous arms dealer wanted by several governments for selling weapons to the wrong people."

"Ah. But the wrong people according to whom? Intellectually, I have difficulty accepting the concept that one nation may decide which other nations are entitled to purchase defense. Therefore I chose to ignore politics. In my view, there are no wrong people, only customers." He placed his elbows on the balustrade and smiled at her. "Are you one of those who believe attorneys should represent only the innocent? Who believe that guns are more deadly than the people holding them?"

Meg drew back from his dazzling smile. Outrage warred with disbelief across her features. "What on earth makes you think I'm willing to stand here and politely converse with someone who *kidnapped* me?"

He laughed and patted her fingers. "I've explained that unfortunate circumstance. Perhaps I can calm you by showing you my weapons room. I'm quite proud of it. My collection is impressive if I do say so myself. I have an authentic Medieval suit of armor and a gold-hilted sword presented to Napoleon in 1797."

Meg shook her head. "I know very little about guns and I don't want to know more." She narrowed her eyes and met his gaze. "Mr. Chango—Martin—for the moment let's set aside how I got here and talk about why. Why am I here?"

"To reunite our great-great-grandfathers' maps, of course."

Meg's lips formed a circle of astonishment. She knew she must have looked thunderstruck. "I beg your pardon?"

He straightened and stared down at her. "You are Meg Mayfair Wolff, aren't you? Of course, you are. You have the Mayfair coloring and the Mayfair nose and chin." When she still looked uncomprehending, he said slowly, "Your great-great-grandfather was Joseph Mayfair. My great-great-grandfather was Walter Bates. They were part of the ship's crew who stole the Peruvian treasure under the pretext of saving the treasure from Bolívar's revolutionary forces. They drew a map of—"

Meg waved a limp hand. "I know all that. But I thought . . . Sam told me that *he* was Walter Bates's great-great-grandson."

"I should have guessed. Livingston is a liar," Chango said flatly. "Three years ago, I lost my half of the map to Livingston in a poker game. It was the single most ill-advised moment in an otherwise blameless life," he added with a thin smile that failed to reach his eyes. "I cannot tell you how often or how fervently I have regretted that evening. But I can assure you that Livingston is not now nor was he ever even remotely related to Walter Bates."

Meg stared at him, speechless.

Martin Chango tucked her hand around his arm and led her away from the terrace and eventually into his study. Animal heads crowded the paneled walls, everything from a massive buffalo head to the more delicate heads of gazelles and deer. Meg glanced away from them with a grimace of distaste and accepted a chair in front of Chango's ornately carved cherrywood desk. He spread an array of papers before her.

"This is my family genealogy. Notice this entry, recording the marriage of Elizabeth Bates to Anthony Chango in

1905. Here are family letters and portraits. I call your attention to this miniature in particular." He opened a locket and placed it on the desk top. "This is Joseph Mayfair, your great-great-grandfather."

Meg wouldn't have believed Martin Chango if he had said the sun set in the west. She had no idea if the portrait was of her great-great-grandfather. It could be anyone. All she could think about was Sam's lies. Had he told the truth about anything? Sudden tears glistened in her eyes, embarrassing her. Despite all evidence to the contrary, she had really wanted Sam to be one of the good guys. She had wanted to believe there was a reasonable explanation for his lies. But all he had done was spin a tissue of fabrication.

Chango studied her expression, then poured whiskey into a heavy crystal tumbler and pressed it into her hand. "This has shocked you." It wasn't a question.

After draining the glass of Scotch, Meg drew a breath and gazed up at him. "So. You want my half of the map."

The smile he gave her was intended to disarm any lingering doubts. "Restoring the map seems fated, does it not? Here you are and here I am, the Mayfair and Bates families reunited."

Meg lifted her hands and glanced at the room's luxurious appointments. "Why on earth would you be interested in a treasure that is probably nothing more than an inflated legend? You're a wealthy man."

Something behind his beautiful dark eyes turned flat and hard. "One hundred million dollars is a tempting proposition even to a man of means." When she didn't comment, he shrugged and refilled their glasses from a decanter on the drink cart.

"Arms are expensive, my dear. Often they are purchased through a credit arrangement. Unfortunately a country that is credit worthy today may be under a new government and broke tomorrow." A sigh lifted his shoulders. "By extending credit to several Latin American countries, perhaps unwisely, I find myself in a cash poor position at present."

"Surely you can collect the money owed to you."

He smiled another humorless smile. "As my customers wish to continue purchasing arms on credit, they assert certain pressures on the Costa Rican officials, which allows me to maintain residence here. Should I press for payment, these same customers might find it expedient to urge Costa Rica to deport me and thus avoid repayment altogether."

Meg tilted her head. "And those governments that decide who the wrong people are would then imprison you?"

He held her glance. "Something like that, yes."

"You need a hundred million dollars to pay your bills?"

He laughed and sat across from her. "Ordinarily, no. But I find myself in the awkward position of owing a great deal of money to my suppliers, a cartel of rather unpleasant men who are becoming increasingly impatient for payment. As you can judge from this brief explanation, my dilemma has assumed an edge of urgency. Therefore, our reunited map becomes of compelling and immediate interest. One might say critical, in fact."

"I see." And she did. Sort of. "Two thoughts come to mind. You appear to be pinning a lot of hope on a treasure that may not exist. And second, doesn't Sam have your half of the map?"

"The treasure definitely exists. There are in fact, three authenticated treasure troves proven to have been concealed on Cocos Island." Chango was as unshakably convinced of this as Sam. "As for Livingston, he has the original map, but naturally I made a copy." He regarded her for several moments, his gaze appreciative. "Now, my dear, I think we should discuss your half of the map."

Another moment elapsed before Meg responded. "Confusing events have happened very fast, Martin. As you said, your revelations are a shock." She met his gaze. "Frankly, I don't know what to believe." She waved a slim hand at the papers on his desk. "All of this could be faked and I wouldn't know the difference."

"Nothing is faked," he said evenly.

"The point is, it could be and I wouldn't know."

"I see. Perhaps you should consider Enrico Riale as you ponder who is telling the truth."

Meg's body twitched. "You know about Riale's murder?"

"Of course. I was notified immediately after the police established his identity."

Meg rubbed her temples. Her head was spinning. "Forgive me if I sound stupid. But why would the police notify you?"

"Because Riale was my employee. The instant I was informed of your whereabouts, I sent Riale to Denver to offer you a considerable sum for your half of the Bates/Mayfair map. Livingston killed him. Who else could it have been?"

"No," Meg whispered. "That isn't possible. At the time Riale was murdered, Sam and I were having dinner."

A hint of superiority underlay Chango's smile. "My dear, the time of death is a variable which can be manipulated. Riale's body was found in your kitchen, correct? And in your kitchen there is an oven, is that not also correct? If your oven had a timer, the timer could be set to operate the oven at high temperature until a few minutes before you were scheduled to return." His white linen shoulders moved in a shrug. "Such an alteration would affect the time-of-death estimate as that estimate depends to a large degree on the temperature of the body." He looked at her. "I submit that your oven door was ajar when Riale's body was found. Is this not so?"

"I don't know." Sam had found Enrico's body. And Sam could have closed the oven door, covering his tracks before Meg even knew a dead body was in her kitchen. She swallowed hard, then spoke in a whisper that was almost a plea. "Do you really believe Sam murdered Riale?"

He shrugged. "Livingston was there. He had opportunity and motive."

And Chango had explained how Sam might have adjusted the oven to provide himself an alibi for the time of death. "Martin, what motive would Sam have for killing Riale?"

"To obtain your half of the map before I did." He met her eyes. "By the way, did you reach an agreement with Livingston about your half of the map? Does he have it?"

"No."

"Excellent." The lines smoothed from his brow. "Livingston is as interested in the hundred million dollar treasure as I am. His loan on the greenhouses has been called. Unless Livingston finds an infusion of money rather quickly, he stands to lose the half a million he has already sunk into his project. I imagine Cocos Island exerts a rather urgent appeal...."

Meg felt sick inside. "Can you prove any of this, or is it just speculation?"

"Part is subject to immediate proof, my dear. Carlos Mendoza, president of the Banco de Blanca, is one of our dinner guests this evening. He is also responsible for calling in Livingston's bridge loan. Perhaps you would find it informative to have a chat with Carlos." Standing, he adjusted his tie, then smiled and offered Meg his arm. "Don't decide anything tonight, my dear, Meg. Tomorrow will be soon enough."

Meg blinked and swallowed. "Tomorrow?"

"I believe I mentioned there is some urgency attached to the matter. We'll want to proceed with our plans as swiftly as possible." He extended his arm. "Our dinner guests are waiting."

"I'M SORRY, SAM, but the decision wasn't mine to make. Two years of planning have gone into this operation, you know that. We're this close to the finish line. We can't afford a mistake."

Sam glanced at Howard Westin, then shoved his hands into the back pockets of his jeans and stared down the hillside at the frames of his greenhouses.

"I disagree. Meg deserves to know what she's gotten herself into the middle of. For God's sake, Howard, Enrico turned up dead in her kitchen! Now she's here in Costa Rica right under Chango's nose. Do you really think she'll settle for a 'trust me' and a pat on the back and then quietly go away?" He made a face. "You don't know the lady. She's smart and she's stubborn. She says she isn't adventurous, but she's adventuresome enough to show up here demanding answers. And she deserves them."

Howard rocked back on his heels and watched the construction crews swarming over the greenhouse site. "Sounds like you have a personal interest."

"Hell, yes, I do." Sam frowned and thought about that. He eased away from the memory of long shapely legs and cheekbones like porcelain. "I feel responsible for her. I got her into this mess. Call your people back and tell them she has to know everything. Put the blame on me. Tell them I'll withdraw unless we play fair with Meg Wolff."

"No way. As it happens, I agree with the decision not to involve Miss Wolff."

"Howard, she *is* involved. Up to her gorgeous eyebrows! And she isn't going to part with her half of the map until she gets the whole story!"

"We don't really need her map. All we need is for Chango to believe we have it. Actually, Miss Wolff appearing in Costa Rica works well for us. We'll put out the word that she hand delivered her map." Howard slid him a look. "Did she bring it, by the way? Did you look for it?"

Sam pressed his lips together and scuffed his boot across a smear of raw red dirt. "Parts of this business are really lousy, you know that? Yeah, I looked for it. And I didn't find it."

For a moment they stood in silence, watching a cement truck maneuver into position. When the project was completed, Sam would have three acres of greenhouses maintained by state-of-the-art equipment. It would be the culmination of several years of meticulous planning.

"You're putting Miss Wolff on the plane back to Denver tonight?"

"Yeah," Sam said without enthusiasm. He knew it was necessary to get her out of Costa Rica, but it would have been nice to show Meg the greenhouse project, to have her as his guest for a week or so and get to know her better. Maybe in the next lifetime.

"Good. Then you'll depart for Cocos Island on Thursday as planned. Everything's ready, isn't it?"

"*¡Señor!*" Manuel Cama leaned out of the construction shed and beckoned to Sam. "*Teléfono,*" he shouted.

"Excuse me a second." Sam left Howard standing on the hillside as he walked down to the shed. He thanked Manuel, then picked up the phone. An excited voice shouted in his ear. He listened, his face darkening, then he hung up and sprinted back up the hillside.

He gave Howard an icy scowl. "The rules just changed, Westin. An hour ago Meg was kidnapped out of my house at gunpoint."

"Chango." Howard pushed a hand through a shock of thick gray hair and swore steadily. "Okay. I'll call my people."

"You tell your *people* that if Meg gets so much as a broken fingernail out of this, I'll raise so much hell they'll still be talking about it a decade from now. And Howard, I'm going to tell her everything whether your people approve or not. No argument, that's how it's going to be."

Howard nodded, his expression grim. "I'll tell her myself. Everything just changed." He placed a hand on Sam's sleeve. "We've got some time, Sam. Chango isn't going to harm her. Not yet, anyway. Not until he gets her half of the map. If she plays it as cagey with Chango as she's done with you, she'll be safe. For a while."

THE MEN WERE charming and amusing; the women reminded Meg of bright blossoms bending and bowing and exuding expensive perfume. Everyone at the table but Meg wore designs fashioned in Paris or Milan. The conversation sparkled with an international flavor as intriguingly spiced as the silver platters flowing from Martin Chango's French kitchen.

Throughout the entrée and the salad, Meg cast continual glances toward Carlos Mendoza, a pink and balding man with a daunting dignity who didn't converse so much as pronounce. Each time Meg attempted to maneuver Mendoza into a discussion of finances in general and Sam Livingston's finances in particular, Mendoza's cool steady appraisal sent her questions veering in another direction.

It occurred to her that Mendoza was not the type of man to reveal a client's financial problems to a stranger. Which of course, Martin Chango knew.

Sitting back in disappointment, trying to think of another way to obtain proof of Sam's motives, Meg watched Estoban approach the head of the table and bend to murmur in Martin Chango's ear. They both looked at Meg as Chango appeared to hesitate. Then he nodded and Estoban moved around the table. He leaned to one side of Meg's high-backed chair.

"There is a telephone call for you, *señorita,*" Estoban said, speaking in a low voice.

Meg's gaze darted to Chango, who presided over his table like a feudal lord. He smiled and nodded. Frowning, irritated at how quickly she had fallen into the approval-seeking behavior exhibited by Chango's guests and staff, Meg placed her napkin to one side, rose and followed Estoban from the dining room.

She knew who the caller had to be even before she lifted the ivory-handled receiver. "What do you want?" she snapped.

"Thank God, you're all right! Meg, listen to me." Sam's voice boomed in her ear. "Just be cool a little longer. We'll get you out of there. Have you been mistreated in any way?"

Meg cupped her hand around the mouthpiece and whispered in a furious voice. "You lying weasel! Did you tell me the truth about *anything?*"

"Meg, I wish I could explain but—" he sounded helpless.

"I know—you can't. But I should trust you anyway, right? Well, forget it! How could you pretend to be Walter Bates's great-great-grandson? And tell me that we were practically cousins. That was really low, Sam, even for you."

Meg held her breath, annoyed to discover that even now she hoped he would stick to his story and insist that he was indeed Walter Bates's great-great-grandson, that he wasn't lying about that.

"Is anyone monitoring this phone call? Is someone standing right beside you?"

"Of course not. They're treating me like a guest!"

"A guest." A moment of silence lengthened before Sam sighed and said, "I thought you'd be more disposed to sell me your half of the map if you believed I was Walter Bates's great-great-grandson. I'm sorry, Meg. I'm sorry about this whole damned thing."

Meg covered her eyes and leaned against the wall. So Chango was telling the truth about everything; Sam was telling the truth about nothing. Was Chango also correct in his speculation about Enrico Riale's murder?

"Look, Meg, as long as you hang on to your half of the map, there's no reason to suppose Chango will harm you. I'll get you out of there, I promise."

"Forget it, Sam. I'm exactly where I want to be and I'm having a lovely time. I don't need to be rescued, and I sure as hell don't want to see you again!" Meg slammed down the receiver and glared at the phone, feeling a scald of betrayal.

For a brief time she had believed that something wonderful was beginning to happen between herself and Sam Livingston. She had sensed an underlying compatibility, a similarity of ambition and drive. Certainly the chemistry had ignited. During the drive to Puntarenas the air had almost shivered with repressed excitement. And his kiss had knocked her socks off. All of this went to prove how greatly a woman could delude herself when she really wanted to. Suddenly Meg felt like weeping.

"Is there a problem, my dear?" Martin Chango appeared at her side and placed a hand on her arm. He had a better manicure than Meg did, she noticed. "You look upset."

"Why do liars always believe they should be forgiven when they're found out?" The phone rang again and Estoban appeared. "If that is for me, Estoban, please inform the gentleman that I'm not accepting his calls. Not now, not ever."

"As you wish, *señorita.*"

It seemed that Estoban and Chango exchanged a brief smile, but Meg wasn't sure and she didn't care anyway. So much had happened recently that her mind was numb. She had a suspicion that she wasn't thinking clearly about anything.

Martin Chango gave her a long flirtatious glance and seemed disappointed when Meg frowned and looked away. "Shall we rejoin our guests, my dear? They're all enchanted by you. You've made a conquest of Sheik Ben Dulla, he's utterly besotted." Chango's dark eyes sparkled. "I can confidently predict the position of third wife is yours if you want it."

"No offense intended, but all I want to do is go home and forget I ever heard of any of you."

Chango wrapped her hand around his arm but hesitated before he escorted her to the west terrace for after-dinner drinks. "Please believe me when I say that I deeply regret having to abduct you. I hope you'll forgive me. As for Livingston, are you disappointed?" he asked curiously.

Meg ducked her shining head and bit her lip. For a while she had enjoyed a dozen exciting fantasies about Sam.

There was a certain rough charm about him. And God knew he was sexual dynamite. As furious as she was at him, the sound of his deep voice in her ear had sent a secret heat zinging through her system. It was hard to deny that Sam had an effect on her.

"I'm disappointed. And furious," she said finally. A lump formed in her throat and she swallowed with difficulty. "I was beginning to think of Sam as a friend."

"Enrico Riale felt the same way, once," Chango reminded her.

Chapter Five

Sam paced in front of his desk and shouted into the phone. "She thinks she's Chango's guest!"

"Everything is under control. We've got the Villa Estes under surveillance. Go to bed, Sam, nothing's going to happen tonight."

"I'm telling you, Howard—"

"We'll take care of her tomorrow, and I want you ready. When things start to happen, they'll happen fast. This means advancing our schedule. As of noon tomorrow, you need to be on your launch prepared to sail for Cocos Island at a moment's notice."

"Wait a minute! Are you saying...?"

"Look, I don't like it, either, but this is the only way. We've run half a dozen scenarios on this and believe me, Sam, this is the best of the lot."

Sam let a silence develop. He raked a hand through his hair and glared out his study window at moonlight dancing on the Pacific. "You'd better be right, Howard," he said threateningly.

After he hung up, too restless to do anything but pace, he made himself a drink and carried it out to the terrace. Regret pinched his expression.

Eventually, because there was nothing else he could do, he told himself that Meg was as much to blame for what was going to happen to her as anyone. After all, no one had invited her to Costa Rica. It had been her decision to tempt fate.

But still. He was sorry it had come to this.

MEG AWOKE to a glorious sunshiny morning. When Lena brought her breakfast tray, Meg carried it to the glass table on the balcony, enjoying hot croissants and a pot of café au lait while Lena ran her bath and laid out a freshly pressed cotton blouse and skirt.

From this vantage Meg could glimpse distant sails bobbing on the ocean beyond the cliffs. Gulls looped against the sky. For all she could see of it, Puntarenas might not have existed. This was fine with her. The rooftops of Puntarenas would have reminded her of Sam and she didn't want to think about him. Every time she did, a furious heat pulsed in her cheeks.

Of course, ordering herself not to think about Sam made it impossible to think of anything else. Meg had always believed she was too smart to be easily suckered. But Sam had given her one of those craggy lopsided smiles and she had believed whatever fell out of his well-shaped, lying lips. His wildly exciting, kissable lips. A blush of anger and embarrassment warmed her throat.

She made a sound of disgust, then stood abruptly and went inside to bathe. She needed to stop thinking about Sam Livingston and start thinking about how she was going to escape Martin Chango.

"GOOD MORNING," Martin Chango called. Dressed in white slacks and pullover, he descended a flight of stone steps and joined Meg beside the tennis court. An instant later, a servant appeared with iced fruit punch and a tray of small cakes.

"Perhaps you'd like a game later," Chango suggested, indicating the immaculately groomed court. "Did you find the pool and the stables?" Taking Meg's elbow, he led her to a courtside table shaded by a royal poinciana.

"You live very well for a man who's pleading poverty," Meg commented, raising an eyebrow.

Chango laughed, displaying a dazzling white smile. "One must maintain appearances." He let his dark eyes travel slowly from Meg's open collar to the halo of honey blond hair that framed her face. "I like your hair loose. Sunlight becomes you."

Meg forced her lips into a faint smile, but she didn't respond to his compliment. Behind Martin Chango's easy charm lay something cold and ruthless, sensed rather than fully seen. But it was there and strong enough that adrenaline pumped into her system at the sight of him.

"Are you ready to talk business?" Chango asked in a pleasant tone.

Meg nodded. She lowered her head and sipped her fruit punch. It wasn't difficult to guess what was coming, only the details were a mystery.

"I propose we combine our halves of the Bates/Mayfair map."

"I rather expected you would."

"I further propose that you sail my yacht to Cocos Island and head an expedition to locate and retrieve the Peruvian treasure."

Meg's head snapped up and she stared. "I beg your pardon? You want *me* to organize and lead a treasure-hunting expedition?"

Again the dazzling smile. "The yacht is equipped and ready to sail. All you need to do is supervise the search and digging operation."

"Martin, I'm the last person you should select to lead a treasure-hunting expedition." Meg leaned forward over the table. She hadn't seen this one coming. Even Sam had recognized that she wasn't suited for treasure hunting. She drew a breath and tried to sound persuasive. "First, I'm not convinced the treasure is there. Second, I'm not an adventurous type...traipsing through a jungle is definitely not my cup of tea. Third, there is no Denver ocean. I don't know anything about yachts or sailing. And finally...why don't *you* lead the expedition?"

He touched his collar and glanced away from her. "Cocos Island lies in excess of three hundred miles southwest of Costa Rica." After a pause he met her eyes. "It would be folly for me to venture outside Costa Rican territorial waters, my dear. I'm not in the habit of tempting fate."

"I see." But she didn't, not entirely.

"As half the treasure will be yours, I trust you to lead the expedition and protect our joint interests." A hard kernel of greed flickered in the dark depths of his eyes. "The treasure is still there, you may be sure of that," he added in a soft voice. "Waiting." He gazed deeply into Meg's eyes. "You do have your half of the map, do you not?"

"Merely because your people have been unable to find it, doesn't mean I don't have it."

Chango waved a slim manicured hand and a slight smile brushed his lips. "I apologize if my people have been clumsily obvious in their search," he said without a trace of embarrassment. "I can't help wondering if Livingston found the map when he slashed your luggage...."

So Chango had searched her belongings. But Sam was the one who had savaged her luggage. Another block of betrayal stacked atop the list building in Meg's mind.

She turned her face toward a drift of crimson hibiscus. "I have the map."

"Actually I never doubted it," Chango said in a casual tone intended to disarm. He snapped his fingers and a servant appeared out of nowhere to refill the punch pitcher. "You impress me as an intelligent woman. I doubt you would sail to Cocos without the complete map."

"I don't want to go to Cocos Island at all."

"Nonsense, my dear. All you have to do is interpret the united map and tell my men where to go and where to dig. Point to the spot, then stand back. My men will do the rest. Then you and the captain bring the treasure to Puntarenas, where I will be waiting to congratulate you."

It took a moment for Meg to grasp what he had said. She frowned. "The captain and I? What about the others? The men who do the actual digging and loading?"

Chango's voice was smooth as cream. "Don't concern yourself with them, my dear. Rather than risk a mutiny and the loss of the treasure, it seems prudent to leave the laborers behind. To be picked up a day or so after your departure. This is for your protection, of course."

Right. There was virtually no chance that the laborers who unearthed the treasure would ever leave Cocos Island.

"I need to think about this," Meg said, stalling.

A line appeared between Chango's dark eyebrows. "I don't wish to rush you, my dear, but my situation grows more urgent by the minute. If we're agreed, the expedition should depart no later than tomorrow. I fail to see what there is to think about."

"Do you truly believe I can stick together the two halves of our map, stroll into the jungle, point to a spot, and the treasure will actually be there?"

"I have no reason to think otherwise. No one else has enjoyed the advantage of possessing a genuinely authentic map drawn by two men who were present when the Peruvian treasure was concealed."

Another silence developed before Meg met his gaze. "Suppose I don't want to lead an expedition to Cocos Island? Do I have a choice, Martin?"

"Of course you do, my dear." She heard the hesitation before he answered. "But it wouldn't be prudent for me to lead the expedition, naturally I hope you'll agree to do it. There's no one else whom we can trust."

It was time to discover exactly where she stood.

"You've given me a lot to consider. If you don't mind, I'd like to drive into Puntarenas and do a little shopping." Meg gave him a dazzling smile of her own. "I think best when I'm shopping." Chango impressed her as the type of man who basically saw women as ornaments. He would believe such a silly statement. Still smiling, Meg waited to discover if he would agree to let her leave the villa, or if, despite his assurances to the contrary, she was his prisoner.

His frown deepened. When he finally replied, Chango spoke in a slow, measured tone. "As you wish, my dear." The pretense of warmth vanished from his eyes. "But when you return...I shall expect a firm answer. Do we understand each other?"

"I think we're beginning to," Meg replied, holding his gaze. It would be Chango's way or no way.

Twenty minutes later Chango handed her into the long white limousine that lacked interior door handles. He stood on the steps in front of the Villa Estes, watching until the limo curved into the cedar-lined drive leading away from the mansion.

Meg sat in the back seat, biting her lips and trying to decide what to do. She had a disorienting sense that life was spinning her upside down.

Lead a treasure-hunting expedition? It was insane. If she hadn't recalled the veiled threat in Chango's eyes, she would have laughed aloud at the idea. But it wasn't a laughing matter to Martin Chango. He genuinely expected a woman who knew nothing about the tropics or about treasure hunting to sail off into nowhere and return with a priceless treasure.

Meg nibbled her thumbnail and frowned out the tinted windows. Dark menace lurked beneath Martin Chango's facile charm. She doubted he responded well to failure. His own or others'. If she failed to return with the treasure, what would he do? Would he believe she had found it but had somehow stolen it from him? This scenario impressed her as a distinct possibility. He was so positive the treasure existed.

"What are you thinking about?" she muttered beneath her breath. There was no way Meg would ever agree to do as Chango asked. She had to find a way to escape.

"Stop here," she called to the driver, rapping on the glass partition.

The limo glided to a halt in front of a luxury boutique displaying swimwear in the street window. As Meg could not open the door herself, she waited for the driver to release her. As expected, Chango's driver followed her into the boutique, sticking close to her elbow. There was no chance at all that she could wander off on her own.

Meg bought a pair of sandals she didn't want, feeling more depressed by the minute. Obviously she had spoken too soon when she'd told Sam she didn't need to be rescued. While she wasn't exactly a prisoner, she certainly wasn't at liberty, either.

Silently she followed Chango's limo driver back to the car. Sam Livingston was a bold-faced liar, but Chango possessed an underlying menace that was frightening. There were no options with Martin Chango. He was accustomed to having things his way and Meg was no exception. Moreover, time was running out.

When she was three steps from the white limo, walking with her head down, trying to formulate an escape plan, several men dashed forward, springing out of nowhere. All of them carried guns. Two men grabbed the limo driver and slammed him against the hood of the limo, jabbing a gun barrel into his ribs. Two others snatched Meg.

It happened in less time than it would have taken to tell about it. Before she could open her mouth to scream, she had been thrust into the back seat of a dark sedan. With a squeal of tires, the sedan sped away, heading toward the docks.

When Meg caught her breath, shoved down her skirt, and pushed back the hair that had fallen over her face, she discovered she was seated beside a deeply tanned, prematurely gray-haired man who was studying her with unconcealed interest.

"Miss Wolff? I'm Howard Westin." He extended his hand.

Meg stared. Her heart banged against her ribcage and she was shaking all over. Her voice was high and stammering.

"You w-want to sh-shake my hand? I don't believe this! Hasn't anyone in Costa Rica ever heard of conventional introductions? Is kidnapping the standard way to meet people here?"

Westin's smile didn't warm his gaze. "I apologize if we frightened you."

"*If* you frightened me?" She rubbed at the goose bumps on her arms. "*Of course* I was frightened!"

"Unfortunately you've wandered into the middle of a complicated situation."

Meg's fingers shook like loose bones and her heart continued to pound. "Look, whatever's going on, I'm not part of it, I promise you. I don't know anything about anything. I'm an American and all I want to do is go home." Despite the fact that Howard Westin had abducted her off a public street, he didn't have a threatening demeanor. Westin reminded Meg of a benign accountant, someone who might listen to reason. "Look, you've made a mistake. Just let me out at the next corner, okay? I won't tell anyone about this."

"I'm sorry, Miss Wolff. I think you know I can't do that."

Her heart lurched. "You aren't going to hurt me, are you?"

"Hurt you?" He looked shocked. "Miss Wolff, this is a rescue, not an abduction. My men and I have been following you since you left Villa Estes, waiting for an opportunity. I'm a friend of Sam Livingston's."

She stared at him, then her face tightened into an expression of accusation. "You're one of Sam's men!"

"Not exactly." Westin held up a hand. "I'm going to explain everything." He met his driver's eyes in the rearview mirror. "Keep driving, no pattern. Stay near the water. Len and his men should be right behind us. Keep them in sight."

"So explain. And this better be good!"

"All right, Miss Wolff," he said, looking at her. "I'm with the United States Justice Department." He showed her a badge. "Justice has been trying to nail Martin Chango for more years than I care to remember. Chango is charged with illegal arms dealing, extortion, conspiracy to murder, and at least two dozen lesser counts."

"Murder?" Meg whispered.

"Murder," Westin repeated firmly. "The problem is, we can't touch Chango unless Costa Rica agrees to extradite him. Unfortunately, Costa Rica has powerful neighbors who are exerting pressure against extradition. Chango and the arms he sells are valuable to them. They don't want him in prison. For years we've been waiting for Chango to take a vacation or a business trip, to leave Costa Rica. He hasn't done it.

"About three years ago the department learned Chango is the great-great-grandson of Walter Bates and was in possession of half of the famous Bates/Mayfair map. We set up a poker game and made sure one of our people won that map."

Meg blinked. "Sam Livingston is a Justice agent?"

"An ex-agent. Sam agreed to reactivate on a one-time basis. He's local, he's known Chango for years, he and Chango belong to the same social club, and Chango doesn't know Sam was an agent." Westin didn't look happy about revealing this information. "When Sam won Chango's half of the map in the poker game, we had a different operation in mind, something that didn't pan out. When we recently learned of Chango's worsening financial squeeze, we saw how the Bates/Mayfair map might be used to draw Chango out."

"I can guess where this is leading."

Westin nodded and peered out the rear windshield of the sedan. "We put a trace on Joseph Mayfair's heirs, looking for the other half of the map. That's where you turned up.

"Chango needs cash. Millions of dollars of cash. If the Bates/Mayfair map was reunited, we figured Chango would convince himself the treasure exists because he needs it to exist and that with the reunited map it could be found."

Meg stared at him. "*You* put Chango on my trail?"

"We leaked the information that the Mayfair heir had been found, yes." Westin had the grace to look uncomfortable. "The only way this operation would succeed is if Chango knew the Mayfair half of the map had surfaced."

"When I've had time to think about all this," Meg said slowly, "I think I'm going to be damned furious at the United States Justice Department." She scowled. "Do you people really think the treasure exists?"

"All that matters is that Chango believes it exists and that he fears someone else is about to find it. To control the operation, we needed someone to sail to Cocos in a blaze of publicity. According to our analysis, Chango would follow—he wouldn't trust anyone else but himself. The minute he sailed into international waters, we'd pick him up."

"Sam was designated as the lure?"

"Exactly." Westin met her eyes. "Sam was instructed to buy your half of the map and make sure the sale generated a lot of publicity so Chango would learn Sam had the reunited map. Then everything else would fall into place. End of story."

Meg rubbed her temples. "Where did Enrico Riale fit into all this?"

"We're working on that. Our best guess at this point is that Chango's men murdered Riale and tossed your place looking for your half of the map." Westin shrugged. "From Chango's point of view, it's easier and more cost-effective to steal your map rather than buy it outright." He looked at her. "Did you give or sell it to him?"

"No." Meg shoved back her hair and glared at him. "Why should I believe any of this, Mr. Westin?"

"If we had time, I could show you a pile of documentation that's two feet tall." He gave her a rueful smile. "We didn't figure on you, Miss Wolff. Certainly, we didn't anticipate that you would turn up in Costa Rica. Moreover, it didn't occur to anyone that you would resist releasing your half of the map. At the time we put a green light to this operation you had a successful business, a busy, eventful life. There was no reason to suppose you'd have the time or the interest to pursue treasure hunting. And, of course, we didn't anticipate Riale's murder."

"I *don't* have any interest in treasure hunting, you're right about that." Meg dusted her hands together with a brisk movement, then leveled a bright, artificial smile in his direction. "Well. Thank you for explaining, Mr. Westin. Now if you'll have someone drive me to the airport, I'll get out of your hair and you can carry on."

He leaned forward and tapped the driver's shoulder. The driver nodded and turned the sedan toward the wharves.

"I'm afraid it's too late for that, Miss Wolff. At the risk of sounding like a bit of dialogue from a B movie, you know too much. For your own protection, I can't have you running around loose until this operation is over."

Meg stiffened. "That isn't fair. I know too much only because you told me!"

"Sam insisted that you be told the full truth. I'm telling you because he didn't think you'd believe him if he told you."

"That's for damned sure."

Meg groaned. Sam Livingston was an enormous thorn in her side. She'd had nothing but trouble since laying eyes on him. An anxious thought darted through her mind, wondering where all this would end.

"The only hope to salvage this operation is to proceed immediately. Regrettably, you are now part of it. If you and Sam depart for Cocos Island at once, Chango will believe the two of you have reunited the map and are only days away from finding the treasure. Chango will follow you and we'll pick him up the minute he crosses into international waters. This operation can still be a success."

Meg gasped and her eyes widened with horror. "You expect me to sail off to Cocos with Sam? Now?"

Westin gave her a smile that was intended to be reassuring. "You won't be in any danger, Miss Wolff. All you have to do is enjoy a nice sail, have a picnic on Chatham Beach, then turn around and sail back to Puntarenas. Four days from now, five at the most, you should be on a plane back to Denver. A little tanner, maybe, but otherwise no worse for wear."

Meg stared at him. "You're serious! Look, I don't want to do this. I want to go home!"

"I can't risk Chango getting hold of you again. He has to believe Sam has the reunited map. I'm sorry, Miss Wolff. You were lucky this time, but if Chango picked you up again ... well, let's just say it's much better to handle it this way."

The sedan braked to a halt as did the backup car. Four men jumped from the other car and immediately formed a block around Meg when she stepped from the cool interior into the heat of the sun. One of the men took her arm and escorted her toward an oversize launch idling at the dock.

Meg glared over her shoulder at Westin. "This is another kidnapping! You can't do this! I'll report you."

Howard stood beside the sedan and waved at her. "Have a nice voyage, Miss Wolff."

The men rushed her to the dock and up a gangplank. Sam stood waiting, gorgeously handsome in jeans and an open-collared blue shirt. "Hi," he said, smiling. "Welcome aboard."

Before Meg could tell him what she thought about being kidnapped yet again, another car sped along the wharf, braking to a halt in a spray of loose gravel. Two men jumped out, carrying Meg's luggage.

"How...?" she started to ask as they ran toward the *Lemon Tree* and tossed her luggage aboard. Her ruined bags were tied together with twine.

Sam's smile widened into an appealing grin. "Don't ask. But we couldn't leave your luggage at Chango's. That may be where you hid the map."

"By now everyone in Costa Rica should know there is no map in that luggage. Is there anyone who hasn't searched it?" Meg continued to stare at her luggage. "It's in shreds."

"We can't leave any loose ends. Chango has to believe we have your half of the map."

Meg stared hard at his darkly tanned face and twinkling blue eyes. It infuriated her that he looked so heart-stoppingly handsome, so damned confident and sure of himself. Stepping forward, she drew back her hand and slapped him across the cheek as hard as she could.

"That's for lying to me!"

Sam raised a hand to his cheek and blinked. "Didn't Howard explain? Meg, I didn't have a choice. This is a confidential government operation."

She slapped his other cheek, furious. "And that's for everything else!"

"What else?"

"The aggravation. Getting kidnapped—twice! At gunpoint, for God's sake. For scaring me half to death. For destroying my luggage and my peace of mind. For bringing me aboard this launch against my will. For not letting me go home. For everything!"

"Wait a minute. It was *your* decision to come to Costa Rica. Nobody forced you. I wanted you to stay in Denver, remember? I didn't want you involved in any of this!"

Howard Westin honked the horn of the sedan, glared, and made a shooing motion with his hands. Sam scowled down at Meg, then turned on his heel and entered the wheelhouse. At once the engine accelerated from a low idle to a steady rumble and the launch eased out of her slip.

Meg approached the railing and gripped it, swearing under her breath as Westin and his men slid into the distance and a fuller view of the shoreline appeared.

There was no escape. Like it or not, she was on her way to Cocos Island. If she understood the plan, very soon Martin Chango would be chasing them. And after him, the United States Justice Department. Not for one minute did Meg believe Howard Westin's assurances that this operation was going to be a picnic.

She bit her lip and glanced toward the wheelhouse where Sam was talking to a thirtyish Costa Rican. She had a feeling she was about to find out just how right she was.

Chapter Six

The first order of business was to change clothes. Skirts and sea breezes didn't go together. Holding down her skirt, Meg eyed her luggage with a frown, trying to recall if she had packed anything casual that might be suitable for an unplanned cruise.

She hauled the roped-together luggage down a flight of steps to the cabin below and cut the twine with a knife she found next to a small sink. When the Justice agents stole her luggage from the Villa Estes, they had been too rushed to be discriminating. The designer gowns Chango had provided for her sprang from her suitcases when the twine popped away. Meg tossed them aside with a sigh. They were about as useful as a parka.

The only halfway-suitable items were a pair of badly wrinkled linen slacks and a couple of silk blouses. Luckily she still had the sandals she had purchased an hour or so ago or she would have been trying to balance on deck in a pair of high-heeled pumps.

Meg removed her skirt and blouse and was standing in a blue bra and panties when she heard a discreet cough behind her and spun to see Sam filling the cabin doorway.

"Go ahead," he said, grinning. "Don't mind me."

Meg clutched the silk blouse against her body, acutely aware that the scrap of material covered the vital spots, but left her shoulders and long legs bare. Essentially she was naked. One look at Sam's steady appreciative gaze told her the same thought had crossed his mind.

"How long have you been standing there?" she demanded hotly. The overheated air in the small cabin quivered with the tension of anger and their joint sexual awareness.

"Long enough to see that I was right about you. You're as pale as a new moon. There's a tube of sunscreen in the compartment beside the bed. Use it." When he walked past her, trying to be casual, it seemed to Meg that tiny fingers of lightning flashed from her naked skin to his large body. Despite everything, she thought with a sigh of despair, the chemistry was still there. She bit her lip, and gripped the silk against her body as Sam leaned into a small fridge behind the sink.

"Beer?" he asked. His jeans pulled tight, defining heavy thighs and well-shaped buttocks.

Meg stepped backward and snapped a reply. "No thank you!"

Suddenly she was aware of how small and confining the cabin was, and how Sam's presence made the humid air seem hotter. Her mouth went dry as she looked at the bits of ice sliding down the beer bottle he extended toward her.

Sam shrugged. "Suit yourself." After removing the bottle cap, he drank thirstily, then thumbed his hat back and rolled the cold beer bottle across his forehead. Desire smoldered in the slow gaze that swept her nearly naked body. "You want me to turn around?"

His look made Meg's knees suddenly go weak. She had to remind herself that she was furious at him. "I want you to leave!"

"We need to talk," he said. He turned his back to her, standing wide-legged, facing the bulkhead. "Get dressed."

Keeping a wary eye on him, Meg hastily stepped into the linen slacks then shoved her arms into the silk blouse. Watching him every minute, she buttoned her blouse and tucked it in, then smoothed back her hair.

"Okay. You can turn around." Pride wouldn't let her change her mind about the cold beer. "Say what you have to say."

"It will be cooler on deck. We'll get the breeze."

She also wouldn't feel so trapped and overpowered by his large body and sexy eyes. Jumping on his suggestion, and noticing that she was already perspiring, Meg silently followed him topside. Sam was right; it was a little cooler on deck. The shore was still visible but swiftly slipping away. Soon they would be surrounded only by water.

"You do know how to navigate this boat, don't you?" Meg asked uneasily.

Sam leaned against the railing, holding the beer loosely in one hand. Meg hadn't seen him this relaxed since she had met him. "I practically grew up on the sea, and so did Julian." He nodded toward the man in the wheelhouse. "Don't worry. There's no bad weather expected, it's an easy ride. How are you doing? Any queasiness?"

Meg's stomach was a little uneasy, but she would have swallowed nails before she admitted it to him. "How long will the trip take?"

"We should arrive about midafternoon tomorrow."

"Tomorrow," Meg repeated, unhappily watching the shoreline recede. She refused to think about Sam seeing her almost naked. "Why do we have to go to Cocos Island? Why can't we just sail to some little town down the coast and hide out in a hotel for a day or so? What difference would it make?"

"Maybe none." Sam took a pull from the beer bottle and shrugged. "But that's not the plan. Look, Meg, don't underestimate Martin Chango. He has informants everywhere. If we went to your little town, it's possible Chango would know about it before you checked into a hotel. If there was a hotel. Then a once-only opportunity and a lot of planning would go down the drain." He studied her hair rippling in the sea breeze like a pale ribbon. "Why are you so resistant to go to Cocos Island?"

"I'll tell you why," she said, turning to face him with blazing dark eyes. "Cocos Island has been a curse on the Mayfair family! A destructive obsession! My great-great-grandfather drove himself crazy trying—and failing—to get back to Cocos Island. He died a raving lunatic, babbling about treasure. My great-grandfather inherited the quest. He made it to Cocos all right, but he didn't find the treasure. He found a tropical fever that eventually killed him. My grandfather, when it was his turn, went to Cocos, too. A shark attacked him in Chatham Bay. He died a few feet from shore while my grandmother watched."

"I'm sorry. I didn't know any of this."

"Then there's my father. He spent most of his life raising money for Cocos Island expeditions. You can imagine how that made my mother feel. She wanted roots, a home and a normal life, but my father wanted adventure and treasure. It was a family tradition. He sank every dime he could get his hands on into funding one treasure hunt after another, sure that he would find millions this time. My parents were arguing about his latest plan when their car crashed. The accident killed both of them and put me in a hospital for six months." Meg stared into Sam's clear blue eyes. "Does *that* explain why I have no interest in seeing Cocos Island or even hearing about it?"

"Look—"

"No, Sam, *you* look. The obsession with Cocos Island destroyed four generations of my family. I had a lot of time to think while I was lying in that hospital. And I swore that I would be the Mayfair who beat the curse. And I did. I used Cocos Island and its legends as the basis for Treasure Trove. My game sold like hotcakes and I made a bundle of money. I'm the only Mayfair who profited a dime from Cocos Island." She planted her fists on her hips and leaned close enough that she caught a whiff of his after-shave. "I'm through with treasure hunting. Do you understand? I'd rather be anywhere in the world except here, on my way to that cursed island!"

Turning, Sam leaned his elbows on the railing and looked toward the horizon.

"As you know, I'm not part of the Bates family."

"Right. You lied . . . cousin."

He ignored the comment. "But I grew up with tales of the Cocos Island treasures just as you did. Most of the expeditions depart from Puntarenas. As a boy, I'd ride my horse down to the docks and watch them depart. I'd dream that someday I'd have my own expedition and I'd be the one who found the Peruvian treasure."

Meg made a face. "Come on. We're beyond this kind of nonsense, aren't we? This operation has to do with catching Chango, not finding treasure." She stared up at him. "Or does it? Are you still lying to me?"

"Howard told you the truth."

She frowned, trying to think it through. "Why should I accept the word of a liar that someone else is telling the truth? Maybe that was a fake badge." Her mind went into a slow spin.

"Look, Meg, I'm sorry I had to lie to you." Sam's deep stare held her eyes. "If it had been up to me, I'd have been square with you from the start. But it wasn't my decision to make. Are you going to let some unavoidable lies form a wedge between us?''

"Enrico Riale." The two words blurted from her lips. "You and Westin claim Chango's men killed Riale, Chango says *you* did." Staring at him all the while, she related Chango's theory about the oven and the temperature and the time of death.

Sam swore. "That's sheer bull! The oven door was not open when I found Enrico. It wasn't even on."

"That's what I'd expect you to say. Since you found the body initially, I only have your word for it."

Sam thought a moment. "There's a problem with Chango's theory," he said finally.

"Oh?" She couldn't help it. Her tone was sarcastic.

"Think about it. What happens to dead bodies in the tropics? Heat accelerates the decomposition process, it doesn't retard it."

Meg frowned. When Chango laid out his theory, it had made sense to her. But Sam's rebuttal made sense, too. She rubbed a hand across her forehead and sighed. "I don't know what to believe," she said finally. She closed her eyes. "I wish I were back in Denver, putting my life in order. I wish I'd never heard of Cocos Island. Or of Sam Livingston."

"That's the part I regret most of all," Sam said quietly.

When Meg opened her eyes, he was striding away from her toward the wheelhouse.

TO MEG'S SURPRISE, Sam was a terrific cook. For dinner, he served shrimp Newburg, green beans au gratin, a salad, and fresh strawberries. Confident of Julian's ability at the wheel, Sam refilled Meg's wineglass and his own, then settled back in a deck chair to watch the sun burst into layers of brilliant color as it slowly sank beneath a calm sea.

"Not talking?" he asked eventually. "You're giving me the silent treatment?"

Meg had tied her hair back with a piece of the twine that had bound her ruined luggage. The evening breeze tugged a few tendrils loose and they fluttered around her face. She kept waiting for Sam to make some snide comment about her sun-pink cheeks, but he didn't.

"What is there to say?" she asked, not looking at him.

He was silent a moment. "You could tell me what you plan to do with your life now that Wolff Games is gone."

Although it wasn't as blistering hot as it had been earlier, enough heat lingered to cause Meg's silk blouse to stick to her ribs and upper arms. Tomorrow she would have to swallow her pride and ask Sam if she could borrow one of his cotton shirts.

"I don't know," she said finally, sipping her wine. "I enjoy development and marketing. Maybe I'll start another company. Maybe I'll take a long vacation. Write a book. Plant a garden. I haven't thought that far ahead."

"If you decide on development and marketing, let me know. I could use some advice about marketing orchids."

She tilted her head, watching the sunset colors play over his craggy features. "Chango said you'd lost your bridge loan. Is that true?"

"No." He smiled. "What else did Chango tell you about me?"

Meg pushed a blond tendril off her cheek and sighed, the movement stressing the silk over her breasts. "The problem with liars is you never know when they might be telling the truth."

"I thought we put all that behind us. There will be no more lies, Meg. You can trust what I say."

"Right." They watched the sunset for several minutes. "You didn't tell me you used to be a Justice agent."

"I used to be a Justice agent."

"That's it? That's all you're going to say?"

"I'm not at liberty to discuss that part of my life except to say it's behind me." He gazed into his wineglass. "A few years ago I was in a hospital, too. A gunshot wound." Unconsciously he touched his shoulder. "I had some time to think about what I really wanted. The answer surprised me."

Meg lifted an eyebrow. "What do you want?"

"The same things your mother wanted. Roots. A home and a family. I'm not saying those items are off limits to government agents, but life isn't easy for an agent's family. Right now Howard's wife doesn't know where he is or how long he'll be gone. I don't want that kind of uncertainty for my family. When I get one."

"You continually surprise me."

"Why? Because I want the same things most people do?"

Her laugh was light and genuine. "You aren't like most people. You aren't like anyone I know. Most people don't involve themselves in James Bond-type adventures. Most people don't grow orchids. Most people don't kidnap other people or turn their lives upside down."

Most men didn't look like a bronzed statue or had eyes that silently spoke of passion and exotic pleasures. Most men didn't speak in a deep voice that sent thrills of pleasure down a woman's spine. But Meg didn't mention these distinctions.

Sam smiled. "This operation is a one-time shot. A favor to a friend. After all, I don't have a family yet, so what the hell. Besides, it's the right thing to do."

Meg tilted her head and studied his face. "Plus, you're enjoying yourself. Admit it. You like this swash and buckle stuff."

Sam's laughter rumbled up from his chest, a deep comfortable sound. "Maybe. Growing coffee and orchids isn't the most exciting profession a man could choose."

"Sam . . . are we as safe as Howard Westin promised?"

"Absolutely." He hesitated. "Unless something goes wrong."

Alarm widened her dark eyes. "What can go wrong?"

"I'm sure nothing will."

Sam's smile curved toward a frown. He didn't seem able to avoid lying to this woman. But he'd been with the department too long not to know that few operations unfolded smoothly. There was always a glitch. Always. He could hope the Chango operation would be the exception. Because if a single hair on Meg Wolff's head was harmed, he'd have Howard's scalp. She'd been through too much already.

"It's going to be a long day tomorrow, we might as well turn in early. You take the bed in the cabin. Julian and I will sleep on deck."

They stood at the same moment and Sam caught the clean scent of Meg's hair, felt the radiant warmth of her body. The memory of her standing in her bra and panties flashed into his mind. Blue strips across creamy-silken skin. A long, shapely expanse of leg. The curve of her waist.

Surprised at standing so close together, neither of them moved. Enough light fell from the wheelhouse door that Sam could see her parted lips and the movement of her breasts at a quick intake of breath.

She must have guessed he was thinking about kissing her because she placed a light, restraining hand on his chest.

"Please don't," she whispered. "In a lot of ways, you scare me more than Chango."

He traced his fingertips along her cheek, feeling the lingering heat of the day, feeling the porcelain smoothness. "I don't want to scare you."

"I can't get a fix on you, Sam. You're like a chameleon, one thing one moment, something else the next moment. I trusted Mark Gerard to be what he said he was . . . and he stole my company. I won't make the same mistake again." She drew a breath. "Maybe you're on the level now, but maybe you aren't. So let's keep our association impersonal, okay?"

He thought he heard regret in her tone, but he dropped his hand away from her cheek. However, neither of them stepped back. They continued to stand close enough that he imagined he could feel her breath on his skin, felt the tug of her body like a magnet.

"What do I have to do to prove myself to you, Meg?"

"I don't know," she said in a low voice.

"Can we start over?"

Biting her lip, she glanced toward the light from the wheelhouse door. "I'm sorry, Sam. I wish we could, but . . . I could never trust you."

Turning, she walked away from him, descending the steps to the cabin. She didn't look back.

COCOS ISLAND rose from the sea like a glistening green jewel. Meg pushed up the sleeves of the cotton shirt she had borrowed from Sam, then shaded her eyes and watched as the *Lemon Tree* set a course for Chatham Bay, one of two deep bays on the north side of the island.

The island was much smaller than Meg had imagined, perhaps three miles wide by four miles long. No wonder it had gone undiscovered for so long. During the afternoon rains, a ship could pass within a mile of Cocos and never notice its existence. She cast a glance of grudging admiration toward the wheelhouse. Being a landlubber, it impressed her as just short of miraculous that Sam and Julian had managed to find this tiny speck.

Another surprise was the terrain, the steep mountainous peaks and ramparts of unscalable rock. The soaring conical island appeared to rise vertically out of the sea. Meg doubted there were three square feet of level land anywhere on the whole island.

"Surprised?" Sam asked, appearing beside her. He leaned his elbows on the railing and drew on a cigar.

"I pictured gentle slopes, not steep mountains." There were thousands of clefts and crevasses, folds and cutbacks. Meg began to understand how hundreds of expeditions had failed to find anything on Cocos. Not only was the terrain brutal, it was covered with a dense, impenetrable jungle foliage.

"Have you been here before?" she asked after Sam and Julian brought the *Lemon Tree* into the mouth of Chatham Bay.

"Once. Years ago. Some treasure seekers ran into trouble and needed rescue. It's a formidable place, isn't it?"

Meg steeled herself, waiting for Sam to explain that Cocos was named for the multitude of coconut palms on the island, that pirates had put in here regularly to hunt wild boar and take on fresh water. That a Costa Rican penitentiary had been situated on Cocos in the late 1800s. That the island was volcanic in origin, had seven rivers, and a grand waterfall that dropped six hundred feet along with many other smaller waterfalls. She waited, scowling, prepared to jump on him for patronizing her.

He leaned against the railing, smoked his cigar and said nothing.

When he sensed her watching him, Sam gave her a wink. "Considering the research you've done, I imagine there are things you could tell me about Cocos Island."

Meg released a breath. "Men like you drive women crazy," she muttered. He didn't do anything she expected him to.

"What?"

"Never mind. Are we dropping anchor?" Meg knew neither of the island's two harbors were hospitable to anything larger than a rowboat, but she had supposed they could take the launch closer than a mile.

"We're three-quarters of a mile offshore," Sam said. "High tide was about two o'clock." He consulted his watch. "It's four o'clock now. All you can see of the rocks and boulders littering the bay are a few tips. If we took the launch in closer we'd risk tearing out the bottom."

Meg accepted the binoculars he extended and scanned the shore.

Her first impression was one of almost desolate isolation. If anything moved on the beach or in the dense foliage, Meg didn't see it. The island appeared deserted and steaming in the heat, timeless.

Chatham Bay was nearly a mile wide from tip to tip. There was a stretch of level ground in the center, but trees and foliage grew down to the high watermark everywhere else. The beach, growing larger as the tide slowly receded, was empty and deserted except for the emerging stones and boulders, some of them huge.

Perhaps it was the scorching heat that smothered her like a hot blanket when the launch stopped moving, or perhaps it was the lonely cry of sea gulls, but Meg felt an oppressiveness settle over her spirits. Spotting a shark's fin near the shore didn't help. She thought of her grandfather and the awful way he had died.

Silently she returned the binoculars to Sam.

"Not a very welcoming place, is it?" he asked. Starting at one tip of the bay, he slowly and carefully scanned the shore.

"Are you looking for something in particular?" Meg asked, curious.

"I don't spot any sign of Howard's men."

Meg thought about his comment. "Why would Howard's men be here?" she asked finally. "Aren't they laying in wait to nab Chango when he sails into international waters?"

"That's a large section of ocean to cover. The backup plan is to have people here in case they miss Chango on the water. But I don't see anyone." He finished his surveillance. "Of course, I'm not supposed to see anyone." But he looked uneasy. "Maybe they put in at Wafer Bay."

"Or maybe they aren't here yet," Meg suggested, peering at the shoreline.

"That's what's worrying me. They should be."

"What do we do next?"

Sam smiled down at her and suddenly Meg was conscious of how ridiculous she must look. She wore one of Julian's baseball caps to shade her forehead and nose, which was coated with zinc oxide. The shirt she had borrowed from Sam was so large the cuffs would have hung below her fingertips if she hadn't rolled up the sleeves. Under that she wore the white linen slacks that were now a crumpled mass of wrinkles. To top things off, the Justice agents hadn't packed her makeup or toiletries. Meg didn't need the amusement dancing in Sam's blue eyes to know she looked a far cry from the cool sophisticated image she usually projected.

"Would you like to go exploring?" Sam asked.

"Stop looking at me like that! I know I look awful."
Her chin jutted and her dark eyes narrowed, daring him to
laugh aloud. Even though she suspected makeup would
have melted in the heat, and even though she didn't give a
damn what Sam Livingston thought, Meg would have
given everything she owned to put her hands on a tube of
lipstick and a mascara wand.

His grin widened. "You look great. About twelve years
old."

"Once a liar, always a liar."

"So, how about it? The tide's still high enough that we
could take a rowboat in."

Meg crossed her arms over her chest and scowled at the
shoreline. As soon as she understood she was on her way
to Cocos Island like it or not, she had made up her mind
that she would remain on the launch and not step foot on
shore. There was too much family tragedy associated with
this place. It had a forbidding reputation and ambience.
She didn't believe in mythical treasures. She wasn't interested, period.

But now that she was actually here...

Curiosity began as a tiny kernel and swelled into a sudden raging desire to explore the site that had obsessed and
eventually consumed the Mayfair family.

She studied Sam from beneath the bill of her baseball
cap. "We row in, have a look around, then row back.
Right? We don't hang around. No stupid treasure hunting."

"Whatever you want."

"Okay." But he headed for the wheelhouse instead of
lowering the rowboat. "What are you doing?" She could
see he was putting together a collection of supplies. Water
canteens, a collapsible shovel, a can of insect repellent, and
what looked like a tent.

"Be Prepared, the guiding principle of the Boy Scouts of America and the United States Justice Department."

When Meg saw him strap on a shoulder harness, her gaze dropped to the gun gleaming in the holster and her heart lurched and banged against her ribcage.

There was not a soul on the deserted beach. The ocean was empty. As far as Meg knew, she, Sam and Julian were the only people within three hundred miles. A person could scream her head off and not a soul would hear.

It didn't require any particular genius to figure out that Sam didn't need a gun for a brief sight-seeing tour. Nor was it any mental leap to realize that at this point Meg Mayfair Wolff had become expendable. The Justice Department, if any of that was true, and Sam, no longer needed her.

Damn it! Her attraction for Sam had occupied her mind and lulled her into forgetting how dangerous he was. She had been a monumental fool. Once again she had fallen for Sam's lies.

Gripping the rail, Meg turned wild eyes toward the beach. Legend insisted there were at least a dozen bodies buried on Cocos Island. Was she about to become Cocos Island's next secret?

Sam looked up from placing the supplies in the rowboat and frowned at her. "What's the matter with you? You're as white as that stuff on your nose."

Meg couldn't take her eyes off the butt of his gun. The dull metallic color seemed to absorb the relentless sunlight. Waves of heat pounded her head and made her feel dizzy.

"Why do you need a gun? Who do you plan to shoot?" she whispered.

Suddenly she believed she knew who had murdered Enrico Riale.

Chapter Seven

Meg stumbled backward across the deck of the launch as Sam moved toward her. Wildly, she looked around for something she could use as a weapon.

Sam halted and stared at her. "Oh, for God's sake." He shoved back the brim of his Panama hat, put his fists on his hips and scowled. His eyes narrowed to blue slits. "Right now I'd like to strangle you for being such an idiot."

"If you lay a hand on me, I'll . . ."

He bellowed at her, "This gun is for protection in case a wild boar charges us! They're all over the damned island. What . . . did you think I was going to shoot *you*?" He glared at her, then burst into a steady stream of swearing. "You did think that, didn't you? Damn it, Meg. How can I convince you that I'm one of the good guys?"

Meg swallowed hard. She couldn't take her eyes off the gun. After wetting her lips, she spread her hands. "You have a gun. You packed a shovel in the rowboat. . . ."

"So automatically that means I intend to shoot you and bury you on the beach?" He made a sound of disgust. "Women! And this is one of the brighter ones!" he said to Julian, who leaned from the wheelhouse, grinning. "Well, to hell with you, Miss Wolff." Spinning on his heel, his face thunderous, Sam strode to the rowboat and began lowering it toward the water. "Stay here if you fear you're going to end up as crab food if you go ashore with me. I don't give a damn what you do!"

Instantly Meg felt like an idiot. She smoothed her hands over her fluttering shirttail. She tugged on the bill of the baseball cap and cast Julian an imploring look.

"Okay," she finally admitted. "Maybe I jumped to conclusions."

"Listen, you've had a mad-on ever since I met you!" Sam turned to her with a hard expression. "Well, I'm getting mad, too. I've said I was sorry for misleading you, I've apologized, I asked Howard to explain everything. I don't know what more I can do. I tried to protect your place in Denver. I organized your rescue from Chango. What's it going to take to get it through your thick skull that you can trust me?"

Her chin jutted. "Maybe trusting you isn't a good idea. I haven't been too lucky trusting men."

"I'm not Charles Wolff, and I'm not Mark Gerard. Don't blame me because a long-ago marriage failed or because Gerard screwed you out of your company. If you want to talk about grievances, I've got a couple myself. How about you setting me up with that phony map? How about you believing a sleazebucket like Martin Chango instead of me?"

He disappeared over the side of the launch, climbing down a rope ladder to the rowboat.

Meg hesitated, made fists with both her hands, then drew a long breath and followed him over the side and dropped into the rowboat.

"I figured you'd steal my map and you did. That's why I set you up with a phony. As for Chango, I didn't believe him until *you* confirmed he was telling the truth about who he was. *You're* the admitted liar!'' She sat in the prow of the rowboat, glaring at him.

"I had no choice." He frowned at her, flexed his shoulders, then took up the oars and dug them into the water. The rowboat shot forward. "You don't see me holding it against you," he said, applying himself to the oars. "I'm not blaming you for doing what you felt you had to do. I'm willing to accept the circumstances and start over."

"So what are you saying? That you're a better, more noble person than I am?"

"If the shoe fits . . ."

Meg narrowed her eyes and ground her teeth together. "Like hell! And I am *not* blaming you for Mark Gerard's faults! You have plenty of your own faults!"

Without taking his eyes off her face, Sam let go of the oars, withdrew his pistol and fired at the water. "I don't mind accepting responsibility for my faults, but I'll be damned if I'll be blamed for the faults of every man you knew before me." He shoved the pistol back into the holster, then noticed her horrified expression. "Damn it, I wasn't trying to scare you," he muttered, picking up the oars. "It was a shark."

"Where?" Gripping the edges of the boat, Meg whipped her head around. "Did you kill it?"

Sam rolled his eyes. "No, I didn't kill it. But I hope I discouraged it from investigating us too closely."

Meg didn't speak again until the bottom of the rowboat scraped the hard sand of the beach. Silently she cursed herself for getting involved with Sam Livingston, for deciding to fly to Costa Rica, and for agreeing to jump in the rowboat for a closer look at Cocos Island. It was an awful place.

First, there were an alarming number of sharks close in. Second, the heavy heat was damp, scorching, and relentless. Already she was drenched in perspiration. Third, the instant she stepped out of the rowboat, a swarm of insects surrounded her, attacking her throat and ankles. The terrain was rocky, mostly vertical and inhospitable.

Sam pulled the rowboat up the sand and out of the water, then handed her a can of insect repellent. After waiting to see that she used it, he set off toward an old, dry streambed and began assembling the tent in a sheltered spot between two boulders the size of small cottages.

"Why do we need a tent? I thought you agreed we would have a quick look around then return to the launch."

"I plan to spend tomorrow exploring." He glanced up from driving a peg into the yellow clay and gave her a distracted smile. "You can stay on the launch if you want to, but since I'm here, I intend to explore the place. The tent will offer some shade."

Meg watched for a moment, wondering how he could bear to work in the energy-draining heat. Sweat plastered his shirt to his back. Damp spots appeared at his waist and behind his knees. Almost feeling sorry for him, Meg waved at the insects swarming in front of her, then turned to have a look around.

The prominent feature along the shore were the hundreds of rocks and boulders crowding the beach and emerging as the tide receded. All were carved with names and/or dates. Curious, Meg wandered among the huge stones, reading the inscriptions.

Many of the carvings remembered the names of ships, others commemorated visitors to the island. The earliest date Meg located was 1702. After thirty minutes of aimless wandering, she came upon a needle-shaped rock uncovered by the tide that bore the name, Joseph Mayfair, 1821. With trembling fingers, she traced the name cut into the wet glistening rock, pushing aside bits of algae and weed.

"Find anything interesting?" Sam asked, appearing behind her. Pulling a bandanna from the back pocket of his jeans, he mopped the sweat from his forehead and throat.

"My great-great-grandfather...he was really here," Meg whispered. She had accepted the family legend, but she hadn't genuinely believed it. Until now.

Pushing up the bill of her baseball cap, Meg scanned the beach and the thick stands of coconut palms, the dense foliage that intruded on the shoreline. Her great-great-grandfather, her great-grandfather, her grandfather, and her father had all explored this beach. Perhaps they had stood where she was standing now. She had a sudden absurd idea that if she squinted, if she concentrated hard enough, she might see ghost echoes of her family.

"I never knew them," she said in a low voice. For most of her life Meg had dismissed her forebears as eccentrics, as irresponsible dreamers.

Until now she hadn't thought of them as real people, not even her father. But there was his name carved into the boulder facing her. Tears blurred her vision. What had her father been thinking as he sweated in the tropical sun to carve his name in the tide-wet rock? Had he thought about his young daughter? Had he thought about ponies and dolls and tea sets and all the small delights he might buy her if he found the treasure? Had he ever guessed that she wanted his time and his love, not the items he might buy for her?

"It's like a guest book written in stone, isn't it?" Sam remarked, gazing at the names and dates gouged into the rocks. Then he saw her face. "Hey, are you all right?"

GET A FREE TEDDY BEAR . . .

You'll love this plush, cuddly Teddy Bear, an adorable accessory for your dressing table, bookcase or desk. Measuring 5½" tall, he's soft and brown and has a bright red ribbon around his neck—he's completely captivating! And he's yours *absolutely free,* when you accept this no-risk offer!

AND FOUR FREE BOOKS!

Here's a chance to get **four free Harlequin Intrigue® novels** from the Harlequin Reader Service®—so you can see for yourself that we're like **no ordinary book club!**

We'll send you four free books . . . but you never have to buy anything or remain a member any longer than you choose. You could even accept the free books and cancel immediately. In that case, you'll owe nothing and be under **no obligation!**

Find out for yourself why thousands of readers enjoy receiving books by mail from the Harlequin Reader Service. They like the **convenience of home delivery** . . . they like getting the best new novels . . . and they love our **discount prices!**

Try us and see! Return this card promptly. We'll send your free books and a free Teddy Bear, under the terms explained on the back. We hope you'll want to remain with the reader service— but the choice is always yours!

181 CIH AJA3 (U-H-I-06/93)

NAME

ADDRESS   APT

CITY   STATE   ZIP

Offer not valid to current Harlequin Intrigue® subscribers. All orders subject to approval.
© 1993 HARLEQUIN ENTERPRISES LIMITED   Printed in the U.S.A.

▼ CLAIM YOUR FREE BOOKS AND FREE GIFT! RETURN THIS CARD TODAY! ▼

NO OBLIGATION TO BUY!

Meg shoved her dark glasses back in place and lifted her eyes to the craggy peaks covered in dense green. Gulls, divers, and petrels screamed overhead and foraged along the damp sand. The heat made it difficult to breathe.

"For a moment I was overcome by my own history. So much of it is tied to this island."

Meg tugged her gaze from the tall conical hill dubbed Observation Hill by a long-ago treasure seeker. It was carpeted by thick saw grass that grew as tall as Sam. At the top was a sparse collection of wind-shaped palms. Wafer Bay lay on the other side, as inhospitable as this bay.

After giving her head a shake, Meg looked at Sam. "Did you find anything?"

"A few odds and ends of machinery, a couple of rusted shovels, a sheet of corrugated roofing." He shrugged. "Nothing very interesting."

Meg leaned against the boulder and studied the profusion of tropical growth. Here and there a gap appeared in the wall of green, the path of a stream falling out of the mountains, or the rock-strewn, dry bed of a rivulet that had altered its course over the centuries.

"Sam...what if the treasure really does exist?" she asked in a dreamy voice. "What if all the old stories are true?"

"A lot of people believe they are," he said. A slow grin began at the corners of his lips. "Are you getting treasure fever?"

A blush added to the pink heating her cheeks. "Like you said...since we're here, anyway, we might as well see where the united map takes us. That doesn't mean I have treasure fever, it just means I'm here and I'm curious, that's all."

Sam laughed and walked farther up the shore, toward the spot where once a stream had tumbled down from the high peaks. Now the wide sandy bed was dry, a thick scatter of stones showing where it had once separated into three runs during its final dash to the sea.

"You know something, Ms. Wolff?" he called back to her. "You're a fraud."

"What the hell is that supposed to mean?" Meg demanded. Bending, she rolled up the cuffs of her slacks then followed after him, scattering birds picking at the sand and seaweed.

"All that bull about you not being an adventurous type." Smiling, he held up a hand and ticked down his fingers. "You don't think it's an adventure to start your own company? With an adventure game, I might add. Or to jump on a plane and fly to a country where the only person you know is a man you don't trust? Now look at you. Your mind is racing at the speed of light. You're thinking: They wouldn't bury it here. Gold is too heavy, it would sink in the sand. Is that bedrock over there? Wouldn't a spot near bedrock be a better choice?" His grin widened.

Another infusion of pink glowed on Meg's cheeks. Her chin lifted. "All right. Maybe I'm more adventurous than I realized. So what?"

"So, what are we going to do about it?" His grin was now ear to ear. "We won't find anything, you know. But treasure hunting will help pass the time until we can leave."

"How can you be so sure we won't find anything? You're the guy who believes there are fabulous treasures buried here just waiting to be plucked from the ground."

Sam laughed aloud, the deep rich sound startling a few birds into the air. "I think the tales of treasure are probably apocryphal. Man has a natural need to account for the disappearance of something as fabulous as the Peruvian treasure. Or maybe some seaman buried a sack of coins here during a stop-over long ago. And the tales just grew and grew.''

"So you lied about that, too. You don't believe there's any treasure here.''

He winced. "Well, if there was, don't you think someone would have found it?'' A large hand swept across his chest in an all-encompassing wave. "See those pits? See that boulder that's been dynamited? That cliff face that's been hacked away? Assuming you weren't fool enough to carry heavy loads of gold up a mountain in this heat or through foliage that dense, where would you hide a few tons of gold? You'd bury it close in where you could retrieve it easily. But take a look, Meg. There isn't a square inch of this beach that hasn't been searched and picked over a hundred times. If there was treasure here, someone would have found it.''

"What about the map?'' she asked stubbornly. She couldn't believe she was arguing in favor of the treasure's existence. Had the sun fried her brain? "Why would Joseph Mayfair and Walter Bates bother to make a map if there wasn't something valuable here that they intended to retrieve some day?''

Sam shrugged. "Who knows? Maybe they buried a few coins. Maybe they found a little trove left behind by someone before them. Maybe it was a bid for fame. Maybe it was a hoax from the beginning.''

"Or maybe they were part of the crew that plundered the Peruvian treasure exactly as they claimed and history confirms.''

"Maybe. But unlikely, don't you think?'' he said, looking at her. "You've got it bad, kiddo.'' The grin returned.

"The Peruvian treasure *was* stolen and it *did* vanish! That much is fact. No one questions it. The treasure has never turned up. It *could* be here. Just like history and legend says it is!''

Sam lifted his hat and ran his fingers through heat-damp curls. ''Let's hope Chango thinks so. If he does, this operation ought to be a slam dunk.'' He settled his hat and smiled at her. ''Hey, I'm game. Tomorrow morning we'll put the halves of the map together and pace it off. All I'm saying is don't get your hopes too high.''

Although it was unreasonable, Meg felt a pang of disappointment. Secretly she had relished the image of Sam as a modern-day pirate consumed by glittering chests of treasure. He looked the part, that was for sure. He was big, heavily muscled, possessed a commanding presence, and was afraid of nothing. Take away the modern jeans and sunglasses, add breeches and an eye patch and he'd be Meg's conception of the ideal pirate. Sexy, confident, there was even a hint of a swagger in his step. An unconscious sigh collapsed her shoulders.

''I really thought you believed in the treasure. Did you tell me anything that wasn't a lie?''

The smile vanished from Sam's lips. His clear turquoise eyes swept her body then narrowed. In three strides he crossed the sandy distance between them and caught her around the waist, pulling her hard against his body.

''This isn't a lie,'' he said in a rough voice.

His mouth came down on hers in a hard, hungry kiss. Meg was so startled that she didn't resist. Then, as his tongue pushed inside her mouth and explored within, she couldn't resist. She had wanted this, too.

In an explosion of sensation, curiosity, and sudden leaping passion, she wrapped her arms around Sam's neck and returned his kiss. His mouth was hot on hers, his body even hotter. Hard, flat muscle pressed against soft flesh. One hand clasped her waist, the other spread points of heat across her back. Her mind reeled. And where he touched her, her skin tingled and shot tiny thrills toward her spine.

When he released her, Meg's knees sagged before she caught her balance. Racing blood pulsed in her temples and at the base of her throat. Slowly she lifted her fingertips to her lips and stared at him.

"I thought we agreed to keep this impersonal," she whispered. The implied accusation wasn't entirely fair as she hadn't put up any resistance. But then, she hadn't known a simple kiss could leave her feeling so shaken.

"That was your idea, not mine," he said, returning her stare. "There's no way you and I can be impersonal, Meg. This became personal the minute I walked into your office. I think you know that."

Meg wet her lips. Somewhere behind the veil of tropical green an animal snorted and crashed through brambles and lianas. She didn't notice. She couldn't look away from his blue eyes and sunburned face.

"I damned near went crazy when I learned Chango's men had taken you at gunpoint! That's when I knew just how personal this had become. If Chango had harmed you, I would have killed him with my bare hands."

Right now Sam looked like a man who could carry out such a threat. The coiled-spring tension Meg had noticed when they'd first met had returned. This was not the type of man to make idle conversation; he meant what he said. It scared her a little, thrilled her a little.

"I admit there's a strong physical attraction between us," she said, speaking slowly. It was useless to deny the obvious. Her lips still burned with the taste of his kiss and her skin fizzed and tingled where he had touched her. It wasn't just the sun that made her feel hot all over.

"What are we going to do about it, Meg?"

"Nothing. I'm sorry, but there's too much water under the bridge. Too many lies and not enough trust. Sam, I feel like a fool about this, and I apologize, but an hour ago I felt certain you were going to shoot me." Her gaze dipped to the butt of the gun gleaming in his shoulder holster. "Without trust, a relationship can't go anywhere. And that's where we are." She shrugged. "Maybe if we'd started differently...maybe if you hadn't been forced to lie...but that's not how it happened."

He was silent for a full minute, then he turned to face the foliage and squinted, trying to pierce its impenetrable depths. "At least you acknowledge I was 'forced' to lie. That's a beginning."

Meg hesitated, wanting to kiss him again, hating herself for such idiocy. "Don't make too much out of it," she said finally. She paused. "What are you looking for?"

Absently he swatted at the ubiquitous swarms of insects. "I don't understand why Howard's men haven't made contact."

"Is that what this inspection trip is all about?"

"I thought you'd like a look around. But I also thought Howard's men would use our arrival on the beach to show themselves and let us know they're here."

Meg peered at the dense growth. The crashing noises deeper inside had ceased. There was only the buzzing of insects, the occasional cry of a bird, and the silky whisper of the sea. She rubbed at the goose bumps rising under the sleeves of Sam's borrowed shirt.

"I'd hate to be stranded here," she murmured. The air seemed charged with heat and dark secrets. After a minute she added, "Maybe Howard's people haven't arrived yet."

Sam frowned. "They were supposed to arrive before we did. Chango won't be more than a day behind us. If he slips the net and eludes the Justice launches, he'll show up here. The plan was to have at least ten well-armed men waiting to pick him up. Just in case."

Suddenly Meg felt as if a dozen eyes silently watched from behind the ferns and thick vines. Without thinking about what she was doing, she edged a little closer to Sam. "Maybe they're here but they don't want to make themselves known."

"That's possible," he agreed slowly. "But not likely. There's no reason to remain hidden at this point."

Yesterday Meg would have wagered the earth that she'd feel safer on solid ground than on a boat. But right now she wanted to escape the oppressive heat and menacing silence of Cocos Island. Turning on the heels of her sandals, she walked away from Sam toward the beached rowboat.

"I'm getting hungry, aren't you?" she called over her shoulder. "Let's return to the launch and see what we can scare up for dinner." If the Justice agents intended to show themselves, they would have done so before now. If they chose to remain hidden, that was okay with Meg. She was waffling between wanting to uncover a few of the island's secrets and wanting to sail away from here as fast as they could.

After a moment Sam followed and they dragged the rowboat through the rocks.

FOLLOWING A QUICK shower in the cramped bathroom of the cabin, Meg donned a light cotton blouse and skirt and joined Sam and Julian on deck. Julian had prepared grilled tuna, corn on the cob, rice, and champagne sherbet for dessert.

She told herself she had chosen a skirt because the faint sea breeze would be cooler on her bare legs. But when she saw the smoldering speculation in Sam's eyes, she wasn't as sure of her motives. When it came to Sam, she wasn't sure of anything.

All he said was, "You should keep the zinc oxide on your nose and cheeks until the sun goes down."

Julian was more complimentary. He raised his wineglass and smiled at her, displaying a row of even white teeth. "To our beautiful guest."

Meg laughed. With no makeup and her nose already beginning to peel, with her hair artlessly arranged, she didn't feel very beautiful. Still, she slid a glance toward Sam to see his reaction. Sam stared out at the ocean, he seemed to be fighting looking at her. "Are you a Justice agent, too?" she asked Julian.

He shook his head. "Me? No, *señorita.*"

"Julian is an old friend," Sam explained, still not looking at her. "We grew up together."

While Sam and Julian reminisced about youthful high jinks, Meg ate her champagne sherbet and studied Sam's face, bathed by the golden rays of sunset.

Here was a man who loved delicate plants and who wanted a home and a family. Yet he was also a man accustomed to carrying a gun and who had spent time in a hospital recovering from a gunshot wound. He was as comfortable in the midst of a dangerous operation as he was in one of his greenhouses. This was a quiet man who filled his home with books and plants and beautiful objects, a man who professed himself tongue-tied at the prospect of small talk. At the same time he was charismatic, intimidating, afraid of nothing, and not averse to using violence or subterfuge to get what he wanted. No man's kiss had ever thrilled Meg the way Sam's had, yet he was the wrong man.

Meg sighed, thinking of the contradictions that existed within Sam Livingston. She turned her face toward the dying sun, bit her lip and wished she could stop thinking about him. Wondering about him. Wanting him.

It seemed she possessed a few contradictions of her own.

MORNING MIST softened the island's high peaks and lingered in the interior valleys. Meg stood at the rail of the launch, sipping a mug of Julian's coffee, listening to the scream of birds and the thunder of waves crashing against the island's rocky barriers.

The tide was at its lowest point, exposing about one hundred yards of wet rocks covered by thousands of birds seeking breakfast. The skeletal remains of boats with ripped bottoms lay here and there among the exposed rocks, debris left by those who had not guessed the existence of the jagged boulders submerged at high tide.

"Ready to seek our fortunes?" Sam asked, coming up beside her to lower the rowboat. Meg noticed droplets of water still clung to his hair from his shower. She also noticed that he had taken time to shave. He looked like a macho model in a yachting ad, too handsome and sun bronzed to be real.

"As ready as I'll ever be," Meg said finally, looking away from him. Last night she had washed her slacks and borrowed shirt and hung them across the outside railing. They had not dried completely and the dampness felt cool against her skin. Already it was scorching hot.

"You have your half of the map?" Sam asked, running a glance over her. She wasn't carrying anything except the picnic basket Julian had packed for them.

Meg nodded.

"If you say so," Sam said after a minute. "I hope you don't mind a little work before we get started. We'll need to pull the rowboat up to the high watermark. In this heat it's going to feel like we're dragging a tractor.''

He was right. By the time they hauled the rowboat through the boulders onto dry sand, Meg was panting and puffing, gasping for gulps of humid air. Sweat poured from her.

''Sit down and rest,'' Sam ordered.

Yesterday he had dug a trench around the tent and filled it with oil to trap insects and crawling bugs. The tent was a relatively insect-free site to store their picnic basket and water canteens. When he finished unloading their supplies, Sam sat on a rock beside her and lifted a canteen to his lips.

''Okay, me fine wench,'' he said after a moment's rest. '''Tis truth time. Time to produce your half of the famous Bates/Mayfair map.''

Meg tilted her head back and gazed at him from beneath the bill of the baseball cap. ''Two million people have played my video game, Treasure Trove. But you haven't. Right?''

Puzzled, he frowned at her. ''What does your game have to do with actual treasure hunting?''

She smiled. ''If you had purchased a copy of Treasure Trove, you'd have my half of the map. The map forms the backdrop for the introduction to the game, and there's a full clear copy in the instruction booklet. I had to guess what the Bates half contained, but the information on the Mayfair half is accurate.''

Sam stared. ''Good God. Are you saying that two million people have the map that serious treasure hunters have been seeking for more than a century?''

''I'm afraid so.'' She grinned. ''You and Chango could have had my half simply by walking into a video store and plunking down thirty-five bucks.''

"I don't believe it." He shook his head, then laughed aloud. "Actually I do have a copy of the game. But I never dreamed the game map was the *real* map. Maybe you haven't noticed, but there's no way to hook up a video game here. Do you have a copy of your half?"

Meg tapped her temple. "It's all here. I spent so many months working with that map that I know it by rote." Leaning forward, she picked up a twig and made a hasty sketch in the wet sand. "My half contains the overall shape of the island and the written clues. I figure your map overlays mine and lays out direction arrows and number of paces, that kind of thing. Am I right?"

"You've got it." Kneeling beside her drawing, Sam studied it a moment and nodded before he jabbed a finger at a spot near the bottom. "This is Chatham Bay. You are here. So what happens next?"

"Here's where it gets tricky." She accepted the water canteen, took a long drink and patted some drops on her throat, conscious that Sam watched her fingertips on her breast. "One of the written clues says the treasure is hidden in a cave or cleft in the face of a huge bald rock about a mile from shore."

Sam turned away from her toward the curtain of vegetation and frowned. "There's no place on this island that provides enough of a vantage to see if a bald rock exists or not."

Meg nodded. "I spotted the problem yesterday." She drew a breath. "Now that I've actually seen the island, I think false clues are interspersed among the real ones."

"Great." Sam made a face. "How are we supposed to know which is which?"

"Trial and error?"

His face relaxed when he smiled. "Atta girl, Ms. Wolff. I should have known you weren't a quitter."

For a long moment their eyes met and held. A hollow space opened in Meg's stomach and filled with butterflies before she cleared her throat, closed her eyes, and made herself remember what they were doing. She quoted: "Begin at the mark of the K. Follow the arrows." She opened her eyes. "So. Any idea what the mark of the K might be?"

"The mark of the K," Sam repeated, frowning. "It must be a rock carving. Good thing we decided to explore at low tide."

They stood at the same moment, but before they moved out to inspect the rocks, Meg briefly touched his arm.

"Sam, you seem jumpy today. You keep looking around. Are you still watching for someone from the Justice Department?"

"I can't understand why they haven't shown themselves."

Meg searched his expression. "What are the chances that Martin Chango will elude the sea operation and actually show up here?"

Sam's shrug indicated a casualness that Meg suspected he didn't feel. "Who knows? But I'd breathe easier if I knew for sure the backup was in place. Just in case."

Meg scanned the foliage drooping in the heavy heat. "No offense, but I think the whole plan is off base. Chango is too smart to be lured outside territorial waters. He won't risk following us. I wouldn't if I were him."

"I hope you're wrong. I hope Chango is desperate enough to commit this one mistake. I'd like to hear from Howard that his men picked up Chango this morning and he's on his way to a holding prison in Miami."

They walked around the boulders exposed by low tide.

"How long are we supposed to stay on Cocos Island?" Meg called.

"If Chango took the bait and if he set out immediately and if he slipped through the cordon . . . he could show up here sometime today." Sam avoided Meg's startled look.

"Today?"

"In the unlikely event that happens, all you and I have to do is stay out of the way and let Howard's men do their job. They'll nab Chango, then everybody can go home." He scanned the palm-studded hill that separated Chatham and Wafer bays. "If Chango doesn't show up, we'll wait another day or so, then head back."

"Do you think he will? Show up?"

Sam bent to examine the inscription carved on a rock. "If he does, it means something went very wrong."

The conversation was sobering enough that Meg almost forgot their examination of the rock faces had a purpose. Until she found what they were looking for.

"I found it!" Her voice rose with excitement. "Look! Here's the K! And an arrow!" Time and water had eroded the markings but they were still visible. "Quick! Come here, come here!" She lifted an eager face. "What do we do now? That info must be on your part of the map. Which direction? How many paces?"

Sam approached slowly, his mind still focused on the Justice operation and what might have gone wrong, that none of Howard's men seemed to be in place on the island. When he reached Meg, he stared down at her. Wearing a shapeless shirt and a smear of zinc oxide, smelling of insect repellent, her hair and forehead damp with perspiration, she shouldn't have impressed him as beautiful. But she did. The excitement dancing in her dark eyes sparked a definite response in him. Her lovely mouth seemed to cry out for kisses. It occurred to him that he was falling for her. Hard.

"You look like a beachcomber. Do you have any idea how truly beautiful you are?"

She blinked, then laughed. "I think you've been standing in the sun too long." But she met his gaze and their eyes locked. Finally her gaze dropped to his mouth. She blushed violently and gave him a self-conscious poke on the arm before she turned aside. "The arrows appear to end here. So where do we go next?"

"North," he said in a gruff voice. "There are twelve dots on my map. I assume they indicate twelve paces."

"Great. Let's go."

Meg turned right. Sam turned left. They stopped and looked back at each other.

"Which north do you want to try first?" Sam asked, grinning.

"Your north is going to run smack into a condominium-size boulder at about six paces. My north has a clear shot toward the foliage."

"So we take the north of least resistance even though it's south?" Sam grinned. "Partner, I think we're in trouble here."

"Could be." Meg laughed. "Since we can't even agree on the starting point."

"How about this. We'll follow your interpretation until noon. After lunch, we'll follow my interpretation. Okay?"

Meg gazed at him for a long moment. "I expected you to argue. You always surprise me."

"That's because you always expect the worst of me."

They didn't move for a minute, both remembering yesterday's passionate kiss. Meg was the first to break eye contact. She pulled down the bill of her hat, cleared her throat self-consciously, then struck off twelve paces. Sam followed. His twelve paces ended about three yards in front of her.

He looked over his shoulder. "Would you happen to know whether Bates and Mayfair were my size or your size?"

Meg bit the inside of her cheek and absently swatted at a cloud of insects. "This gets complicated pretty fast."

"If it were easy, someone would have found the treasure before us."

"I know." But caught up in treasure fever, and having the famed map finally reunited, Meg had dared to secretly hope it would simply be a matter of following instructions. Certainly she had not expected the interpretation to be this confusing.

Their combined clues eventually brought them to a riverbed. After studying the obstacles ahead, Sam silently returned to the tent, reappearing with his machete.

"Just in case your interpretation takes us into the underbrush," he explained.

"The way I figure it, we have to walk up the riverbed," Meg said uncertainly.

"That's what I was afraid you were going to say." Sam eyed the rivulet of tumbling water, then drew a breath and stepped into the rushing stream.

It was tough going. The riverbed was composed of loose rocks and gravel. They both slipped, slid, and fell a half-dozen times before they had progressed more than a few feet up the mountainside. Adding to the discomfort of uncertain footing, the water gushing out of the high peaks was surprisingly cold on Meg's bare feet.

"You said forty yards?" she called, looking down at the sandals she carried. She might as well have worn them. They were soaked from her last fall. "I think we've come about forty yards." Or ten miles—she couldn't tell the difference. Meg felt as though she'd been loading concrete for eight hours, carrying it straight up. "My clue says, 'Into the green wall.'"

While they put their shoes back on, they eyed the thick interlocking foliage. It was daunting. Unlike the cedar forests higher up, this area was densely covered with vines, bushes, tree ferns, and thorny brambles. Without Sam's machete, they wouldn't have had a prayer of penetrating the green thickness.

The difficulties didn't abate even after Sam had hacked a narrow path. Following him uphill, trying to avoid the brambles, Meg watched the sweat pour off his body and soak his clothing. The heat trapped in the thicket of growth seemed even worse than the heat on the exposed beach. She stumbled over vines as thick as a man's thigh, slapped at millions of mosquitoes disturbed by the swing of the machete.

At one o'clock, too fatigued to speak, they silently returned to the tent on the shore. Their canteens were nearly empty and they were famished, but both were too exhausted to do more than pick at the items in the picnic basket.

Afterward they sat in the shade of a boulder, drenched in their own sweat. Sam lit a thin cigar. Meg leaned her head against the rock and watched the returning tide swirl up the yellow beach. Only the top quarter of the needle-shaped rock on which her great-great-grandfather had carved his name was visible.

"Ready to try my north?" Sam asked without opening his eyes.

"Pacing through a boulder can't be any more difficult than what we've already been through."

"You know something? You're a damned good sport for someone who isn't adventurous." Sam pushed to his feet, then extended a large hand to help her up.

For a moment Meg thought he would kiss her again, maybe she hoped he would. But he patted her shoulder instead, stretched, then pointed to about a foot of rock extending above the surface of the waves.

"If I remember right, that was the K rock. Over there is the boulder we ran into at six paces. Walk around the boulder in your imagination and resume pacing on the other side. That puts us about there." He indicated a spot on the water. "What was the next clue?"

Knowing their measurements were wildly imprecise, they followed the clues as best they could. Twice they nearly fell into deep pits dug by previous treasure hunters, pits almost impossible to see until one was practically on top of them. They followed another streambed uphill, dry this time. They argued over which was harder to negotiate, a streambed gushing water or a dry bed strewn with treacherous loose stones.

By the time they returned to the tent, about five o'clock, Meg counted herself among the walking dead. The only way she knew she was still alive was by the burning pain of insect bites circling her ankles, her wrists, and around her neck.

"Assuming we have the energy to row ourselves back to the launch, the first and only thing I'm going to do is fall into bed and sleep like the dead!"

Sam halted beside her and stared at the sea. "As they say in the movies, it looks like we've got company."

"What?" Meg's head snapped up. She shaded her eyes and peered toward the mouth of the bay. A sleek white yacht lay at anchor about sixty yards from Sam's *Lemon Tree*. "Chango!" Her exhaustion vanished in a burst of adrenaline.

"That's my guess," Sam confirmed. His tone was grim. They studied two men standing on the deck of the yacht looking at them through binoculars.

Meg cast a glance behind her. "Isn't this the moment when a dozen Justice men jump out of the vines waving machine guns and shouting 'Gotcha'? What are they waiting for?"

Sam didn't answer. He kept his eyes on Chango's yacht.

Two men lowered a rowboat off the rear of the yacht and rowed to the *Lemon Tree.* As Meg and Sam watched helplessly from shore, the men boarded Sam's ship and one of them attacked Julian.

Instantly Sam's gun appeared in his hand, but the fighting figures were too far away for an accurate or clean shot. Tight-jawed with frustration, he lowered his arm, swearing steadily through clenched teeth.

"Julian is a pacifist," he explained to Meg in a hoarse voice. "He refuses to carry a weapon." Fury, impatience, and helplessness roughened his tone.

The incoming tide swirled around Meg's ankles but she didn't notice. Her attention was riveted on the drama unfolding on the decks of the *Lemon Tree.* She could see Julian fighting with Chango's henchman, then Julian disappeared.

Nothing happened for several long minutes. Presumably Chango's men were searching the *Lemon Tree.* Then the men reappeared, returned to the yacht and climbed aboard. An eerie silence spread across the water, a dark sense of vague expectancy. Meg and Sam swung their staring eyes back to the *Lemon Tree.*

"Come on, Julian. Damn you, come on," Sam chanted. "Where are you? Get off that boat. Now. Now, Julian. Come on!"

"Where is he?" Meg asked, wringing her hands. "What did they do to him?"

"Come on, buddy! Come on, Julian."

The sky split in a deafening explosion. One moment the *Lemon Tree* rocked at anchor in the unnatural silence, the next moment it exploded in an eruption of fire and flying debris.

Meg's knees collapsed and she dropped into the wet surge. Her mouth fell open in disbelief. She stared unblinking at the smoke and flaming ship without actually registering what she was seeing. It was impossible. This couldn't be happening.

When she finally turned tear-blurred eyes toward the yacht, she discovered the man with the binoculars had not moved. Sam's burning boat did not interest him. He was watching them.

Chapter Eight

"Meg, get on your feet!"

"Oh, my God! Julian! He..." Tears streamed down her face as she stared at the burning launch. "They killed him!"

Bending, Sam caught her in his arms and, running, carried her higher up the beach to a boulder near the tent. They were not as exposed here, but could still see the yacht. Sam lowered her to the sand and gently pressed her against the boulder.

"Oh, my God! I can't..."

"Meg, listen to me." Kneeling, Sam cupped her chin in his large callused hand, lifted her face and forced her to meet his eyes. "Don't think about it. Put it out of your mind."

"Put it...Sam, they blew up your launch and they murdered Julian!" Tears welled in her eyes and spilled over her cheeks. She was shaking.

"I know. Chango will pay for what he did to Enrico and Julian." For a moment Sam was deadly silent. Knots rose like small hard stones along his jawline. "Later there'll be time to mourn Julian, and we will. Right now, Meg, we need to think about us."

"Us?" Her mind wasn't functioning. Sam's boat had burned to the waterline. Flames reflected on the waves flowing into Chatham Bay, stretching toward them like fingers of fire and light.

Sam gripped her shoulders and gave her a gentle shake. "Meg, snap out of it. I need that fine mind of yours."

Meg stared at him. Her eyes felt as wide and round as dinner plates. Tears scalded her lids. Her hands wouldn't stop shaking.

"The plan has gone exactly as Howard and I hoped it would," Sam said, looking into her eyes. He didn't blink. "Chango followed us."

"But—"

"But something went wrong. Chango slipped through the cordon, and the backup people aren't here. We're on our own."

Meg's wide gaze swung back to the flames on the sea and the man watching through binoculars. Martin Chango. Fear turned her skin the same chalky color as the zinc oxide that lay sweat-caked across her nose and upper cheeks.

"Oh, my God. We're alone and trapped."

"Howard knows we're here. Meg, are you listening? Howard will get here as fast as he can. He's on his way right now."

"You don't know that for sure. Meanwhile, we're sitting ducks!" Meg shifted against the boulder to stare into Sam's turquoise eyes. "We don't have any way off this island! We can't radio for help!"

Sam tilted his head toward the oily smoke rising from the waves. "I think that was the idea."

Meg wiped her eyes and wrenched her mind away from Julian. Deliberately she made herself focus on their predicament.

"All right. What happens next?" she asked after a minute.

"You tell me," he said, watching her intently for signs of hysteria. "Define the situation."

Pride kicked in and Meg squared her shoulders and her thoughts. "Okay." She frowned, concentrating. "Chango doesn't know about the Justice operation. He thinks we're seriously looking for the treasure. He doesn't know whether or not we've found it." She thought a minute. "He's pinned us down. Taken away our ability to escape or radio for help. If we've found the treasure, we're expendable." Resolutely she kept her thoughts from Julian. "If we haven't found the treasure, we're still expendable, but not until he gets the reunited map."

"So what do you suggest?" Sam's hands loosened their grip on her shoulders and he sat back on his heels.

"Are you absolutely positive that Howard is on his way?"

Sam ducked his head. "Right now I'm not positive about anything except that we have a serious problem here. I hope like hell that Howard is on his way. Certainly he knows by now that we've got trouble."

"Wait a minute." Meg's mind darted and raced. "I was wrong. Even if Chango thinks we've found the treasure, we're not expendable until we tell him where it is. It's a huge treasure, Sam. He knows none of it was aboard the *Lemon Tree*. So we might have marked the spot somehow and left it where we found it."

"Your point?"

"Don't you see? It comes back to the map. What Chango really needs is the reunited map. Not us—the map! I could tell him about the video game. Better yet, I could draw out my half of the map and we give him the damned thing!"

"Meg, Chango is going to come after us. You had it right the first time. We're expendable no matter how you slice this pie. He wants the reunited map, he wants the treasure, and he doesn't want any witnesses. His next move is to get the map and get rid of us."

In her heart, Meg knew he was right.

"Do you think a man as sophisticated as Martin Chango would believe your half of the map is part of a game? He won't believe that for a minute. He expects the original map, a piece of old paper. And we don't have that map to give to him. If you draw up something, he won't buy it. He won't believe you gave him the correct clues, especially when he runs across one of the false leads. In the end, it won't matter. We know his men killed Julian. Chango isn't going to leave us alive to talk about it."

His words hung in the hot air. Meg turned her face toward a spectacular sunset, marred by the coil of dark smoke rising from what was left of Sam's boat.

"I'm sorry, Meg. The last thing I ever intended was to involve you in a showdown with Martin Chango."

She looked deep into his long-lashed eyes and recognized the truth. "I know," she whispered. Reaching inside, she found the strength for a wobbly smile. "You said from the beginning that I was the last person you'd want to have on a treasure hunt. I just didn't realize it was because people get killed hunting treasure."

He returned her smile. "Looks like I'm stuck with you."

It suddenly occurred to Meg that the situation wouldn't be half as complicated for Sam if she weren't with him. Earlier today she had seen that he was no stranger to a machete or to a jungle environment. He had faced life-threatening situations before. He had the experience and the skills to survive.

None of these descriptions applied to her. She was a city girl with no skills for surviving in the wild. No experience with thugs and murderers. She didn't know a banana palm from a coconut palm. She was a fragile-boned woman with a low endurance rate. As Sam had guessed, the last time Meg had been involved with the wilderness she had been twelve years old and wearing a Girl Scout uniform. To the best of her knowledge, she was the only girl in the history of scouting who had failed to earn a single badge.

On his own, Sam would have faded into the undergrowth, lived off the land, and waited for Howard's cavalry to arrive and save the day.

She grasped his arm, feeling the hard muscle beneath her fingertips. "Sam...there's something that has to be said." She gazed into his eyes. "There's an easy solution for you. Chango has the Bates's half of the map. All he really needs is my half. You could hand me over to him, then disappear into the underbrush until Howard's men arrive."

He stared at her from stony, glittering eyes. "You don't trust me even now?"

"Are you claiming that solution hasn't occurred to you?"

"Not once." He gripped her shoulders and shook her hard. "Listen to me, you little fool. I think I started falling for you the minute you ordered me out of your office. I am *not* going to turn you over to Martin Chango, and I am not going to abandon you. You're my responsibility. I got you into this mess and I'll get you out! Got that?"

"Sam—"

"If you don't believe me...if you still can't trust me, then the hell with you, Meg. I give up. Climb into that rowboat and row yourself out to Chango's yacht! If you think your chances are better with Martin Chango, go for it!"

"I didn't say I *wanted* to give myself up to Chango, I was only—"

"If you do, you're as good as dead. And I'll wonder for the rest of my life how I could have been so stupid as to fall for an absolute idiot!"

He released her so abruptly that she almost rolled backward. Fuming, he stood and strode down the beach away from her.

Meg scratched the insect bites on her neck and looked after him. He believed he was falling in love with her. She shook her head in amazement. From Sam's point of view, she had been nothing but a pain in the neck from the beginning. She had been obstinate from day one. She had refused to sell him her half of the map. She had followed him to Costa Rica and messed up the plans of the Justice Department. He'd had to rescue her from Chango's grasp. Now he was trapped on a tropical island with a woman who didn't know north from south. In spite of these handicaps, he thought he was falling for her and that it was his job to keep them both alive until Howard's men arrived.

Standing, Meg drew a breath, then cupped her hands around her mouth and shouted, "I hate this, but I'm attracted to you, too!"

He turned and scowled at her across a surge of water that foamed up the beach.

"But you don't trust me, right? I might kill you any minute. Or sacrifice you to save myself. But you're attracted to me, anyway. What the hell does that mean? A tentative declaration of a temporary aberration?" Long shadows softened his glare. "Hell, no wonder you've had bad luck with men."

"I always fall for the bad apple in the bunch." She sent him a weak grin. Then she realized they were standing exposed on the beach. "Does Chango have a weapon with enough range to pick us off at this distance?"

"He's an arms dealer. He could blow up this whole island if he wanted to. Go hide behind a rock or something, will you? I need to think about our next move."

Meg walked toward the tent in the swiftly descending darkness. Admitting they felt something for each other didn't seem like much of a defense against a man who could blow up an entire island if he chose to. Nevertheless, she felt a little better.

A FEW MINUTES before full darkness descended, Chango addressed them through a bullhorn. A man stood on deck beside him watching the shore through a pair of binoculars.

"As it appears the *Lemon Tree* has suffered an unfortunate accident, I invite you and your charming companion to accept the hospitality of my yacht. We'll have dinner and talk."

Sam swore between his teeth, lifted his arm, and made a rude gesture toward the yacht.

"I'll give you tonight to think over your position, Livingston. We'll talk again at first light. We can do this the easy way or the hard way, but let me remind you that you're outmanned and outgunned. Think about it."

"WHY HASN'T CHANGO sent someone after us?" Meg asked.

They sat inside the sweltering tent in the tropical darkness, their shoulders touching, slapping insects off their legs and necks and picking at the remains of their picnic lunch.

"We aren't going anywhere," Sam said, tossing a chicken bone out the tent flap, hoping it would draw bugs and insects away from them. His oil-filled ditch stopped most of the ants and crawling insects but was no barricade against the flying kind. "He can afford to wait until daylight."

"Is it possible that Chango found out about the Justice operation and therefore circumvented the cordon? Could he have interfered somehow and that's why none of Howard's men are here on the island?"

The same unpleasant questions had occurred to Sam. "I don't know," he said after a minute. "It's possible, I suppose. That would explain a lot."

He glanced through the flap at the string of lights outlining the yacht. Male voices floated on the night air too far away to be distinguishable, but the laughter was distinct and recognizable. Acid poured into Sam's stomach. Julian was dead and that bastard and his thugs were laughing.

If he had been alone, he might have risked rowing out to the yacht and attempting to pick off Chango's men during the night. Such a plan was out of the question now. If he failed and was caught or killed, Meg would be alone and defenseless.

He thrust his fingers into the sand and gripped hard. By now he had formed a good guess as to what had gone wrong with the operation. As with so many things, the problem was timing.

Meg's kidnapping and subsequent rescue had accelerated the timing of the operation. There had been no choice. After the fact, Howard would have had to clear the change of plans with Washington. Sam had served with the department long enough to imagine the foot dragging and delays as the desk jockeys in Washington analyzed the new situation. This took time. Then they would insist on a background check on Meg. This, too, required time. Then they would want confirmation that Chango had taken the bait despite the altered circumstances. More time. And it was possible, he supposed, that Chango had a plant in the Justice Department, someone paid to arrange a strategic delay.

A grim smile touched Sam's lips as he imagined Howard tearing his hair and burning up the long-distance lines between Puntarenas and Washington, D.C.

"Sam? Chango's going to kill us, isn't he?"

"As long as we have the map, we have some bargaining power."

"But in the end—he's going to kill us."

"He's going to try."

He watched Meg lean into a patch of moonlight to scratch her ankles. They had used the last of the insect repellent earlier in the day. By noon tomorrow, they were both going to be a mass of angry, burning welts.

She kept her head down. "What are we going to do?"

He supposed he should be glad that she was turning to him for advice and comfort. It indicated at least a little trust. He wished he had something positive to tell her.

"Are you rested?"

She blinked at him. "Are you kidding? Never in my life have I been this physically and emotionally exhausted! If I wasn't too frightened to sleep, I'd be out like a light." A full minute elapsed before she shifted position and faced him. "Why?"

"Never mind."

"Why, Sam?"

From where he sat he could see part of the rocky promontory that rose like a huge ebony blot against the night sky. For a moment he considered holding his tongue. Then he decided Meg deserved better than silence or a patronizing reply.

"I'd like to have a look at Wafer Bay. Maybe the instructions got screwed up. Maybe Howard's men put in on the other side."

For a moment she didn't speak. When she finally did, her voice was carefully expressionless. "If Howard's men are camped in Wafer Bay...wouldn't they have heard your launch blowing up?"

"Probably." A half-dozen unpleasant implications hovered behind that one word. None of which Sam wanted to examine right now.

"Sam...are you suggesting that we climb that mountain—in the dark—and go to Wafer Bay? Now?"

He nodded toward the distant yacht. "We can't row around the promontory without passing within a few yards of Chango's lookouts. The only way to Wafer Bay is up and over."

"There's another reason, too, isn't there? It wouldn't be wise to be caught sitting here on the beach come morning." She was tracking his thoughts.

"That's how I see it. So, are you up for a night hike?"

A long silence ensued. Then she sighed, pushed to her feet and pulled on her sandals.

Her voice was glum. "Let's go."

Sam slit the back of the tent with his machete so they could crawl out without being seen by anyone watching through binoculars. He wanted Chango's men to believe they were still in the tent. Keeping to the shadows, they crept along the beach foliage searching for the path that led up the promontory.

VIEWED BY DAYLIGHT, Observation Hill looked deceptively easy to climb. In fact, it was not. At night, with only the dim glow of moonlight to guide them, it was a daunting undertaking.

Within minutes Sam realized the path that appeared so clear-cut from a distance was actually faint and over-grown with vines and clutching brambles. At times the track through the underbrush ended at a stand of saw grass and picked up on the other side. Assuming one could find it again.

Three long frustrating hours passed before they reached the stunted palms on top of the hill. They rested there, leaning their backs against the rough trunks, gasping and panting for breath.

"You okay?" Sam asked when he could speak. He passed the canteen to Meg.

"My legs weigh two tons apiece," she whispered, her eyes closed. "My lungs are burning and I ache all over. If I ever get home again, the first thing I'm going to do is throw out my stair machine and join a real exercise club. Stair machines don't prepare you for fighting through a jungle. I had no idea I was so out of shape."

"Your shape looks fine to me."

"You must be alive. You can still make jokes." She took another pull from the canteen, then handed it back to him. "I hurt in places I didn't know I had. A corpse has more energy than I do. How much farther do we have to go?"

Sam summoned the energy to stand and walk through a scatter of boulders. He found a spot where the distant north edge of Wafer Bay was visible in the moonlight.

"Bad news," he announced, frowning.

"Somehow I'm not surprised."

"There's no path on this side. It's saw grass most of the way down." The saw grass was as tall as he was and about as friendly as a forest of blades. He hefted the machete. "I'll take the point position. Tear off your shirttail and wrap your hands and ankles or the grass will flay you alive."

Behind him, he heard the sound of ripping cloth. He tore his own shirt and did what he could to pad areas of exposed skin.

Then he swung his machete at the tough grass and began.

It was nearly dawn before they staggered out of the undergrowth onto a patch of hard pebble beach. Sam's machete arm was numb and trembled with fatigue. The machete itself weighed a thousand pounds.

Without speaking, they stumbled to the black edge of the water and knelt in the surge to bathe scratches, bruises and stinging insect bites. Sam's jeans were torn in a dozen spots but had fared better than Meg's linen slacks. Her slacks hung in ribbons from just above her knees. Even in the dim light he could see that the saw grass and brambles had inflicted deep scratches down her legs.

"Listen, are you—"

"Look!" Excitement gave her the energy to raise her arm and point a trembling finger.

When Sam turned, he saw two small tents pitched above the high watermark clearly visible in the waning moonlight. At once, he, too, felt a surge of energy.

Followed by a pang of concern.

He and Meg had made enough noise crashing down the hillside to alert even the soundest sleeper. So why weren't the tent's occupants waiting to see who was about to invade their campsite?

He placed a hand on Meg's arm and drew his gun from the shoulder holster, checking the chambers. "Get behind that rock and wait here."

She stared at the gun, then lifted her head. "Sam, what are you doing? It has to be Howard's men. They'll have a radio and fresh water and—"

"Wait here!" he repeated, his voice sharp.

After he positioned her behind a concealing rock, he willed the fatigue out of his mind and darted toward the deeper shadows defining the wall of vegetation. Although he strained to hear noises within the tents, he heard nothing but the drone of insects and the wash of water licking the shore.

When he was close enough to notice the flaps of the tents had foolishly been left open, he selected a couple of stones and lobbed them at the tents, holding his gun ready.

Nothing happened. He tried again but there was no response.

Sitting back on his heels, Sam studied the camp. It was conspicuously laid out like a fishing camp. Too conspicuously.

Then he noticed—and recognized—the smell.

Standing, dreading what he now knew he would find, he walked to the first tent. Silently he thanked God that he had insisted Meg remain behind.

"Hello?" he called in a low voice, leaning into the first tent. He expected no answer and there was none.

After shoving his gun back into the shoulder holster, Sam withdrew his cigar lighter, stepped farther into the tent and steeled himself, then flicked the lighter flame as high as it would go.

"WHAT DID YOU FIND? Is it them? The Justice men?" Meg darted out of the shadows as he crossed the beach toward her. The pink glow of dawn illuminated her anxious face.

"Sit down, Meg."

Her dark eyes swept toward the tents, then swung back to him. Slowly she sank to a sitting position on the sand, not taking her eyes from his face.

"It's something terrible, isn't it?"

He nodded.

"Tell me, Sam. Don't hold anything back. I have a right to know."

Suddenly he felt as if he were a hundred years old, tired and heavy, worn out. He had believed he was finished with this kind of thing after he left the department. You never got used to it.

"There's four men inside the tents. They're all dead." He didn't tell her their throats had been slashed, didn't mention the blood and insects.

Meg dropped her head into her hands. The baseball cap fell onto the sand. "Oh, my God! Were they Howard's men?"

"I recognized one of them." Just barely.

They sat in silence, their shoulders pressed together, watching streaks of pink and gold rise out of the waves.

"Chango?" Meg asked after a while.

"Who else."

"When?"

"Probably before he showed up in Chatham Bay." Sam rested his forearms on his knees, letting his hands dangle. "If the agents came here by boat, the boat's at the bottom of the bay. Or maybe they were flown in by helicopter." He shrugged. It didn't matter now. "They had a radio. It's smashed."

"Did Chango know they were agents?"

"Hard to say. But that would be my guess."

Meg struck the packed sand with her fists. Tears ran down her cheeks.

Sam let her cry for a couple of minutes, then he dropped his arm around her and held her against his chest, stroking her tangled hair. When her shoulders stopped shaking, he lifted her face and gently kissed her wet eyelids.

"Get some rest."

Anxiety flared in her eyes. "Where are you going?"

He met her gaze. "There are things that need to be done."

"Oh." Understanding flared in her eyes and she shot a quick look toward the tents. "I...do you need any help?"

"I'll handle it. You try to get some sleep before it gets too hot. Later, after...we'll see if there's anything in the tents that we can use."

Resistance tightened her expression before fading to resignation. She nodded, touched his cheek, then looked around for a level spot to stretch out.

Standing, Sam made himself return to the tents. There was a camp shovel stuck in the sand outside the flap of the tent nearest the water. Sandy eyed from exhaustion, he examined the shovel and decided it was sturdy enough to dig four graves.

With a stamina fueled by hatred for Martin Chango, he moved down the beach and stabbed the shovel into the hard clay under a palm tree.

When he had finished burying the agents and had thoroughly cleaned one of the tents, Sam shook Meg awake and half led, half carried her inside the tent. They fell onto the cots and were instantly asleep.

WHEN MEG AWOKE, it was midafternoon and the interior of the tent was about as comfortable as a steam bath. She rubbed at gritty eyes, then stumbled outside and down to the water's edge to wash her face. When she stood up, finger combing her hair, she spotted Sam sitting in the shade of the tent awning. He'd made a fire and a pot hung over it. Something smelled wonderful.

"There's coffee," he called, nodding toward a pot sitting on the edge of the fire ring. "And stew if you're hungry."

"I'm famished."

"I found a first-aid kit. Before you do anything else, pour some of this calamine lotion on your bites. There's also a can of disinfectant."

"Thanks. Now if you'll just tell me where the shower is..." She would have given anything for a bar of soap and a shower. Her torn shirt was stiff with dried perspiration. The shreds of her slacks stuck to bloody scratches. The bay tempted her, except for the threat of sharks and the idea of salt water drying on her skin and leaving an itchy residue. Meg sighed and studied the calamine lotion coating parts of Sam's face and throat and the backs of his large, capable hands. "You look like a spotted pony. How can you drink coffee in this heat?"

"Beggars can't be choosers," he said, watching her spray disinfectant on her legs through the long tears in her slacks. When she took the camp chair beside him, he ladled stew onto a plastic plate. "Canned, but not bad." He glanced at her peeling forehead and nose. "I didn't find any sunscreen or zinc oxide. And where are your sunglasses? You should be wearing them."

"I lost them last night. Where are your sunglasses?"

He shrugged. "Same place as yours, I imagine."

Meg fell on the food, trying to remember when they had eaten last. As she ate, she inspected their surroundings.

Aside from the pebbled patch of ground where they had emerged last night, the shore along Wafer Bay was composed of clean yellow sand attractively shaded by graceful palms. Beyond the mouth of the bay, crashing waves thundered against the rocks, but within the bay, the waves were gentle, washing the beach with a pleasant hissing sound. The tumbledown remains of explorer's shacks formed a picturesque backdrop.

"This is what people imagine when they think of an island paradise," Meg murmured appreciatively. Or when they thought about honeymoons. Unfortunately the jagged rocks hidden by the tide were deadly to incoming vessels. As a harbor, Wafer was even more treacherous than Chatham Bay.

"We have to talk, Meg."

She knew it. And she dreaded it. Immediately the events of last night rushed back into her mind. Meg winced and lowered her head.

Sam stretched his long legs out in front of him and squinted at the birds strutting along the shore. "This operation has turned into a monumental screwup. I can't even guess why Howard's agents set up here in Wafer instead of in Chatham Bay. As near as I can tell—and it's only a guess—they probably arrived the day before we did and probably by helicopter."

"Since we arrived earlier than expected, they weren't looking for us."

"Very likely they were an advance unit sent to make sure there weren't any real fishermen here or any unauthorized treasure hunters. They weren't heavily armed, so I doubt they were designated as part of Chango's welcome party. I'm guessing they planned to leave on the launch that was supposed to deliver Howard's men."

"Chango's men got to them first." Meg hated to say it out loud. She resolutely kept her face turned away from the four mounds beneath the banana palm.

"With the radio smashed, there's no way to establish outside contact." He gazed at the rocks exposed by low tide. "My guess is Howard assumes we've made contact with these men and that we're safe and in no immediate danger."

Meg finished the stew and set her plate on the sand. Almost immediately it was covered by a swarm of red ants.

"So, what do we do now?"

"We return to Chatham Bay."

"What?" She blinked at him in astonishment. "Sam, in case you haven't noticed, there's no gunboat disguised as a yacht sitting in the mouth of *this* bay! We're safe here. Why on earth would we want to go back to Chatham and put ourselves in Chango's gunsights?"

"Several reasons. From here, we can't see what Chango is doing. Second, what happens if Chango sends a few men overland? They'd be on top of us before we even knew they were coming. If someone started firing at us from the hillside, where would you run? Into the bay?"

Meg's gaze fastened on a gray fin cruising the bay waters and she shuddered.

"From the Chatham side, we can retreat into the island's interior if we have to. It's more accessible from there. Plus, I think we'll buy some time if Chango sees us looking for the treasure."

Meg sat up straight and stared. "A bunch of ruthless killers want to murder us and *you* think we should just blithely continue to look for the treasure? Come on, Sam."

"Meg, consider this from Chango's viewpoint. Would you rather hack around in the heat and the jungle looking for treasure, or would you rather let someone else do it for you?"

She turned her face to the water and didn't answer, dreading a return hike up Observation Hill.

"Chango will figure we're searching for the treasure to use it as a bargaining chip for our lives. That will make sense to him. And it will buy us some time."

"Unless he's figured out these were not simple fishermen, but were agents waiting to get him."

"I forget how smart you are."

"If he figures these men were agents, then he'll be in a hurry to get the treasure and get out of here. He's not going to let us stall him.'' Meg turned and looked into his eyes. ''He'll kill you and capture me. The minute he gets my half of the map, he'll kill me, too, then turn his men loose to find the treasure.''

She saw in Sam's gaze that he was thinking the same thing.

''Okay, what do *you* suggest we do?''

A large sigh lifted her shoulders. ''You're probably right about returning to Chatham Bay,'' she eventually conceded, waiting for Sam to say ''I told you so.'' He didn't. ''You made a good point about the possibility of getting trapped here. I admit I'd feel better if I could see what Chango's up to. But the treasure hunting part stinks. I suggest we find a place to hide out and we stay there until the cavalry arrives.''

''All right. Agreed.''

She blinked at him. ''Just like that? No argument?''

Sam touched her cheek with the back of his hand. ''My primary concern is your safety and well-being.''

Sudden tears brimmed in her eyes. ''Oh, Sam. I'm so damned scared.''

''So am I,'' he said, kneeling in front of her.

''No, you're not. You're furious. If I wasn't holding you back, you'd have a dozen plans to get those guys, wouldn't you?''

''Maybe.'' He put his large hands on her waist and looked into her calamine-smeared face. ''You've been a hell of a good sport, Meg. You've been through more than anyone should have to endure and you haven't complained once. I appreciate it more than I can say.''

She looked into his sun-bronzed face and frowned. ''What did you expect? That I'd whine and complain every step of the way?''

''Frankly?'' He grinned at her. ''Yes.''

She stared at him, then laughed. "To tell the truth, that would have been my guess, too. But what's the point of complaining? We can't do anything about the heat or the insects or Chango or Howard's men not being where they're supposed to be." She cocked an eyebrow and tried to sound pleased with herself. "Maybe I'm tougher than either of us thought I was."

His grin widened. "What did I tell you? You're an okay broad." Rocking back on his heels, he glanced around him. "I think I've packed everything we can carry, which isn't much in this heat. I've put together some apples, bananas, another canteen, extra shells, a couple of cans of stew, a few other things. So. Are you ready for a hike?"

Meg eyed the hobo sacks he'd tied together. Just looking at them made her shoulder muscles ache. In the sweltering humidity, each sack was going to feel as if it weighed a ton.

"I've saved the good news for last." A twinkle appeared in his eyes as he got to his feet. "There's an easy path running from Wafer to Chatham Bay. We should reach the other side in about an hour and a half."

"*What?*"

"We missed it in the darkness."

"An hour and a half?" Meg thought of the seemingly endless trek through the blackness and the lethal saw grass. It had taken them nearly six hours. Standing, she pushed back a wave of hair, glanced at the deep scratches on her legs and the back of her hands, then swallowed a string of swear words. Right now she felt as if the island itself were malevolent. She looked up at Sam.

"I'd like you to hold me," she said softly. Wordlessly he opened his arms and she stepped forward, pressing her head against his broad shoulder as his arms closed around her.

"We're going to get through this, Meg. I promise you," he murmured in a gruff voice against her hair.

"I know." She loved the feel of his solid strength, of his heart beating steadily against her ear. With Sam's arms around her, holding her close, she could almost believe that everything was going to work out.

"When this is over, I'm going to buy you the biggest lobster dinner in Puntarenas, then I'm going to take you dancing and show you off."

"Dancing?" She smiled against his soiled shirtfront. He was starting to smell a little ripe, but so was she. "You like to dance? No man likes to dance."

"I do a rumba that's so sexy it scorches the dance floor. Women faint with passion over my merengue. You'll be putty in my hands. Mine for the taking."

Meg laughed and tilted her head back. "Shut up and kiss me while I still have the energy to enjoy it."

His kiss took her breath away. It began slowly, gently, a deliberate, unhurried exploration that swiftly deepened to the hunger and urgency of desire. Meg felt his heart beating against the thunder of her own, responded to the heat of his large hands framing her hips. Sam's kiss repeated the contradictions inherent in the man. Gentle yet demanding. Tender but possessive. Soft and hard at the same instant.

Meg was trembling when she stepped back and met his eyes. "Wow," she said softly. "You weren't kidding about turning women to putty." Despite the heat and their circumstances, she wanted him, wanted the passion promised in his kiss. The dark intensity in his eyes told her that he wanted her, too.

"The timing for everything about this operation is lousy," Sam said in a hoarse voice. "The last thing I want to do at this moment is go for a hike." A smoldering gaze traveled her body.

"I know." Meg gave herself a shake and glanced at the sun that was sinking behind the promontory. Once they arrived on the other side, there would be a dozen urgent items to occupy their attention. They had to find a hiding spot. And set up a primitive camp. Check on Chango's activities. She ran her fingertips over the heavy stubble sprouting on Sam's chin and cheeks, surprised by how soft it was, then spoke with reluctance. "We'd better get moving."

Two hours later, drenched in perspiration and panting, they emerged on the beach at Chatham Bay. The path Sam had found was smoother going than what they had experienced the night before, but not easy by any stretch of the imagination. The mosquitoes they disturbed were the size of bombers.

They paused behind a boulder above the high watermark and shared the canteen, then cautiously looked to see if anything had changed since yesterday.

The yacht was still anchored at the mouth of the bay. Music drifted across the slowly receding tide. Someone stood at the yacht's railing, scanning the shore through a pair of binoculars.

The man with the binoculars raised the bullhorn and spoke in a bored voice, as if he had repeated the same words a dozen times before.

"We'll find you eventually so you might as well give yourselves up. Mr. Chango only wants to talk to you."

"Right," Meg muttered. "Look." Her fingers tightened on Sam's arm. Their rowboat had been slammed down over a jagged rock. Nothing remained of their tent but scorch marks on the sand.

Sam cursed. "We should have hidden the rowboat." He turned hard eyes to the jungle growth behind them. "Let's find a hiding spot while we still have some light."

Penetrating the bramble and dense growth was about as easy as walking through a concrete wall.

Chapter Nine

When it was dark enough to assume the people on the yacht could no longer see them, they abandoned an exhausting climb through the underbrush and cut back to a streambed. They climbed through the gushing water until Meg's feet were numb with the cold and her stubbed toes were bleeding. Twice they lost ground when Meg had to chase her hobo sack downstream, having lost her grip when she stumbled and fell in the darkness.

Near midnight, Sam used his machete to clear a narrow path to a patch of almost level ground. There he stamped down a circle of ferns and created a nest.

Meg dropped like a rock to the bed of ferns. Without a word, she curled into a ball and was asleep within seconds.

Gently Sam eased the baseball cap off her head and laid it aside. After shaking the items out of his sack, he untied it and spread the sheet over her sleeping form.

Then he sat against a palm trunk, lit his last cigar and listened to the sounds of night foragers rustling through the underbrush.

Before he permitted himself to doze, he emptied Meg's sack and studied the items with a frown. He ground his teeth together and cursed himself for unforgivably bad planning.

Since all the items were weighty, he had distributed the load to give Meg the less bulky items. Unfortunately he had given her the can opener and the box of shells. Now they were lost somewhere beneath the rushing water of the stream they had climbed in near blackness.

Swearing softly, Sam scrubbed a hand over his eyes. If he used his machete to open the cans of stew, he would do so at the expense of the blade, which was already becoming dulled and less effective.

The bullets were irreplaceable.

For a brief instant he looked at Meg and wanted to throttle her. Except the loss was really his fault. He should have kept the shells with him. Should have, could have, would have. The three excuses that inevitably followed disaster.

After a while he returned to the tree trunk, closed his eyes, and tried not to think about their increasingly perilous situation.

MEG DREAMED THAT Martin Chango was torturing her. He had her tied to a chair while his men pushed hot needles into her arms and legs. She awoke in a panic and discovered a swarm of red ants covered her body.

Jumping up, she stamped her feet, shook ants out of her hair, frantically brushed and swatted at her ragged clothing. She was covered with stinging, burning bites. One eye was swollen so badly it was almost closed.

That didn't concern her as much as discovering she was alone. She didn't see Sam anywhere.

Panicked, she spun in a circle that left her facing the bay. Fresh shock diverted her attention from the stinging insect bites as she realized how little distance they had covered last night. Despite all the hours and the torturous climb, she was within easy shouting distance of Chatham Beach.

Instantly Meg sank into a crouch, ducking beneath the level of the foliage, listening to her heart pound.

Where was Sam? Had he deserted her? No, she told herself firmly. Sam would not desert her. If she let herself believe that he would, she was lost.

"Ahoy the shore."

It was the bullhorn on the yacht. Cautiously, Meg raised her head and peered over the vegetation. Two men stood at the rail of the yacht. One scanned the jungle growth with binoculars. The other was obviously Chango, dressed in white and holding the bullhorn.

"I'm tiring of this game of hide-and-seek," Chango said into the bullhorn. "I'll give you until noon to show yourselves and agree to negotiate. After that..." he paused, "my men will find you. Give yourselves up now. Spare yourself any further unpleasantness."

Meg's heart stopped as she heard a crashing noise moving through the underbrush. Wildly, she sought for a branch with which to defend herself.

When Sam stepped into the small clearing, she almost wept with relief. "Where have you been?" she demanded angrily. Then she threw herself into his arms. "Don't do that again!"

"Do what?"

"Sneak off without telling me where you're going!"

He smoothed a clump of tangled, sweat-matted hair off her forehead and studied her face. Most of the calamine lotion had washed off during one of her spills into the stream last night. Her face was burned and peeling. The eye that wasn't swollen was reddened from squinting against the sun. Insect bites and hard, red welts covered her from head to toe. A couple of the scratches on her legs were inflamed and looked infected. Sam swore.

"No offense, but you look like hell," he said softly.

"You aren't going to win any beauty contests, either, pal."

The stubble on Sam's cheeks and chin had thickened into a short, scraggly beard. His eyes were reddened from the sun. He was covered by insect bites that stung and itched and had risen into welts the size of quarters. They both wore tattered, stained clothing that had turned to rags with astonishing swiftness.

They grinned at each other, then Meg asked, "Where did you go?"

"I went to the deli to buy us some breakfast. Sorry, but they were out of newspapers." Kneeling, he used his machete to slice the top off two ripe coconuts. "If you've never drunk coconut milk fresh from the container, you're in for a treat."

He was right. Holding the hairy coconut with both hands, Meg tilted it to her lips and drank the milk inside. It was sweet, refreshing, and surprisingly cool. Afterward, she used a sharpened branch to dig out hunks of damp, chewy coconut.

"Maybe you haven't noticed, but we're within a stone's throw of the beach," she said, casting a discouraged glance toward the yacht. "All those hours and all that hiking and I doubt we climbed a hundred yards." Actually, it wasn't too surprising. The terrain was so steep that climbing it was like trying to walk up the wall of a house.

Sam waited until they had eaten their fill of bananas and coconut, then he repacked the hobo sacks, leaving behind the cans of stew.

"The can opener is missing," Meg noticed suddenly. "And the can of disinfectant and the calamine lotion!"

Her fingers fluttered to her mouth. "Oh, God! I lost them, didn't I?" When Sam didn't say anything, she bit her lip. "I'm sorry. We'll go back, I'll find them."

"Forget it, Meg. We don't have time to waste. Come on, there're a couple of things I want to show you."

Silently flogging herself for having lost such essential items, Meg followed him to the stream and would have headed up the mountain if Sam hadn't stopped her. She stared at him. "We're going back to the beach?"

"Briefly."

"Sam, they're watching us. They'll see us."

"This is important."

For a long moment Meg gazed into his eyes, fighting her instincts, which were to flee as far from the beach as possible and as fast as her exhausted legs would carry her.

"All right," she said finally, walking through the water toward him, heading downstream.

"Thank you, Meg," Sam said softly.

"For what?"

"For trusting me." Their eyes held, then they descended the stream until it broke from the foliage and split into two rivulets that ran across the beach and emptied into the bay.

Meg paused at the edge of the foliage, her heart pounding. "I feel like someone is watching through the cross hairs of a gun. Do we have to go out onto the beach?"

"There's something I need to show you."

Feeling like a slow-moving target, aware they were being watched, Meg swallowed hard and followed him onto the rock-strewn beach. Sam led her to a spot not far from the stream.

"See these seashells?"

Meg nodded. Two reddish shells were thrust into the sand, placed about three feet apart.

"Good. Now follow a straight line about ten feet forward. Do you see a matching set of red shells?" When Meg nodded, Sam directed her attention to either side of the path between the shells. "Do you notice anything different about the sand here?"

Meg tried to concentrate. "What am I supposed to be seeing?"

He looked pleased. "Think back. Remember the pits dug by previous treasure hunters? You're looking at two side-by-side pits about nine feet deep. I've covered them over with twigs and leaves and tossed sand and weed over the top."

"You've built a trap!"

"Right. If you walk on a straight line from this set of shells to that set of shells, you'll be safe. Anyone on either side of you will fall into the pits."

Meg frowned at him, squinting in the blazing morning sun. "Why are you telling me this, Sam?"

He met her eyes. "If we should get separated, you may need to know it."

"When did you do this?"

"Last night. While you were sleeping. Over here is a leg snare, let me show you."

Silently she followed, sneaking peeks at the yacht from the corner of her swollen eye. When Sam pointed, she stared at a cluster of stones beneath the water of the stream.

"A step above those rocks is a snare. Remember where it is."

"I lost the extra bullets, too, didn't I?" Meg asked in a low voice. She closed her eyes. "I don't know what to say. I feel like an idiot."

"Ahoy the shore." They both turned to look at the yacht. "We're coming in to talk." Two men lowered a rowboat over the side.

Meg pulled the bill of her hat over her eyes. "Give them our *no comment* sign, then let's get the hell out of here."

Sam lifted his arm, repeated his rude gesture, then they dashed for the streambed, plunged into the water, and struggled upward. "Where are we going?" Meg called over her shoulder.

"Up. As far and as fast as you can."

Within five minutes, Meg was panting like a dog. Her lungs were on fire, her feet felt like chunks of marble. Sweat plastered her clothing to her skin. When she slipped and fell, Sam pulled her up. She knew he was exercising enormous patience not to shout at her or urge her to hurry.

In a shorter time than she would have imagined possible, Meg heard men's shouts on the beach.

She had to rest or her lungs would burst. Stopping, she pitched forward, gripped her knees and gulped the heavy humid air. Black dots danced in front of her eyes. "How far behind us?" she gasped.

"Not far. A few minutes." He sounded resigned.

She turned her head and noticed Sam had stripped to fighting stance. He had abandoned the hobo sacks and carried his gun in one hand, his machete in the other. His expression was hard, but composed, waiting for the showdown.

"We aren't ready for that yet," Meg managed to say between gasps for breath. She pointed. "See that switchback up ahead? Grab our sacks and come on."

She dug down deep and found the energy to continue fighting up the riverbed, stopping when she reached the bend in the stream. Leaning down, Meg spread her arms to part a stand of saw grass, wincing when the sharp blades cut through her sleeves and into her flesh. "Lean past me and cut us a path. Don't disturb the blades I'm holding out of the way."

In a flash Sam understood. He leaned over her, swinging the machete well past the tall grass Meg held aside. Behind her, she heard the noise of splashing and men's cursing, close enough to raise goose bumps on her bleeding arms.

Sam stepped over the grass she pushed to one side, then he bent and held the blades apart for her as she jumped into the tiny spot he had cleared. Sam let the blades spring back upright and they both dropped to their knees, trying to restrain their heavy breathing.

Two minutes later a man ran past them. Meg couldn't believe it. He was as surefooted as a mountain goat. Behind him followed two others, cursing and swearing at the treacherous footing, but still a hundred times faster than Meg had been. All three men carried machine guns.

"Good thinking," Sam whispered when the men's voices had receded. He squeezed her shoulder.

"Now what? We hide here until they give up and return to the yacht?"

Already Meg's legs ached from crouching. Ants crawled over her sandals and snacked their way up her ankles. Every time she shifted weight, the saw grass sliced at her. The damp heat trapped in the foliage made her feel faint.

Before Sam could respond, they heard a rooting, grunting noise, and something crashed through the vegetation. The heavy saw grass distorted the sound, it was impossible to isolate which direction the noise came from. The sounds of snorting grew louder.

As they slowly stood in the tall grass, Sam swore and squinted, trying to penetrate the thick stand of grass and brambles. He raised his gun, uncertain where to point.

"What is it?" Meg whispered. Beneath the soles of her sandals she felt the ground vibrate. Something heavy was smashing through the vegetation, running toward them.

"A wild boar. Don't move."

He didn't need to tell her twice. Meg stood paralyzed, listening to the terrifying sounds crashing nearer. Then, through the blades of saw grass she spotted a flash of dark hairy brown. She sucked in a breath and her jaw locked. The sound of thunder hammered behind her temples.

The boar was running right at them. Meg saw tiny enraged red eyes and the gleam of wickedly sharp tusks, a sight that would haunt her nightmares for a long, long time. She clapped her hands to her ears as Sam aimed and fired.

The boar screamed and snorted, thrashing through the blades of grass. Then he sprang to his feet, maddened, and renewed his charge. Meg stood as though rooted to the ground. The boar was heavy and fast, and seemed to focus on her. Raw fear shook her body. There was no way she could hope to elude him. He was almost on top of her before Sam fired again. This time the boar dropped at Meg's feet.

The boar was close enough to her sandals that Meg could smell his rank odor. Her heart pounded so hard she thought it would fly through her chest. The shots still rang in her ears. Mesmerized, she stared at the boar's sharp tusks, thinking of the lethal damage they could have inflicted. Her bones turned to straw and her stomach quivered.

Sam almost jerked her off her feet when he grabbed her hand and said, "They know where we are. Run!"

For an instant Meg's mind didn't function. She was still shaking from the near encounter with the wild boar. Then she remembered. Chango's men.

Shielding her face with an arm, stumbling over concealed rocks, Meg hurried after Sam through the razor-like saw grass. Brambles caught at the strips of cloth swinging from her knees. She lost her cap. When they broke out of the saw grass, Meg felt like sobbing with relief, but Sam didn't give her the chance. Without pausing, he plunged into a dense growth of ferns and broad-leafed vegetation, pulling her after him.

Her nails tore and bled as she climbed frantically up a vine-clogged rock slide. At the top of the slide, the ground leveled out for a few feet. Meg threw herself down on the ground, her lungs screaming for rest and oxygen.

"Sorry," she panted. "Must stop. A minute."

Sam crouched beside her, his large hand wrapped around the butt of the gun. He squinted against the relentless sunlight. The yacht was visible in the bay, but reassuringly far away.

In the stillness they heard Chango's men swearing and splashing back down the streambed. When they reached the spot where Sam and Meg had hid, where they had shot the boar, the men sprayed the stand of saw grass with bullets.

Birds and dust shot upward. Shaking, Meg dropped her head and swallowed the sour taste in her mouth. The ceaseless chatter of the machine guns made her feel like vomiting.

It was one thing to calmly state that Chango intended to kill them. It was another thing entirely to listen to the rapid fire of machine guns and accept the reality of it.

"Stay absolutely still, Meg," Sam hissed at her. "Don't make a sound!" He eased back from the edge of the rock slide and lay on the ground beside her, keeping his head down. Meg scooted over and pressed her body against him.

They held their breath and listened as Chango's men searched the saw grass. They heard the men spray the foliage beyond the stand of grass with bullets.

"You two go that way. I'll take this side." Chango's men fanned out and separated.

Meg lay on the ground without breathing, her eyes squeezed shut. An hour might have passed before Sam stroked her shoulder and spoke in a low voice.

"They've given up. I think they're returning to the yacht."

Slowly, Meg rolled over and sat up, her muscles aching. There were probably new insect bites, but she didn't notice. She could no longer isolate small new pains from the larger overall pain that was her whole body.

Sam tore a strip from his shirt, soaked it in water from the canteen and gently washed the dirt from her forehead and cheeks, taking care not to press her swollen eye. "You were terrific, you know. That trick with the grass... and staying quiet."

Meg submitted meekly to his ministrations. His touch was surprisingly gentle. "So much for my theory about Chango wanting my half of the map. Those thugs didn't care about a map. They just wanted us dead."

"We're not the only ones with a plan that got screwed up. Chango probably thought we'd unite our halves of the map, follow a few simple directions and stumble over the treasure. He'd show up, take it away from us, and be home in Puntarenas counting his money a day later. Right now he's got to be getting uneasy that capturing us is taking so long. There's always a risk that a group of fishermen could show up, or a boatload of tourists, or some treasure hunters."

"What would he do?"

Sam looked at her. "What do you think? But Chango's no fool. He'd prefer to avoid a messy situation if he can."

"Is there any chance he'll just give up and sail away?"

"None, Meg. That isn't going to happen. Chango might give up the idea of the treasure, but he's not going to leave here while you and I are alive. The Costa Rican government would dearly love to have a legitimate reason to defy the pressure exerted by her neighbors. As Julian was a Costa Rican national, his murder would provide the government excellent justification for deporting Chango. Or, if they choose, to try him themselves. You and I are eye-witnesses to Julian's murder."

Meg nodded slowly, her eyes fastened to Sam's craggy face. "You're saying Chango's priorities have changed. Killing us has become more important than finding the treasure."

"I'm sure he'd like to obtain both objectives. But, yes. I'd say leaving no witnesses takes priority."

"You're right. This operation has gone bad for him, too," Meg said, thinking out loud. "Chango still has some nasty people closing in on him for the money he owes them, now he could be facing extradition or a murder charge."

Sam stood and extended his hand to Meg. "Howard will be here soon. All we have to do is stay alive a little longer."

Meg shook the insects out of her clothing and wiped the sweat from her forehead. "Sam? How many bullets do you have left?"

"Four."

Aside from the yacht's crew, which remained largely invisible and didn't appear to be a factor, Meg had counted five men including Chango. Five heavily armed men with a plentiful supply of ammunition.

"I hope you're a good marksman," she muttered, following Sam up another rock slide. "By the way...where are we going?"

"We're looking for a hiding place," he called over his shoulder. A moment later he paused atop a rock to mop his forehead. "Here. Take my hat."

"I'm okay."

"No, you're not. You're peeling like a lizard, and the new skin underneath is burning."

"Like a lizard?" Meg glared at him. "I begin to see why you're considered lousy at small talk." She climbed up beside him. The rocks were scalding to the touch. Lifting her fingertips, Meg self-consciously touched the skin peeling on her forehead, nose and chin. For once in her life, she was glad that she didn't have a mirror. She suspected she would have taken one look at herself and screamed.

Without a word she accepted Sam's hat. And ignored his grin.

After they caught their breath, they continued climbing.

ASIDE FROM the legends promising fabulous treasures, Cocos Island was most famed for its spectacular waterfalls.

First they heard the thunder of falling water. A few minutes later they broke out of the cedar forest onto a shelf of rocks rimming a deep gorge. Meg stopped and gasped in delight at the sight of the highest waterfall she had ever seen. Water gushed down from the high peaks and spilled over a lip of rock, pouring almost three hundred feet down onto piles of rainbow-strewn boulders.

It was a scene from Eden. A dozen varieties of parrots and tiny yellow birds similar to canaries darted in and out of the cedars. Brilliantly colored butterflies as large as Meg's hand floated among the clusters of wild orchids that clung to the rocks within reach of the spindrift misting from the waterfall.

Meg gazed covetously at an explosion of lacy ferns draping one of the pools at the bottom of the waterfall. "This is it," she said firmly. "This is as far as I'm going."

They couldn't see the yacht from here, which meant the man with binoculars could not see them. For the first time in days, Meg felt almost safe. It was a false impression and she knew it, as Chango's men could be creeping up behind them even now. Still, she gazed with awe and admiration at the spectacular beauty of the waterfall and the surrounding greenery, and the knot behind her ribs gradually loosened.

"I'm going to have a bath," she announced, her chin lifting. "No power on earth can stop me from climbing down to that pool and jumping in. Don't even try."

Sam laughed and raised his palms. "I wouldn't dare."

"What are you going to do?"

"I'm going to explore for a few minutes, then maybe I'll join you." His gaze held hers for a full minute, then they turned away from each other. Sam strode toward the waterfall and Meg headed down the mountainside.

Meg didn't bother removing her clothing, she simply threw off her sandals and Sam's battered hat, then jumped into the water. The shock of the cool water closing over her burning skin caused her to gasp, first in resistance then with pleasure. After a moment or two, the water didn't seem as cold. It was wonderful. Heavenly.

Once she became accustomed, Meg paddled around for a while, then stood beneath a flow of water pouring over the rocks and scrubbed her hair and lifted her face, letting the cool water stream over her. Eventually she became aware of Sam, sitting on the rocks, watching.

"Come on in. The water's fine," she called. She felt refreshed, renewed. The only thing lacking was a cake of soap.

"Aren't we a little overdressed for a bath?" he asked, grinning.

She looked down at her wet shirt and returned his smile. "I'm doing laundry, too."

Sam pulled off his boots, then made a face and waved a hand in front of his face. "Whew. These socks need to be killed. I think you have a good point about the laundry." Placing his lighter next to his boots, he jumped into the pool, surfaced, and released a long sigh of sheer pleasure. "God, this feels good!"

After he scrubbed his hair and beard under the spillway, they stretched their arms out and floated side by side, holding hands and tilting their faces to the afternoon sunlight.

"This is so perfect," Meg murmured. "I could stay here like this forever."

"Not quite. For perfection, we should be buck naked and cavorting like wood nymphs."

"For perfection, there shouldn't be a bunch of guys with machine guns wanting to use us for target practice." Meg opened her eyes, feeling her hair floating around her face. "You know something? I was trying to remember what I used to worry about. Whatever it was, it wasn't important at all." Turning her head on the water, she gazed at him. "I can't imagine why I was so upset about losing Wolff Games. It doesn't matter. What matters is being alive. Living each day—enjoying it."

Sam smiled at the sky. "You're turning into a philosopher."

"Having a bunch of guys trying to kill you does that to a person." Meg watched a bank of clouds gathering. The rainy season was overdue. It looked as if it was about to begin. "Did you find anything interesting while you were exploring?"

"Sure did. You'll like it."

"What did you find?"

"I'll show you."

But neither moved to climb out of the pool. They continued floating side by side, holding hands and watching the clouds steal across the sky, erasing the blue. It wasn't until an arrow of lightning streaked overhead that they roused themselves and climbed out. Meg wrung the water from her hair and her shirttail, and slipped into her sandals. After pulling on his boots, Sam slipped his lighter into his shirt pocket.

"Is there time to show me your discovery before the rain begins?" she asked. Sam's wet shirt clung to his body, outlining heavy, well-defined muscles. Realizing that her shirt also molded her body, Meg turned slightly away from him, suddenly feeling self-conscious. After all they had been through together, her reaction struck her as ridiculous. Straightening her shoulders, she fit his hat to her damp head and faced him again.

"Come on. Follow me."

Sam led her back up the mountainside, passing the spot where they had emerged from the cedar forest. Smiling, he grabbed her hand and helped her over some rocks to a place where the ground swerved near the edge of the waterfall. Meg gazed at the tons of falling water with an uneasy expression.

"This is a little too close for comfort, don't you think?"

A single false step and the cascading water would sweep one down to the jagged rocks far below.

"Watch this."

Sam walked forward, appeared to step into space, and disappeared. Swallowing a scream, Meg watched. Her hands flew to her mouth.

Reappearing as if by magic, Sam leaned around the misty edges of the waterfall. Grinning, he extended a hand. "There's a ledge back here, and behind it, a nice dry cave. Come on."

"Oh, God. I hate things like this." Round eyed, Meg stared at the water tumbling and roaring in front of her. If she leaned too much to the left when she stepped forward, the water would catch her and hurl her down to a certain death. Biting her lip, she looked around in indecision. Thunder rolled across the dark sky. Raindrops pattered on broad-leafed foliage. In a moment a tropical deluge would ensue.

"I don't want to do this," she whispered, wetting her lips and staring at the waterfall. The roar and the swiftness frightened her, the tons of cascading water.

"Take my hand," Sam urged. His steady eyes said, Trust me.

Meg stared at him. She felt her heart crashing painfully against her ribcage. She imagined falling to the rocks below. Then, as if exercising a will of its own, her hand slowly lifted and reached toward him. Not looking away from his face, Meg held her breath and stepped forward.

Her foot found a wet ledge of rock almost hidden by the falling water. The ledge extended perhaps eight feet in length, perhaps three feet in width. A solid curtain of water formed a wall to Meg's left. On the right was a cave opening into the rock. Slowly she released her breath.

"How in the world did you find this place?"

"There was something in your map clues about a waterfall and in mine about a cave."

"But they were separate clues. I never would have connected them." She frowned. "I'm not sure they're supposed to be connected."

"Put it down to dumb luck."

Sam gave her a gentle push and she ducked and stepped inside the cave. He had spread the floor with cedar boughs, soft and fragrant. When Sam flicked his lighter so she could see, Meg noticed that he had collected a pile of coconuts and ripe bananas plus other plants she didn't recognize. He had also returned for the hobo sacks.

"How deep is the cave?" she asked, peering into the blackness beyond the reach of Sam's lighter. "There aren't any animals in here, are there?"

"No animals, I checked." Sam ducked his head and moved deeper into the cave, holding his lighter out in front of him. Now Meg could see the cave was not large. Just large enough to shelter two people who desperately needed a hiding place.

"Here's what we're going to do next," Sam announced in a brisk voice. Bending, he untied the sacks and shook them open. "We're going to get out of our wet clothing."

Meg straightened and bumped her head on the ceiling of the cave. "We're going to get naked?"

"Nope. We're going to have a toga party. Wrap yourself in this." He tossed her one of the sheets that had held their supplies. "Seriously, Meg. It's cool in here. Sitting around in wet clothes would be asking for trouble."

She knew he was right.

Face flaming, Meg turned aside, unbuttoned her shirt and peeled it off. Without the flame from Sam's lighter, it was dim inside the cave. But the watery shadows weren't enough to completely block her vision. She saw a flash of firm white buttocks as Sam skinned out of his jeans before he wrapped one of the sheets around his waist. He knelt on the cedar floor and began doing something with the plants he had foraged.

Meg used his distraction to tear off the rest of her rags and wrap herself in the sheet. After she hung their wet clothing to dry on protruding rocks, she sat down on the fragrant cedar boughs. Tossing his hat to the ground beside her, she smiled.

"A toga party, huh?"

Sam gestured at her to lay down. When Meg lifted an eyebrow, he said, "I have something for the insect bites."

"No kidding. What did you do? Find a pharmacy?"

"You might say that. I'm a botanist, remember?" He showed her an oily paste he had made against the surface of a flat rock. "This will take the sting away."

"What is it?" Meg peered at the flat rock. Surprisingly, the paste was almost colorless and had a pleasant smell.

"I only know the Latin name, which probably wouldn't mean anything to you. But I guarantee it will feel good. Lay on your stomach."

"Sam . . ."

"On your stomach," he ordered in a no-nonsense voice.

Uneasily, Meg obeyed. Now that she was out of the pool, the welts and insect bites had begun to itch and sting again. The scratches on her arms and legs burned and ached. But she didn't have much faith in Sam's makeshift remedy.

That is, until his large hands began to massage the paste onto her shoulders and down her arms. The paste was like a cool, magic balm. Almost at once the pain of hundreds of tiny bites ebbed away. The fire disappeared from the scratches and cuts left by the saw grass.

"Oh, my God," Meg groaned. "Don't stop. Whatever that stuff is, it's wonderful!"

Sam rubbed the paste on her shoulders and arms, then down the curve of her back. Moving lower, he massaged her feet and ankles, then worked up her legs. When his large strong hands reached her naked thighs, Meg sucked in a soft breath and closed her eyes. Waiting. Beginning to feel warm all over. Waiting and wondering what she would do when . . .

"Turn over."

The last kernel of resistance melted beneath the touch of his warm large hands. The scent of the paste, rich and musky, filled Meg's nostrils. She felt almost as if she were engaged in a dream that she didn't want to end. Releasing any thought of resisting whatever would come next, she moved onto her back and looked up into Sam's bearded face. For an instant their eyes held, asking silent questions, giving silent answers. Then his hands, gentle on her skin, smoothed the paste along her upper arms and throat.

Without a word, he opened the sheet and pushed it aside, exposing her body. Rocking back on his heels, he gazed at her in the dim, liquid light. His eyes closed and a low groan rasped against his throat.

"You're so beautiful!"

He drew a breath, then leaned forward and tenderly massaged the paste around her breasts, down her waist, across her lower belly, and along the tops of her thighs. Neither said a word, but both were aware of the seductive nature of stroking hands, yielding skin. The sound of quickened breath filled the cave.

Before Sam rocked back on his heels and turned away from her, Meg saw the perspiration on his forehead. She closed her eyes and tried to catch her breath, tried to luxuriate in an unexpected sense of well-being and arousal. Her skin tingled from the touch of his hands stroking her body, touching her with gentle intimacy. She hid a smile at the memory of how hard he had tried to seem impersonal and unaffected by what he was doing. It was impossible not to be affected by the slow intimate exploration of another's body. And it was impossible to submit to such touching and caressing without feeling secret fires ignite within.

"My turn," he said in a thick voice, returning with a fresh supply of paste on the flat rock.

"Lay down." Her own voice sounded throaty and slightly breathless.

His skin was warm beneath her palms. The muscles along his shoulders were tight and slow to respond to her kneading fingers. Gradually, she felt his tension ease. Gently, Meg smoothed the paste over his broad shoulders and down the deep ridge of his spine, stopping when she reached the swell of his buttocks. Her mouth dried and a tremor ran through her body.

Shifting position, she applied the paste to his legs, working from his ankles toward heavily muscled thighs. Finally, in a voice that didn't sound like her own, she asked him to roll over.

"I can't," he said hoarsely. "It would be embarrassing."

Meg stared at his broad, glistening back. She had shared so much with this man, a lifetime of experiences packed into a few short days. There were so many things she didn't know about him. But she knew what was important. She knew that Sam Livingston was a good man, a decent, responsible man. She knew him to be thoughtful, dedicated, strong and caring. He didn't complain when things didn't go his way. He was a man who could laugh at himself.

A man she could depend on. A man worthy of a woman's trust.

Deep inside, the last knot loosened, freeing her to act on instinct, to do what she knew was right.

Leaning forward, Meg drew a deep breath, then she kissed the back of his neck, feeling him go tense with surprise. She tasted the paste on her lips. Tasted Sam's warmth and uniqueness. And she knew with absolute certainty that what she was doing was not only right but inevitable.

"Turn over, Sam," she whispered in a husky voice.

He groaned against the cedar boughs. "Are you sure, Meg? I don't want to take advantage of a vulnerable situation."

She opened her sheet and let it fall before she stretched out on the cedar boughs beside him. Lifting her hands, she framed his face, feeling the softness of his beard against her palms, and gazed into his deep blue eyes.

"Then I'll take advantage of you," she murmured, smiling. Dropping a hand, she tugged at the sheet tucked around his waist.

He laughed softly, and then he kissed her. Long before his lips released hers, Meg understood that Sam Livingston would be as masterful and skilled at lovemaking as he was at everything else.

Afterward, they lay quietly in each other's arms, inhaling the mingled scents of paste and crushed cedar and their lovemaking, listening to the thunder and roar of the waterfall and their own hearts.

"Sam?" Meg murmured drowsily.

"Um?"

"Something is digging into my back."

He smiled and kissed the top of her head. "You have to be the least romantic woman I've ever met. You couldn't say, 'Sam, that was wonderful.' Or 'Sam, I've never felt like this before.' No, you have to mention that something is digging into your back. My love, this is a cave. There are rocks under these branches.''

She poked him in the side. "Sam, that was wonderful. Sam, I've never felt like this before. Now will you let me sit up? Something's digging into my back. It doesn't feel like a stone, it feels like something metal.''

"Metal?'' He sat up, too, stretched, then pushed aside the cedar boughs. "You're right. There's something here. Can you reach my lighter?''

Meg flicked on the lighter while Sam brushed at the dirt where she had been laying. She gasped when she saw what was emerging. "It's a handle! Brass, from the look of it.''

Rising to his knees, Sam used both hands to clear the dirt away. When they understood that whatever they had found was embedded in the floor of the cave, Sam reached for his machete and used the blade to pry decades, maybe centuries, of compacted earth away from the artifact.

When he had pried it free, Sam reached into the hole and lifted out a rotting wooden chest.

Chapter Ten

"My God!" Meg breathed. The lighter glowed hot against her fingertips but she didn't flick it off. She was afraid to breathe lest a tiny exhale shatter the fragile chest. Both ends disintegrated when Sam lifted it out of the hole.

Sam pushed aside the cedar boughs, then took the lighter and inspected the rest of the cave floor. "I don't see a hint of anything else. I think we've found all there is to find."

Full darkness had followed the rain and inside the cave it was pitch black. At Sam's suggestion, they waited in the darkness, letting the lighter cool off before they used it again to examine the chest in detail.

"What do you think we found?" Meg asked. "It can't be the fabled Peruvian treasure." She hesitated, thinking what a joke it would be if this small chest were indeed the Peruvian treasure. "Can it?"

"No." In the darkness Meg heard Sam shake his head. "The Peruvian treasure is too well documented. This small chest was probably some seaman's personal trove, buried for safekeeping."

"How long do you think it's been in the ground?"

Sam's shoulder moved against hers in a shrug. "A long time. The wood crumbles to dust at a touch."

"Sam, I just had a thought. Maybe... maybe our combined map isn't a map for the Peruvian treasure. Maybe it's a map leading to Walter Bates's and Joseph Mayfair's share of the treasure. Is that possible?"

"I suppose anything's possible. Except the map didn't lead us to this cave. Two widely separated clues prompted me to look for a cave behind the falls. I'm not even sure if this is the waterfall mentioned in the clues... there are waterfalls all over the island."

After tightening the sheet around her body, Meg touched his arm. "Is the lighter cool yet? Let's see what's inside the chest."

"Treasure fever?" Sam chuckled.

"Don't tell me you aren't interested!"

"Oh, I am, I am."

While Meg held the lighter, Sam tried the brass lock on the chest and found it wouldn't open without a key. This was no obstacle as the wood had deteriorated to such an extent that Sam could easily pry off the lid and set it aside. After smoothing away the loose dirt on the cave floor, he carefully turned the chest upside down, emptying its contents.

Meg gasped and almost dropped the lighter that was again burning her fingers. Excitement leapt in her dark eyes. "Are those emeralds?"

Sam lifted one of the loose stones to the light. "Once these are cut and polished, I'm willing to bet we'll have six high-quality Brazilian emeralds." He waved a hand over a pile of gold coins. "These should be worth something, too."

Age had not diminished the gleaming luster of the coins. Two dozen gold disks captured the light and glowed like small mirrors.

"What do you think this treasure is worth?" Meg lifted one of the coins. The date 1706 was stamped near the rim. Not once had she really believed Cocos Island would yield a treasure. But here it was. Not the fabulous Peruvian treasure or the fabled pirate troves, but a treasure nonetheless. The sight of it thrilled her.

"It's hard to guess at this point." Sam pushed a cracked and brittle leather pouch with his fingertip. It disintegrated at his touch. After he blew aside the fragments, both he and Meg stared at what the pouch had contained.

Lying on the floor of the cave in front of them was a magnificent gold cross studded with flashing emeralds, rubies, and tiny seed pearls.

"It's beautiful!" Meg breathed. After they let the lighter cool and flicked it on again, she lifted the cross in her palm, feeling the weight of the gold chain. "Someone commissioned this piece," she guessed softly, admiring the craftsmanship. "I wonder who it was and if the cross was for himself or intended as a gift."

"It was intended as a gift for you," Sam said firmly. He took the cross from Meg's hand, then lifted the chain over her tangled hair and fastened the clasp at her neck. "It's your good luck piece."

The cross glowed against her breastbone, the weight pleasantly heavy and solid. "I know I can't keep an historical artifact," Meg said in a low voice filled with regret, "but I'll be proud to wear it until we get out of here. What shall we do with the gold and emeralds?"

Sam frowned and leaned his back against the cave wall. He didn't think the flame of his lighter could be seen behind the torrent of water pouring down the rocks outside, but he wasn't a man to take unnecessary chances. Releasing his thumb, he capped the tiny flame, plunging them into darkness.

"You'll think this is strange," he said, speaking into the blackness. "But in our present situation…I'd rather have weapons and a canteen filled with fresh water than emeralds or gold. I vote we leave them here."

Meg understood what he was implying. Gold was heavy. Every ounce of added weight reduced their agility and their ability to move swiftly.

"The emeralds will fit in our pockets. They don't weigh much," she said.

Another silence opened before Sam responded. "Take whatever you think you can handle, Meg," he said finally. "I'll return later for the rest." He didn't add, "if we survive," but the unspoken words hung in the moist air.

They ate bananas and coconuts, made love again, then sat together in the blackness telling stories of their childhoods, sharing significant events in their lives. They did not mention Howard Westin or the Justice Department, they did not talk about the future.

When Meg was certain that Sam slept soundly, she quietly eased from his arms and found his lighter. She flicked it on long enough to locate the six uncut emeralds. Three of the emeralds she placed in Sam's pants pocket and three she placed in the pocket of her ragged linen slacks.

If—no, *when*—Howard and his agents arrived, Meg knew she was not going to feel like climbing a mountain again and she doubted Sam would, either. The only thing they would be thinking about would be rescue and removal from the island. But they had endured so much for the sake of the Cocos Island's treasure. It seemed only fair they should keep a portion of the small trove.

WHEN SAM STEPPED OUT from behind the waterfall onto the lip of rock that swerved close to the hidden ledge, a heavy mist hung below the tops of the cedars. Soon the

mist and the dew weighting down the leaves of the vegetation would evaporate beneath the scorching rays of the
sun, but right now it was early-morning cool. His clothing was still wet from yesterday's plunge in the pool below the waterfall and the dampness against his skin felt
clammy and unpleasant, adding to his growing sense of
unease.

As he moved through the undergrowth searching for
useful plants, he allowed the optimism he maintained for
Meg's sake to wane. Where the hell were Howard and his
men? As the hours had become days, the situation had
evolved from a minor screwup to a monumental disaster.

Halting abruptly, he tightened his grip on his gun and
squinted into the morning fog, straining to hear. A tense
moment passed, then another, before he identified a
grunting rooting sound and recognized the noise was
moving away from him.

Releasing his breath, he shoved his gun into his shoulder holster and thought, Four bullets. Four bullets allowed for no errors.

Every instinct warned the game was nearing its conclu-
sion. Chango didn't have time to play hide-and-seek much
longer. Experience insisted that today Chango would fan
his men out in an organized search. Realistically, it
wouldn't take long for Chango's thugs to find them. They
knew the general area where Sam and Meg must be hiding.

The odds were stacked against them. Eventually Chango
would win. Chango knew it. And Sam knew it.

This thought brought his mind back to Howard. Wher-
ever Howard was, whatever the hell he was doing, he had
to know they were in deep trouble.

At this point the only explanation that made sense was
that Washington had delayed so long it now appeared

pointless to send a patrol to Cocos Island. They would figure Chango had come and gone. They might assume Sam and Meg were already dead. Very likely, the department was setting up a new sea cordon along the territorial line, hoping to snare Chango when he tried to return to Puntarenas.

When Sam took a mental step backward and considered the situation dispassionately, he recognized the plausibility of that reasoning, the probability. The desk jockeys would write off Cocos Island. They would expand the cordon and hope to catch Chango on his way home.

If indeed that was the new plan, then he and Meg were in worse trouble than he had let himself admit. There would be no rescue.

Frowning, he returned to the cave and jumped through the mist onto the lip behind the waterfall, concentrating so deeply on concealing his anxiety that he took no notice of the sharp crack that sounded above the roar of falling water. He heard the noise at the back of his thoughts, but didn't recognize it, didn't connect it to anything that should occupy his attention.

Meg opened her eyes and smiled. "Good morning," she said, stretching on the cedar boughs.

Seen in the light of liquid shadows, with her hair spread over the boughs like a halo and her lush body loosely draped by the sheet, she resembled a lithe, beautiful, otherworldly creature. Sam stood at the mouth of the cave gazing at her, feeling his heart tighten behind his ribs.

She was severely sunburned and ravaged by insect bites. Her legs were a mass of deep scratches, scabs and bruises. Snarls tangled her hair. Her right eye looked better this morning, but it was still swollen.

Sam stared at her and saw none of this. He thought she was the most beautiful woman he had ever seen. Her smile lit the cave and his spirit. Her determination and quiet courage tugged at something deep inside. He wanted to slay a dragon and lay it at her feet.

"Good morning, my love." Bending, he dropped a kiss on her sun-crisped nose, then sorted the plants he had gathered. "If you crush these leaves against the flat rock, you'll get more of the paste we used last night." After separating the leaves into piles, he indicated the second stack. "Mash these and press the pulp against your eyelid. The last of the swelling will diminish in about an hour."

Meg sat up on the cedar boughs, covering herself with the sheet. She released a small sigh as if she knew the answer to her question before she asked it. "Why are you telling me this? You plan to go off by yourself, don't you?"

The hint of accusation in her dark eyes stung him. "I thought I'd return to Wafer Bay and see if Howard's men have shown up. I'll travel faster alone." To break the sudden silence, he added, "Right now I'd trade my finca and greenhouses for two cups of steaming chicory coffee and a pan of Melda's crusty butter-soaked bread."

"If Howard's men show up, Sam, they aren't going to show up in Wafer Bay. It's too late for anything covert. They'll come in on the Chatham side with their guns blazing."

That's what he thought, too, but he had to check it out.

"I want you to stay here, Meg. You'll be safe in the cave." A swift glance assured him that she had the canteen of fresh water and plenty of bananas and coconuts. She'd be protected from the sun and more important, from accidental discovery.

"He also serves who sits and waits," she said after a minute, speaking quietly.

"I beg your pardon?"

"Churchill said it. It means that waiting and worrying is part of the war."

She held his gaze but didn't argue the wisdom of his traveling alone. A rush of appreciation overwhelmed him. She was saying that she would rather have accompanied him, but she didn't ask him to take her along.

"You really are one hell of a woman," he said softly. "How did I get so lucky as to find you?"

"Lucky?" A wry smile touched her lips. "I'm the one who got you in this mess, remember?"

"Not true." Kneeling beside her, he tilted her face for a kiss. "The dye was cast before you jumped into the vat." He grinned at her. "All you did was heat things to boiling."

She returned his smile, then her expression tightened. "You will be careful, won't you?"

"Absolutely." He checked his gun, tucked some chunks of coconut into his pockets, and gripped the machete. "I think I've got everything."

Standing, she wrapped her arms around his waist, offering her warmth and soft promise. When he looked into her eyes he saw how hard it was for her to remain behind.

"It's not easy for me, either," he said softly, smoothing a tendril of hair away from her cheek. He didn't want to think how defenseless she was. But if she stayed in the cave and didn't show herself, he had to believe she would be all right.

"Don't forget to come back, okay?" she said lightly, followed by a light kiss on his lips.

"Not a chance." Her body was warm and yielding beneath his hands and he had to force himself to move away from her. After giving her a mock salute, he stepped into the mist outside the mouth of the cave.

This time his mind was alert and focused. He understood at once what he was hearing and what was happening. The ledge wobbled beneath his feet, feeling spongy now instead of rock solid. The sharp cracking noise reverberated through his brain and shot deep into his nerves and bones. He jumped back into the cave.

"Sam?" Meg's face paled. She, too, had heard the splintering noise.

Kneeling, he examined the rock extending beyond the cave mouth, ran his fingertips along the edges of a widening crack.

The ledge was pulling away from the rock face. In his mind's eye, Sam visualized the jagged wet rocks far below. When he shook the lethal image out of his thoughts, another scenario presented itself. He imagined them trapped in the cave, their supplies gone, with no way to exit. Unless they escaped before the ledge collapsed, their choices would narrow to a swift death on the rocks or a slow death by starvation.

"Meg, get dressed. Quickly."

She nodded silently and scrambled into the rags her clothing had become. Before she joined him at the lip of the cave, she grasped the gold cross at her throat, closed her eyes, and murmured under her breath.

"You understand what's happening?" Sam asked, staring at the crack.

"The ledge is breaking away."

"There's no way to guess how much weight it will withstand before it cracks off. I want you to leave the cave first."

Fear jumped in her eyes. The distance between the waterfall and the ledge to the verge of solid ground was about three feet. Across a sheer vertical drop. Meg could make it without his hand steadying her, but it would be frightening. The rock ledge was wet and slippery. If she slipped on the edge, or if she threw out her arm for balance, the rushing waterfall would snatch her and hurl her to the rocks below. Sam met her eyes and watched these thoughts whirl across Meg's mind as clearly as if she had stated them aloud.

"Sam..." She wet her lips and tried again. "What if the ledge breaks away under my weight and you're trapped in here?" Her dark eyes were the size of saucers.

"We'll worry about that if it happens." He stroked her cheek with the back of his hand. Watery shadows flowed around them. "When you step onto the ledge, Meg, you can't stand there thinking about the jump. You have to run forward and do it."

She stared at the cascading wall of water roaring past the mouth of the cave and she swallowed. "I know. Sam, I—"

He placed a finger across her lips and managed a smile. "As soon as I know you're safe, I'll be right behind you."

For a long moment her gaze held his, then she stepped back and shook the tension out of her arms and did a couple of deep knee bends. She moved her head forward and back, rolled her shoulders. "If the waterfall catches me and throws me down on the rocks—"

"It won't."

"But if it does...then I want you to beat the living hell out of Howard the next time you see him. Okay?"

His smile didn't reach his eyes. "You got it."

"I'm going." But she didn't move. "Last night was fabulous."

"I promise you, Meg. We're going to have a thousand more just like it."

"I know," she whispered. She rubbed her hands together and glanced at the curtain of falling water. "I don't know what I'll do if you get trapped in here. I couldn't bear it.''

"I'll tell you what to do. *You* beat the living hell out of Howard when you see him.''

She smiled, then lifted on her tiptoes and gave him a quick kiss. "See you on the other side.''

Whirling on the balls of her feet, she caught her lower lip between her teeth, focused her concentration, then dashed out of the cave mouth. Sam heard a low, grinding, scraping noise as she flew over the ledge, rock splintering against rock. The ledge sank about a quarter of an inch.

Leaning forward, he peered out of the cave mouth and sucked in a hard breath.

Through the rainbow-studded mist, he saw Meg hanging off the lip of the gorge, clinging to the cliff rocks by her fingertips. Her arms shook beneath the weight of her body. There was nothing beneath her except a three-hundred-foot drop.

"There's a crevice!'' he shouted, cupping his hands around his mouth, praying she could hear him above the thunder of the waterfall. "Just above your right foot!''

An eon elapsed before her foot moved. Her sandal scraped off against the rock and spiraled down and away, snatched by tons of pouring water. Sam watched, grinding his teeth so hard his jaw hurt. Her bare toes banged at the rocks, finally found the crevice and slipped inside, easing some of the weight off her shaking arms. Slowly, agonizingly slowly, she climbed up and finally dragged herself over the top edge.

Sam's heart didn't stop slamming against his chest until Meg crawled away from the edge of the gorge and collapsed on solid ground. She lay on her back, her chest heaving, her limbs trembling violently. Silent tears streaked her bruised face. After several minutes, she pushed up on all fours, then stood, still shaking. Beneath her sunburn, her face was white.

She raised her hands to her mouth, drew a long breath, then shouted, "I felt the ledge drop. It's breaking off, Sam. I don't think—"

"Stand back from the edge." After removing his shoulder holster, he wrapped it in as small, tight a bundle as possible and leaned as far out of the cave as he could without actually stepping onto the ledge. It would be an awkward throw from this angle but he thought he could make it.

He was wrong. He threw the holster and gun but the cascading water snatched them and, cursing, Sam watched his gun and holster vanish into the waterfall. The machete fared better. So did his heavy shoes. This was not the time to think about the loss of his gun. First he had to get out of here himself.

Outside he heard Meg's shout. "Come on! You can make it, I know you can!" Her shout was shrill and terrified.

Straightening his shoulders, he studied the sinking ledge and understood he would have only one chance. If he didn't make it, Meg would be at the mercy of Chango's men. Surely fate would not permit that to happen.

One, two steps and jump. That's all there was to it, all that stood between himself and Meg. He drew a breath, then raced forward.

The ledge split further with a sickening cracking shriek and sank beneath his bare feet. A sensation of falling opened a void in his chest, not helped by the impression of empty space beneath him. Then he was lying sprawled on the rocks on the other side, his chest heaving, his mind disoriented.

Powered by adrenaline, Meg yanked him to his feet and flung herself against him. Tremors ran up and down her body as his arms swept her in a fierce embrace.

"Oh, God!" she gasped against his shoulder. "I've never been so scared in my life!" Her fingers dug into his arms. "First I thought I was a goner, then for a minute it looked like you were, and—"

"We made it." He stroked a tendril of tangled hair behind her ear.

"But your gun, it—"

"We'll manage without it."

"I don't see how. They've got Uzis and automatics. All we've got is—"

He silenced her with a hard, urgent kiss, then held her against him until she stopped trembling.

"I'm sorry," she said in a low voice, pressing her forehead against his shoulder. "I lost it for a minute."

"Are you okay?"

"Yes." After pressing the heels of her palms against her eyes, she looked up at him, squinting against the blazing sunlight. "Sam...what are we going to do?"

"Make you a shoe."

"What?" Dropping her head, she blinked down at her bare foot, only now seeming to notice that she'd lost a sandal.

"Wait here."

Using the machete, and thanking God he still had it, Sam peeled a strip of cedar bark off a tree, then gathered some broad leaves and a length of thin, tough vine. From these materials he fashioned a crude shoe and tied it around her arch and ankle. "Not bad," he said when he finished, pleased with his work.

"Not bad at all," Meg agreed after walking a few paces.

"Listen to me." They sat on the ground in the shade, facing each other. "I forgot to throw the canteen out of the cave. Dehydration is a serious threat in this climate so we'll stay near a stream at all times, okay?"

She nodded. "Okay." Already they were covered with sweat, broiling in the relentless sun. "But won't that make us easy to find?"

"It can't be helped."

"Without the cave, I agree there's no point staying here. Do you still want to go to Wafer Bay?"

Sam glanced at the sky. It was early but he guessed Chango's men were on the island by now. Looking for them. "To reach the path over the promontory, we'll have to return to Chatham Beach," he said slowly, thinking out loud.

Meg bit her lip, not taking her eyes off his bearded face. "That means we have to slip past Chango's men if they're searching the mountainside. Plus we'll be exposed on the beach for a short stretch. Plus, anyone on the yacht will be able to see us on the path."

"You're right, of course." Sam stared at her. "It's too risky."

"If you still want to check Wafer Bay, I think we should wait until it gets dark."

Staying alive until then was the problem. They discussed a half-dozen strategies, none foolproof and none very satisfactory.

"Well, what do you think?"

Meg gave him a humorless smile. "You're the expert here."

"It's your life, too, Meg. More than anything else, I don't want to expose you to any more danger than is necessary."

She thought about it. "What makes our present situation so nerve-racking is that we don't know for sure what Chango is doing. Would you agree?" Sam nodded. "How about this? Let's sneak down the mountain as close as we dare, have a look, then come back up here and wait until it gets dark."

"Better yet. I'll reconnoiter and you wait here."

Meg looked deeply into his eyes. "No, Sam." She spoke quietly but firmly. "You're not leaving me behind, not ever again. Where you go, I go. We're a team. Whatever happens to us, happens to us together."

"That's pretty emphatic." He gave her one of the lopsided smiles she loved so much. "Is this a proposal, Ms. Wolff?"

"What if it is?" Her chin jutted in a stubborn challenging expression.

He laughed out loud. "Then I accept." They smiled at each other before Sam pushed to his feet and extended a hand. "You're covered with bruises. New ones. And your toes got banged up. Does it hurt to walk?"

Meg rolled her eyes and shook her head. "*Of course* it hurts to walk. It hurts to breathe. It hurts to move. I'm a walking mass of hurts. Aren't you? You have bruises all over you, too."

"Yeah, but I'm a macho ex-agent from the Justice Department." He grinned. "You're a fragile desk flower."

"Not anymore, I'm not. Before this is over I'll be as macho as you are!"

"God forbid!"

"Seriously, Sam. Neither of us is operating at full efficiency. That could be dangerous."

He squeezed her arm. "We'll take it slow."

Meg followed him down the mountainside. Neither mentioned it, but both deeply regretted the loss of Sam's gun. Neither had realized how much comfort they derived from their four bullets.

The heat and humidity were intense, the swarms of insects so vicious that even traveling downhill became a trial of endurance. They tried to move quietly but it was nearly impossible. Pebble slides announced every footstep. Each panting breath emerged like a shout. The swish and chop of the machete rang like a clanging beacon.

Here and there, a gap opened in the foliage and they could glimpse Chango's yacht bobbing gently in the mouth of the harbor, could see the field of glistening rocks now exposed by low tide.

The yacht appeared deserted. But when they paused to catch their breath, they heard no evidence of men searching the mountainous terrain. The steaming silence assumed an ominous thickness. Somewhere, Chango's men concealed themselves and waited.

The next time Meg lifted her head to wipe the sweat from her forehead, she caught a quick breath and almost gasped aloud. They were much closer to Chatham Beach than she had imagined. Sam also wore a startled expression.

"This is close enough," he whispered, motioning her down with one hand. "Too close, in fact." Dropping to the ground, he crawled through the underbrush on his elbows, moving up beside her. "Did you hear or see anyone?"

"No."

He frowned. "I don't like this."

The sun pounded on Meg's bare head. She imagined she could feel the heat sinking into her brain, thrusting toward the headache that throbbed behind her temples. Sweat poured off her. She thought about Sam's battered Panama hat, left behind in their haste to leave the cave.

She thought about the stream behind them and would have bartered a portion of her soul for another long, cool drink. For a shower. For a huge bowl of extra-salty potato chips. For clean, crisp sheets and ten hours of uninterrupted safe sleep.

"Stay here."

A burst of panic roused her and she clutched Sam's arm. "Where are you going?"

"Over there." He jerked his head toward a spot a few yards closer to the sand and rocks. "I'll have a clear view of the beach from there. Don't move. Don't make any noise."

"Sam!"

But he was gone, snaking through the underbrush. Meg rocked back on her heels and squeezed her eyes shut, trying to recall if she had ever been this physically exhausted, this physically miserable before. Every muscle twitched and ached. There wasn't an inch of her that wasn't bitten, scraped, bruised, or cut. Her clothing was so soiled and stained that she could no longer remember the original color. Bits of leaves and twigs clung in her hair. Peeling skin came away beneath her ragged fingernails. She wanted to wake up and discover all of this was just a bad dream.

Instead she sneezed.

Immediately she heard an eruption of men's voices and shouts of triumph. Chango's men had been crawling through the underbrush in her direction. She heard them now, crashing toward her. Before she could move or think what to do, Sam shouted from near the beach.

"Over here! I give up."

A burst of gunfire shook Meg from her paralysis. Her body jumped and twitched as if it was she who had been shot. She fell forward, scraping her cheek against a sharp rock.

A voice on the beach shouted, "Don't move!"

Gasping for breath, her heart hammering against her chest, Meg jumped up on her knees and parted the vegetation, straining to see through it. At first she saw nothing.

Birds and crabs foraged in the wet sand exposed by the low tide. Wet, mossy boulders glistened in the sun.

"Come on out, men," the voice shouted. "I've got him!"

"Where's the girl?"

"I'm alone," Sam answered. Meg heard the sneer in his voice and bit her lip. He'd given himself up to save her. Damn, damn. Desperately she tried to think of something she could do to rescue him, but could think of nothing.

The man smashed the butt of the Uzi against Sam's shoulder. Sam grunted and pitched forward, then slowly straightened and ground his teeth together.

"Where is she?"

"She got tired of all this fun. She went home."

The man would have hit Sam again, but another stepped between them. "Wait for Chango," he ordered sharply.

It wouldn't be a long wait. Chango stepped out of the rowboat and began the long walk through the exposed rocks and boulders, skirting tide pools and webs of seaweed.

Meg clasped the gold cross at her throat, wiped the sweat from her eyes, and stared at Chango's face as he crossed the wet sand. Her heart quivered and sank. Any negotiation would be brief. He intended to kill Sam.

He was looking forward to it.

Chapter Eleven

Ignoring the ache in his shoulder, Sam watched his old enemy stride through the boulders across the wet sand. Clean-shaven and fresh, Chango wore his crisp trademark white. His dark hair was slicked back and gleaming, looking wet in the harsh morning sun. As he always had, Chango moved with liquid grace, reminding Sam of a large stalking cat.

Unexpectedly Sam's thoughts flashed backward to a school yard brawl. He remembered a younger Chango and Julian, slugging it out on the baseball field over some girl. Neither had been happy when Sam stepped in to break up the fight. Later, half a dozen of Chango's buddies had jumped Sam for interfering.

From that day forward Julian had never again raised a hand in anger. Chango had gone on to amass an arsenal and arm the world's worst bullies. Sam had entered the Justice Department with the intention of righting wrongs and making a difference. Each to his own inclination.

Now the three had come together again on Cocos Island. It occurred to Sam that their temperaments had not changed much since their high school days. Except this time Chango had killed Julian.

Stopping in front of him, Chango withdrew a cigar from his jacket pocket and clipped the end. One of his men jumped forward with a gold lighter, then Chango exhaled a cloud of smoke into Sam's face.

"I've waited a long time for this," he said softly.

"This is between you and me. Leave Meg out of it."

"You know better than that."

"You'll never find her," he said, hoping to hell Meg was even now scurrying up the mountain, searching for a safe hiding place. Unfortunately a sinking sixth sense suggested she was watching nearby. If so, he prayed she heard what he was saying and understood he was speaking to her, telling her to take off. "You don't think she's stupid enough to hang around here and let herself get caught, do you?" He shot a penetrating glance toward the sun-drenched foliage intruding on the shore. "She's long gone. Meg will never believe that giving herself up would change anything."

"I'll deal with Meg Wolff later." Chango's smile of anticipation made Sam's blood run cold. "Right now, I have you." He inspected the ash growing on the end of his cigar then studied Sam's rugged appearance. "Let's begin, shall we? Did you and Miss Wolff find the Peruvian treasure?"

"No."

Chango nodded to one of the men standing in a half circle behind Sam. The man stepped forward and smashed the butt of his gun into Sam's side. When Sam could breathe again, straightening slowly, Chango spoke in a bored voice.

"Search him."

"You won't find anything, you bastard. The map was worthless. We didn't find a thing."

"Search him."

A burly man shoved Sam against a boulder and prodded him into a spread-eagle position. Another man patted him down, turned out his pockets. Behind him, Sam heard Chango suck in a hard breath.

"Emeralds!"

Dropping his head, Sam closed his eyes and released a slow breath. Meg must have placed the uncut stones in his pocket sometime last night. It was his fault. He should have explained why he was unwilling to share out the treasure. She couldn't have guessed that he had foreseen the possibility of a situation like this and hadn't wanted Chango to conclude they had located the treasure.

Chango spun Sam around to face him. Fire and greed glittered in his dark eyes. "Where is it?"

"The emeralds came from a small find. They have nothing to do with the Peruvian treasure. What you're holding is all there is. That's the truth."

Chango stared at him, his features tight with contempt. After giving a sharp nod to one of his men, he turned aside, holding the emeralds to the sunlight.

It was the worst beating Sam had endured since he'd left the Justice Department. Twice he nearly lost consciousness. At the end, both his eyes were blackened and swelling rapidly, his ears rang. His lips were cracked and bleeding and his ribs felt as if they were on fire. He assumed the only reason he emerged with no broken bones was because Chango wanted him able to lead the way to the site of the treasure. Every part of his body hurt. Inside and outside.

"You always were stubborn, Livingston. Always had to learn things the hard way. Stupid, really. Shall we try again?" Chango spoke in tones of indifference. "Where is the treasure?"

"Go to hell."

Chango examined him through a curl of cigar smoke. Sam would have given ten years of his life for one sip of the ice water Chango now held in his hand. "You're going to tell me eventually. You can spare yourself a great deal of pain by telling me now."

"There is no treasure." Behind his cracked lips, Sam probed his teeth. Two were loose. Even more than he wanted a taste of the ice water, he wanted his fingers around Chango's throat.

"I suppose you just happened to bring three high-quality, uncut emeralds with you on this trip. The emeralds have nothing to do with the treasure, right, Livingston?"

"I told you. It was a small find." The longer they talked, the more time Meg had to escape up the mountain and conceal herself.

"Where's the rest of it?"

It cost him, but Sam managed to shrug and smile. "I've forgotten."

He was prepared for the blow, but still it doubled him over.

When Sam could stand again, gasping and holding his arm to his side, Chango pointed toward the wet rocks stretching toward the waterline.

"Do you see that needle-shaped rock? Perhaps you'll recall that at high tide the tip is about three feet under water..."

WITH A JOLT, Meg realized exactly how sheltered a life she had lived. Never before had she witnessed deliberate violence or experienced the shock of it. She watched in horror as Chango's thug thoroughly and systematically beat Sam. Part of her horror rose at how dispassionately the beating was administered. Chango's thug displayed no emotion whatsoever as he battered Sam; he neither liked nor disliked what he was doing. To him brutality was simply a job like any other.

Meg's deepest horror was reserved for Sam's defenselessness and pain. Frantic, she wrung her hands and savagely chewed her lower lip. Silent tears scalded her cheeks. She needed to *do* something, anything to help him.

But what? She had overheard what he said to Chango and understood the message was for her. Sam was telling her to get the hell out of here and hide. But how could she abandon him when his capture was her fault? And the emeralds. God, the emeralds.

She dropped her head into her hands. If only she had guessed why Sam was so reluctant to accept anything from the trove they had found in the cave. But she hadn't been willing to think about either of them getting captured, and he hadn't wanted to alarm her by mentioning the possibility.

When she again lifted her head and dashed away the tears of frustration and regret, she saw that Chango and his men were leading Sam across the wet sand through the rocks and boulders. Meg's heart flew toward him. Despite the painful beating he had endured, defiance dominated his posture. It must have pained him to stand erect, his shoulders straight, and to walk with a slight swagger. But he did.

Even now, she thought, loving him, with his face swollen and bloodied, his body beaten and battered, Sam Livingston was a thrilling example of virility and male charisma. It was Sam who dominated the scene Meg watched, not Martin Chango in his elegant whites and coiffed hair. Both were handsome men, each powerful in his own arena, but it was Sam who possessed the greater presence. Sam, whose strength and unshakable integrity diminished the others.

Seeing Sam and Chango together, Meg felt a rush of shame that she could ever have doubted Sam or have thought for a second that Chango was anything more than the amoral viper he was.

A frown puckered her peeling forehead. Where were they taking him? To the rowboat, then back to the yacht?

Straining forward, pushing the foliage farther apart, Meg swatted at a cloud of insects and squinted. The blazing sunlight drained the scene of color. Everything looked hot and white.

The men halted when they reached the needle-shaped rock. They shoved Sam forward and tied him against the rock. Meg's frown intensified as she tried to understand the purpose of roping Sam to the needle-shaped rock.

Trying to puzzle it out, she stared at the scene so hard that her eyes began to water. Then she noticed sea foam washing around Sam's boots and her heart stopped. The sweat on her brow turned to ice.

The returning tide!

Frantically, Meg pushed back her ragged sleeve, but her watch had long since disappeared. Shading her eyes, she peered at the sun in the sky, desperately trying to gauge the time. How long before the tide flowed in again and submerged the needle-shaped rock?

And Sam.

Mind racing, she sank back on her heels. The water would slowly climb Sam's body and eventually drown him. If sharks didn't attack him first. Chango would let it happen.

There was nothing Sam could do to save himself. He couldn't tell Chango the location of the treasure because they hadn't found the treasure. Worse yet, because of the emeralds Meg had stupidly placed in Sam's pocket, Chango would never believe they had not discovered the Peruvian treasure.

Sam was going to drown. The man she had grown to love was going to die.

MEG'S IMMEDIATE impulse was to run onto the beach and beg Chango to release Sam. Sweating with the need to act—now!—she forced herself to sit down, clench her fists, and think.

Chango would not release Sam, no matter what Meg said or how eloquently she pleaded. She and Sam had witnessed Julian's murder; letting them live was not an option for Martin Chango. Treasure or no treasure, he intended to kill them both.

It occurred to Meg that their situation was not dissimilar to her video game, Treasure Trove. As with most adventure video games, the basic principle was simple: the game character either conquered the mazes, traps, and villains . . . or died. If the player was killed off, he could begin the game again for another try. The difference here was it was win or die the first time. There wouldn't be any second chances.

If Meg hoped to rescue Sam, she had to structure her game plan in such a way that Chango's men fell victim to the traps, while she avoided them. She had to win. Sam's life and her own depended on her resourcefulness.

Deliberately she emptied her mind of all distractions, ignoring the blazing sun pounding her bare head, the insects attacking her exposed skin, the anxiety of Sam's dilemma, the fear of Chango's men and their fists and guns. Gently rubbing her temples, she concentrated on a plan, visualizing it played out on a game grid. Minutes passed before the plan firmed in her mind. Then she swiftly reviewed the details, searching for flaws.

She found plenty. There were half a dozen spots where her plan could fail.

But there was no choice. She couldn't just sit here and watch Sam drown. She would have to accept the risk that she could fail and consequently make matters worse. And then do everything she could to make sure that didn't happen.

Parting the foliage, she scanned the scene far down the exposed shoreline. Chango was smoking, chatting with his men. Sam was tied spread-eagled against the needle-shaped rock, his back against the carved name of Meg's great-great-grandfather. His chin was up, his expression stoic. Meg could have sworn he was staring directly at her.

The returning tide had almost reached his ankles.

There was no time to waste. Meg let the foliage snap back together and drew a long deep breath, searching inside for strength.

"You can do this," she said fiercely. She had to win.

Crouching, she darted to the right, pushing through the heavy vegetation, not reacting to the brambles and saw grass that sliced at the rags she wore and inflicted new scratches and cuts. Hoping she remembered correctly, she moved swiftly through the tangled undergrowth, disturbing clouds of angry insects that feasted on her arms, legs, and throat. After she reached a point a hundred and fifty yards to the south, she drew another deep breath, then stood and climbed down to Chatham Beach, no longer caring how much noise she made.

When she emerged from the dense foliage near the streambed, Meg saw that Chango and his men had heard her approach and were already walking toward her through the boulders. Sam, too, had heard her crashing down the incline. He wore a look of despair.

What she hoped none of them noticed was her swift searching glance at the sand. She didn't move until she spied the red shells almost at her feet, then she lifted her head and walked forward in a straight line, spotting the second set of red shells from the bottom of her eyes. She halted and waited about fifteen feet beyond the second set of shells, trying not to focus on the guns Chango's men aimed at her, trying not to think about what would happen if her plan didn't work.

Chango's satisfied smile swept her body, beginning at the makeshift shoe Sam had fashioned for her, moving up over the tattered remains of her slacks and torn shirt, skimming her limp, sweat-damp tangle of hair, finally coming to rest on her fiery, peeling face and still swollen eye. His expression suggested he mentally contrasted her present bruised and bitten appearance with the cool sophisticated persona she had presented at the Villa Estes. Evidently the contrast amused him.

"My dear Miss Wolff. It appears you made an unfortunate choice in whom to place your loyalty."

His amusement drew her attention to his spotless elegance, his manicured nails and unruffled composure. No insects penetrated the repellent he wore. He displayed no evidence of discomfort or deprivation. Aside from the wet sand clinging to his white shoes, Chango could have been enjoying his cigar on his own comfortable and secluded terrace.

"It's not too late for us to join forces," Chango suggested in a relaxed voice. His gaze returned to the jeweled gold cross gleaming against Meg's sunburned skin, so incongruous next to the shredded collar of the shirt Sam had lent her an aeon ago. "Perhaps we should return to my yacht, enjoy a glass of Dom Pérignon and discuss a partnership."

Meg knew Sam could overhear most of what was being said. She wished she could reassure him, could tell him to trust her, but she couldn't. Plus, it required a great deal of concentration to wrench her thoughts away from the sleek white yacht bobbing gently at the mouth of the bay. Inside was a shower and clean clothing, medication and good food. Swallowing, Meg scanned the hard faces of Chango's men and glanced at the guns they held in the crooks of their arms. This was what Chango was about, guns and brutality, not partnership deals and generosity. She narrowed her gaze on him.

"How does Julian's murder fit into this proposed partnership?" she asked in her cool boardroom voice. "And what you're doing to Sam?"

Chango smiled and extended a glass that one of his men refilled with ice water. He did not offer a glass to Meg. "The business with Julian is awkward, of course, but nothing we can't work out, my dear. As for Sam..." He shrugged. He didn't seem able to look away from the priceless jeweled cross at her throat. "You found the treasure, didn't you?"

Meg straightened her shoulders and met his speculation squarely. "Yes. We found the treasure." Now was the time to solidify the object of the game. "And Martin... it's more fabulous than any of us dreamed." She injected a quiver of excitement into her voice.

"I knew it!" He wet his lips. "Tell me."

"We found life-size figures sculpted out of solid gold, at least a dozen of them. And there are hundreds of smaller gold figures decorated with precious and semiprecious stones. We found casks of emeralds and rubies. Barrels of gold and silver coins." She continued in great detail, letting her voice rise with excitement as she fed him the famous inventory of the legendary Peruvian treasury.

"That's it!" Dark fire blazed in Chango's black eyes. A possessive lust turned his handsome features into an ugly caricature.

Their rising voices had carried across the deserted sand, and Sam shouted, "Meg, what the hell do you think you're doing?"

Though it made her wince inside to think how painful it had to be for Sam to muster a shout, Meg made herself ignore him. She concentrated on Martin Chango. "Release Sam, and I'll lead you to the treasure."

"I need more than just your word that the treasure exists. Convince me," Chango said, staring at the cross.

Without a word, Meg lifted the heavy gold links over her head and let the chain pool in her palm before she gave the cross over to Chango's inspection. "There's more," she said, digging in her pocket. She gave him her share of the uncut emeralds, adding them to the emeralds he had taken from Sam. "There are as many chests of uncut stones as there are of stones already cut and polished."

Chango scarcely glanced at the emeralds. He continued to stare at the jeweled cross, savoring its heavy weight in his hand. Unconsciously, he licked his lips.

"This is a magnificent piece!"

"There are more like it. Convinced?" Chango didn't need convincing to be persuaded the treasure existed. This discussion was merely a civilized ploy to get his hands on the cross.

When Chango raised his dark head, Meg saw the flame in his black eyes burn hotter. "Take me to the trove."

"I gave you the cross as a gesture of good faith, Martin. Now it's your turn. Release Sam."

"I didn't get where I am by being a fool, my dear Miss Wolff." A smile lifted the corners of his lips. "I'll release Livingston *after* you take me to the treasure."

Although this was the answer Meg had expected, she felt her heart flutter and sink. She didn't have to feign anxiety when she glanced at Sam. The tide water had crept above his ankles. His boots were now submerged.

"I'll agree to your condition if you'll agree to mine," she said, returning to Chango. She sensed Sam's hard stare across the sand, could feel his effort to comprehend what she was doing.

"Which is?"

"No delays. Obviously time is a factor." She drew a breath. "If you cause a delay—for whatever reason—the deal's off. I'm willing to trade the Peruvian treasure for Sam's life. If it appears we cannot reach the treasure with enough time left to return and save Sam...then I won't lead you to it."

The goal was defined, now came the time limit imposed by the returning tide.

Chango's face hardened and his fist closed over the jeweled cross. "Either you take me to the treasure or I'll kill you, Miss Wolff. It's that simple."

Her chin jutted and her eyes narrowed. She leaned forward from the waist. "Not exactly. If you murder Sam, then I'd rather die myself than hand the treasure to you. I'm aware that in all likelihood you'll kill me, anyway. What I'm bargaining for is a little extra time and another chance to elude your thugs. So choose, Chango. Give me a chance to rescue Sam and you can have the treasure. Or you can kill us both now."

She was counting on Chango's assumption that he had caught them once, he could catch them again. If he agreed to her terms, killing them would merely require a little more time than he would have preferred.

He stared at her, judging her determination. "Very well," he said finally. "I agree."

"There will be no delays? For any reason?"

"No delays." Turning, he studied the returning tide tugging at Sam's pant legs. Another slow smile touched his lips. "It would seem prudent to depart immediately."

"My thought exactly."

But before Meg began the game quest, she turned toward the sea and met Sam's gaze across the expanse of sand. For an instant their eyes locked and held. His silence and his hard mouth informed her that he had grasped her intentions. Though Meg could not read his expression because of his swollen eyes and cracked lips, she imagined his silent good luck wish.

"I'll return to cut you loose," she shouted, ignoring Chango's laugh.

"How touching," Chango muttered. "Love on a deserted island."

Clamping her teeth together, Meg turned sharply on her heel and strode forward at a rapid pace. "Follow me." She fastened her gaze on the far pair of red shells and lengthened her stride. This would be the second time they had watched her walk across this section of the beach. There was no reason for them to suspect anything might be amiss.

Once she was well past the red shells, she turned, squared her shoulders, and watched two of Chango's men step forward.

For two horrible moments Meg believed Sam had built the false roof over the pits out of material too sturdy to break. One of Chango's men had almost crossed the concealed pit, the other reached the center of the second pit.

Chango was about to step onto the concealed roof of the first pit when the roof finally gave way.

Both men screamed as the false roofs broke apart under their boots. They dropped nine feet into the pits. One of them involuntarily squeezed the trigger of his gun and bullets sprayed in an indiscriminate pattern as he fell. Broken branches, sand, and dried seaweed poured in on top of him.

Disappointment shook Meg's body. A second more and Chango would also have fallen into the pit. Slowly she opened her fists and crossed her arms over her chest.

Chango looked down at the pit opening just inches from the toes of his shoes. The men inside the pits swore and shouted for assistance. Raising his head, Chango met Meg's steady unwavering gaze.

"Very clever, Miss Wolff."

"No delays, remember?" Fresh sweat broke over her forehead at the sight of Chango's remaining two men. They trained their guns on her; their expressions reflected hatred. Only the flick of Chango's manicured fingers prevented them from punishing her by riddling her body with bullets. She could see they wanted to kill her.

Chango leaned forward to inspect the men in the pits. "Juan broke his leg in the fall."

"Too bad for Juan," Meg snapped. For the first time in her life, she felt no sympathy for another's pain. "If you want to delay and help your men out of the pits, fine. But if you do...our deal's off." She inclined her head in a meaningful nod toward Sam.

If Chango hesitated, it wasn't noticeable. After a shrug of indifference, he walked along the strip of sand between the two pits and joined Meg on the other side. "It seems I underestimated you on several counts. Lead on. You'll understand if I stay right behind you."

They were too far up the beach for Meg to have a clear view of the needle-shaped rock and Sam, there were too many rocks and boulders in the way. But he would have guessed she hadn't forgotten the pits and that she would use them. Meg felt his silent cheer and his pride.

"This way," she said, striking off toward the stream that gushed out of the high peaks and poured across the beach.

Two men down, three to go. If this were an actual video game, she'd be racking up points like crazy. The thought cheered her, but only slightly. The game wasn't over until it was over.

Meg entered the rushing water of the stream. By now she was experienced enough to set and maintain a rapid pace, avoiding the more obvious hazards of the streambed. Darting a glance over her shoulder, she noticed Chango had not bothered to remove his shoes. His white slacks were wet halfway up his calves. Followed by his men, he had dropped several yards behind her, cursing and fighting to remain upright.

When she noticed he attempted to follow exactly in her footsteps, at least as best he could, she slowed slightly to let him catch up to her. For the moment, she wanted him to follow exactly where she led.

Twenty minutes into the climb, Meg found what she had been watching for. Here the water was not as deep. The leg trap Sam had planted seemed painfully obvious to her, she could see it easily through the water. Her hope was that Chango and his men were not expecting a trap, not watching for it. In that case, she could hope they would overlook it.

Stepping over the thin circle of rope, she continued up the streambed, not looking back, although she longed to. Instead she listened, feeling fresh sweat trickle down her sides.

Chango splashed over the trap without stepping into it. So did the thug following him.

Meg bit her lip and felt her heart sink. Then she heard a shout of surprise and a scream, and she smiled. Her luck was holding.

When she turned around, she saw one of the thugs dangling by his ankle from a tree limb that had returned to its original position about ten feet off the ground. She studied his swinging body without trying to hide her smile.

Chango cursed, then withdrew a handgun from his belt and leveled it at her chest. He spoke in a flat tone. "One more trick, Miss Wolff, and you are dead."

Meg stared into his hard, angry eyes. "Are you going to cut your friend down?" At the very least hanging upside down from one ankle was uncomfortable. More likely it was painful. "Or do we go on?"

"Go on," Chango snapped, waving the gun to motion her forward.

Now there were only two men, Chango and one remaining thug. The odds were improving. Still, they had the guns. Meg had only her wits.

And she was fresh out of traps and tricks.

Chapter Twelve

The pace Meg maintained combined with the sun blazing down on her bare head began to make her feel dizzy. Black dots danced in front of her eyes and sweat poured off her body, but she didn't slack off. Even when she developed a stitch in her side and her lungs screamed for rest and oxygen, she made herself keep going.

Every time she believed she simply could not take another step through the heavy foliage, she concentrated on Sam's danger, on the water steadily creeping up his body, and she found the strength to rush onward.

At the top of the rock slide she stopped to wait for Chango and his man to catch up, taking the opportunity to sink to her knees and gulp deep breaths of scorching air. The ubiquitous insects rose in clouds around her. There were fresh bruises and scratches on her legs and arms. She was thirsty and hungry. None of these things mattered. The only thing that mattered now was saving Sam. Deep inside her head Meg imagined she could hear the silky wash and roll of the returning tide.

The minute Chango pulled himself up the rock slide and dropped onto level ground, gasping, Meg leapt to her feet. It was gratifying to see that both men were red faced and panting, reacting to the furious pace she set. Chango no longer looked as pristine as he had on the beach. Somewhere along the way he had discarded his jacket. His pant legs were wrinkled and torn in several places. Sweat plastered his hair to his skull and forehead.

"Let's go," Meg ordered sharply. "You can rest later."

Resentment filled the eyes of Chango's thug and he fingered his Uzi as if he itched to kill her.

"How much farther?" Chango asked, panting the words. Slowly he pushed to his feet.

"Not far." She smiled at the evidence that both men were reeling from the effects of the sweltering heat and heavy humidity. What's more, she guessed neither would suggest a rest period unless she did so first. They were tied into the macho thing; they wouldn't display weakness in front of a woman.

Recognizing how much she had toughened up since her arrival on Cocos Island pleased Meg enormously. She had always considered herself strong mentally and emotionally, but she had never been physically tested. Nor had she particularly wanted to be. It was good to know that when the time came, she had met the challenge.

While she waited for Chango and his thug to get to their feet, Meg cast a quick glance toward the sea. From here she could see Chango's yacht, but she could not glimpse the beach or Sam. How high was the water now? What was he thinking?

Wincing, her expression tight, she whirled on her toes and set off up the mountain, finally entering the blessed shade of the cedar forest. Behind her, she heard Chango's steady cursing and knew he and his thug were at her heels.

Time played tricks on her. When she thought of the returning tide gradually submerging Sam, time seemed to run too swiftly. When she thought about how long she had been leading Chango and his thug up the mountain, time slowed to a sluggish pace. It seemed she'd been fighting the brutal terrain for hours piled on hours before she finally heard the welcome thunder and splash of the waterfall. Meg's knees went weak with relief. Until now she hadn't realized how fearful she had been that maybe she couldn't locate the waterfall and the cave.

"This is it!" Almost running, she emerged from the cedar forest, stopping to catch her breath and gaze up at the long awesome spill of roaring water. She'd never been so glad to see anything in her life.

Without waiting for Chango, Meg gathered her strength and climbed the tumble of rocks rimming the gorge. When she reached the verge of ground that swerved toward the edge of the waterfall, she dropped onto a flat rock and lifted her hot face to the mist, licking cool droplets from her lips.

"Hurry. Up." She shouted when Chango and his thug stumbled out of the cedar forest.

After the two men dragged themselves up the steep incline, Chango dropped to the ground facing her and leaned back against a fern-capped rock. He closed his eyes and jerked open his collar. Like Meg, he lifted his sweating face toward the spindrift misting from the falls.

"I can't imagine anyone carried heavy treasure this far," he said after catching his breath. Opening his eyes, he gave Meg a menacing look. "If this was a wild-goose chase... you are dead."

Once such a threat would have terrified her. But the intensity of the past few days had numbed Meg's reactions. Or maybe the right word was strengthened. She watched Chango push to his feet and approach the edge of the gorge, then stare down at the jagged rocks glistening at the bottom.

"This is where we found the cross and the emeralds," she said in a flat voice, looking at the jeweled cross that Chango wore around his neck. She resented him for taking it from her; he didn't deserve such a splendid artifact.

"Where?"

Meg pointed. "There's a ledge behind the waterfall. There, where the ground swerves closest to the falls, do you see it? The ledge opens into a cave."

Chango had not taken his eyes from her face. "If you're lying..."

"I'm not," Meg stated, returning his stare. "We found the treasure in the cave exactly as the Bates/Mayfair map indicated we would."

When Chango snapped his fingers, his thug heaved to his feet and gingerly approached the edge of the gorge. The thunder of falling water sounded overloud in Meg's ears as the thug leaned as far out as he dared and peered behind the pouring water.

"She's right," he called, shouting to be heard. "There's a rock ledge behind the falls."

Chango still had not looked away from her. Now his expression altered. At hearing the presence of the ledge confirmed, Chango's excitement returned. Tiny pinpoints of lust and greed replaced the suspicion in his eyes.

"Can you see the cave opening?" he shouted.

"I think so."

"Good. Then I'm leaving," Meg said firmly. She dug deep and found the energy to stand. Somehow she would manufacture the strength to reach Sam in time. She had to. "I need a knife. To cut Sam free."

"Not so fast." Chango stepped up beside her. "All I have so far is your word that this is the site. Before you go anywhere, we'll just make sure you're telling the truth, shall we?"

Meg dropped a contemptuous glance to the gun in his hand. Here's where her plan got tricky. Would Chango keep his end of the bargain? Or would he decide it was less hassle to shoot her here and be done with it?

Chango read her expression and laughed, enjoying the tension stiffening her body. "No, Miss Wolff, I'm not going to kill you now . . . not unless I discover you lied to me. I pride myself on being a man of my word."

"Honor among thieves?" Meg suggested.

"Something like that." Another laugh momentarily diminished the greed and eagerness darkening his eyes. "You have a strange way of looking at things."

"You know, of course, that all you've gained is a delay. Regrettably, Sam is right. I can't leave the two of you alive."

Meg stared into his eyes and remembered the animal heads on his study wall. "You're enjoying this, aren't you? It's a game to you, all of it. You don't object to giving us a second chance because you'll enjoy hunting us down again."

When he shrugged and smiled, Meg felt that she stood in the presence of genuine evil. A shudder trembled down her spine and she wondered how many people Martin Chango had murdered, how many lives he had destroyed.

Holding his gun aimed at Meg's chest, Chango shouted at the man waiting on the lip of ground jutting toward the waterfall. "Alvarez! Jump to the ledge and check out the cave."

Meg pressed her lips together and felt a fresh outpouring of sweat appear on her brow and under her arms. The ledge would give way and Alvarez would fall to his death. Chango would realize she had tricked him. Meg wet her lips. She promised herself that Alvarez deserved whatever happened to him. He had been one of the men who murdered Julian.

Still . . .

Despair tightened her chest. She could not stand here and wait for Alvarez to die; she could not cold-bloodedly send a man to his death. A lifetime of conditioning, of decent living, would not permit it, not even to save her own life. Even assuming that Alvarez's death would change her situation, which she suddenly doubted. Chango would still be alive. And he still had a gun. In the end, Alvarez's death would serve no purpose. Meg's shoulders sagged and she ran a hand across her brow, shoving back the tangled hair.

"Don't send Alvarez into the cave, Chango," she said in a low voice. She had played the game well but she lacked the stomach for the finish. That was the difference between herself and a man like Martin Chango. "If he steps onto the ledge, he'll die."

Chango's laugh was genuine. "For the first time I really believe this is actually the site. Now that we're here, you've changed your mind. You don't want us to find the treasure. You want to keep it for yourself." He smiled at her, a cold, rapacious smile that didn't soften the glitter in his black eyes. "Sorry, my dear. Now the treasure belongs to me."

He swung toward Alvarez and shouted at him to do as he was ordered. Now. Because the din of falling water deadened sound, Chango had to repeat the order twice before Alvarez frowned and nodded acknowledgment. Alvarez stared at the solid wall of roaring water for a long moment, then he stepped slowly forward, edging into the spindrift.

"You're sending him to his death," Meg warned.

"So you say."

She was wrong. Alvarez sucked in a deep breath, then jumped across empty space, landing safely on the ledge behind the water. He entered the cave, disappearing from view. If the ledge cracked beneath his weight, the thunder of falling water swallowed the warning.

After shooting Meg a look of triumph, Chango moved higher among the rocks until he stood on the lip of ground nearest the waterfall. Cupping his hands around his mouth, he shouted Alvarez's name. After a moment Alvarez stuck his head out of the cave mouth and answered.

Meg dimly heard Alvarez's shout but she couldn't make out his words. However, she heard Chango's excited response. "God! Show me!"

Two bright disks spun out from behind the waterfall and rolled near Chango's feet. Meg recognized them as gold coins taken from the pile of gold she and Sam had left in the cave.

Chango bent and dug through the ferns to find the coins. He held one in his palm and stared at it with growing agitation. Treasure lust constricted his features. His greed flared to monstrous proportions as blatantly obvious as his impatience to join Alvarez in the cave. Meg understood there was nothing she could say to stop him from stepping onto the cracking ledge.

But conscience made her give it one last try. "I'm telling the truth, Martin. The ledge is unstable. It's breaking away from the cliff face."

"Shut up." Leaning far forward, Chango tried to peer behind the tumbling water and the mist surrounding the falls. He ignored Meg, didn't believe her, anyway. His imagination was on fire with visions of gold figurines and casks of sparkling jewels. He swayed slightly, as if in a trance.

"Martin!" Meg said sharply. She scrambled to reach him and stretched out her hand. "Wait. You promised me a knife." Chango hadn't promised her a thing, but he was so focused on the cave that she hoped he wouldn't remember.

He frowned at her, annoyed. "Alvarez is trying to tell me something. Will you shut up so I can hear?"

Alvarez was probably telling his boss that the cave was small and empty, the treasure only a handful of gold coins.

"I need a knife," Meg repeated. If she couldn't hear Alvarez clearly, neither could Chango. Especially if she was talking. "I kept my end of the bargain. I brought you here, and you've had proof that this is the site." She nodded at the gold coins clutched in his hand. "You promised you would honor your word. So give me a knife and let me leave." The minutes of Sam's life continued to tick away in her head.

"You won't reach Livingston in time," Chango predicted. But he thrust a hand deep into his pocket and brought out a small utility knife. After tossing it in Meg's direction, he shouted to Alvarez.

"Stand aside. I'm coming in." Alvarez tried to wave him back, but Chango ignored the gesture.

Meg found the pocketknife where it had fallen in a clump of ferns. "Greed will kill you," she warned.

"You are a fool, Miss Wolff."

"I'm smart enough not to die for a few gold coins." Another minute ticked off Meg's mental clock, but she couldn't look away from him. She had to know.

Chango moved backward a step, then ran forward and jumped to the ledge. Meg thanked God that she couldn't see his face. Instead she watched him land heavily on the rock ledge, watched his frame stiffen and freeze as the ledge cracked sharply and splintered away from the cliff. Chango flung out his arms.

The unfolding horror happened in a strange, noisy silence. The roar of falling water, the thunder of water crashing against the rocks at the bottom of the gorge filled Meg's ears. The scene itself happened in silence. She saw Alvarez's mouth open as he leaned from the mouth of the cave. But she didn't hear his shout. Chango must have screamed. But Meg heard only the falling water.

For an instant the ledge seemed to hang in space between the waterfall and the wet cliff face. Then it—and Chango—were gone.

All Meg could see was the upper portion of Alvarez's body leaning out of the cave mouth, looking down where the ledge had been. When he finally lifted his head, his face was chalky with the realization that he was trapped behind the falls without food, water, or hope of rescue.

For one terrible moment Alvarez's wild eyes met Meg's cool gaze. Then she spun away from him and ran to the lip of the gorge. Three hundred feet below, Chango's body, broken against the rocks, bobbed like a rag doll in the water.

Meg felt no sorrow over Martin Chango's death. But she took no joy in it, either.

The ticking sound swelled in her mind, reminding her that she had no time to squander. She squeezed her fist around Chango's pocketknife and ground her teeth together.

"Please, God, let me reach Sam in time!"

Then she flexed her muscles, reached deep for strength, and took off running.

AFTERWARD, Meg would remember very little of her headlong dash down the mountainside. She retained a vague memory of running through a cloud of screeching parrots, and stumbling over a family of gigantic rats. Had a faint but terrifying recall of encountering a wild boar whom she startled as much as he startled her. As she didn't have time for panic, she flew past the boar, ignoring him, and plunged into a rushing stream, following it down, down.

When Meg finally broke free of the clutching vines and dense foliage and staggered out onto the scorching beach sand, she felt spent and half dead with fatigue.

But when she shoved the hair back from her feverish face, gasping for air, and saw the shoreline, a burst of fear sent a flood of adrenaline pumping through her heart.

The tide was in and almost at its highest point. Frantic, Meg looked toward the sea and discovered most of the rocks and boulders littering the beach were now submerged and hidden.

"Sam!" Her knees jerked and trembled. "Oh, God. Sam!"

At first she didn't see him. She thought he was dead. She had arrived too late. Then she heard him shout her name, and she squinted, fighting to discover where the shout had come from.

Finally she spotted him. Somehow Sam had managed to slide upward on the needle-shaped rock. Maybe, helped by the rising water, he could have slid the rope all the way up and over the top of the rock. But the rope must have snagged. The only part of Sam's body not submerged beneath the water was his head, tilted backward to allow for breathing, looking up at the sky. He was mere minutes from drowning.

Meg ran forward and dived into the waves. She dug her arms into the water in long powerful strokes she hadn't known she was capable of. Twice she banged into sharp rocks barely covered by the tide waters. Once, she had to stop to get her bearings.

When she reached the center of the bay and Sam, water covered his mouth. He was breathing heavily through his nose.

"Hang on," Meg ordered when he rolled his eyes toward her. Then she gulped a breath and pushed herself underwater. Seaweed and debris made it hard to see. The currents pushed and pulled at her body. By the time she found the ropes tying Sam's hands, her lungs were burning for want of a deep breath.

Savagely she sawed the blade of Chango's pocketknife across the rope. If she hadn't been underwater, Meg would have screamed in frustration at how long it was taking. Bobbing up, she filled her lungs with air and shot below the waves again.

On her third attack, the rope parted and Sam's arms and hands were freed. Thank God.

So tired she was shaking, Meg kicked to the surface for another gulp of air. Before she kicked beneath the surface again, she saw that water lapped just beneath Sam's nostrils. She had a minute to free his legs, maybe two. That was all.

And it wouldn't be enough. The rope was thick; Chango's knife was dull. Fury and frustration thudded in her temples. Part of her shouted, Forget it, you've run out of time. Stay with him, tell him you love him. Another, more primitive part, screamed at her not to give up. Don't let a dead man steal the thing you love most. Don't let Chango win.

Meg gulped a deep breath of air and dived beneath the surface, clinging to the needle-shaped rock, following it down to the rope binding Sam's legs.

As Meg had feared, the rope was too thick to saw through in the time left to her. Clenching her teeth and straining to see through the particles and weed suspended in the water, she followed the rope around the rock. Finally she found where it had twisted and snagged on a protruding bump as Sam had fought to slide upward along with the incoming tide.

At first she didn't see a solution. Panic exploded through her mind. All she could think was that Sam was going to die.

Stop this! Get hold of yourself and use your head! she commanded herself. *How would you handle this if time wasn't crushing you?*

When the answer came, Meg acted on it at once, not pausing to analyze what she would do if the idea failed to work.

Reaching, she grabbed Sam's feet and jerked down hard, pulling him underwater and freeing the rope twists when the cords went slack. Above her, he thrashed and flailed, instinctively fighting to jerk his head above the surface.

A split second before the cords again pulled tight, Meg thrust the knife blade under the rope near the protruding bump.

The rope easily slid up and over the knife blade and cleared the obstruction. Sam's feet kicked free.

When Meg surfaced, her lungs burning and near bursting, Sam's arms flew around her. Holding each other tightly, they pressed against the submerged rock, panting to recover their breath. Tears of relief and thankfulness slipped down Meg's cheeks. She had never felt anything as wonderful as the touch of Sam's trembling arms wrapped around her.

"Talk about the nick of time," Sam said when he could speak. His voice croaked from the beating he had endured. "I thought I was a dead man."

"I love you." Meg wiped at the tears blurring her vision. She kissed his cracked lips, trying not to hurt him but needing to kiss him. "When I thought I was too late, I..."

His large hand brushed a wet tendril off her forehead. "I love you, too, Meg. I loved you the minute I saw you."

She didn't understand. His voice was hoarse but tender, yet Sam didn't look like a man happy to be alive and declaring his love. His expression was that of a man who was saying goodbye.

"What...?" She twisted in his arms, following his gaze across the bay waters.

Two gray fins wove a zigzag course among the submerged rocks between them and the safety of the beach. Immediately Meg thought about her grandmother standing on Chatham Beach helplessly watching as Meg's grandfather was torn apart by sharks.

"Oh, my God!" She wet her lips and her fingers dug into Sam's shoulder. Suddenly the water felt cold.

"Give me the knife, Meg."

Without thinking, she opened seemingly boneless fingers and let him take Chango's knife from her palm.

"Listen to me." Sam braced against the needle-shaped rock. Beneath the water his large hands circled her waist, pulling her close against his body. He looked into her eyes. "I want you to swim like you've never swum before. Do you understand? Don't stop, don't pause. And, Meg— don't look back."

"Sam!" She gripped his shoulders, her fingers digging into his flesh. "What are you saying?"

"I'm saying I love you." He spoke through cracked lips. His eyes were almost swollen shut. But Meg stared at him and saw the arrogantly handsome man who had swaggered into her office a lifetime ago. The man who had forever changed her and who had captured her heart.

Calmly he lifted Chango's knife and slashed a cut across his upper arm. A steady stream of reddish pink flowed into the water.

Meg uttered a tiny scream. Her hands flew to her mouth and she stared at him in horror. "What are you doing!" But she knew.

"When I say go, head for the beach. Swim like hell."

While Meg swam toward the beach, Sam would swim toward the mouth of the bay, toward the sea, his blood drawing the sharks to him and away from Meg.

"No!" She pressed against him, holding him, feeling his heartbeat strong against hers. Hot tears blinded her. Her hands flew over his battered face. "No, Sam! No."

"On the count of three." He stared at her, memorizing her face, his eyes making love to her. "One. I love you, Meg. Remember that."

"No. No! I love you, too!"

"Two. The time I spent with you was unforgettable. The best in my life."

One minute Meg felt frantic and shaking with panic. Her thoughts darted this way and that, desperately seeking a safe solution. The next minute a strange calmness descended over her. She stopped shaking. The din inside her head quieted and she felt almost serene as she gazed into his beloved eyes. Her voice emerged firm and steady.

"No, Sam. I'm not leaving you." The decision was hers to make and it was the right decision. The only decision. A tranquil smile curved her lips. Love glowed in her dark eyes. "You and me—we're a team. Remember?"

"Three. Go!"

Sam pushed her away, but Meg calmly swam back to him. He stared at the fins, closer now, and despair drained the color from his skin.

"Don't do this," he said in a low voice. "I cannot bear the thought of you . . . of the sharks . . ."

Meg ducked beneath his arms, then pressed herself against him and rested her wet head against his shoulder. "There's no guarantee I could have made it to the beach," she said, closing her eyes. When his arms tightened around her, she pressed her mouth against his throat and kissed his wet skin. "I have at least two dozen scratches. They would have come after me, too. I'd rather spend my last minutes with you."

"We could have built a great life together," Sam murmured against her dripping hair.

"I know."

He stroked her hair, held her close to him. "What happened to Chango?"

"He's dead. The ledge broke away when he stepped on it."

She felt Sam nod. "You were fabulous, Meg. Really wonderful." He smiled against the top of her head. "I'll never believe you're not the adventurous type. I wish I could hear how you outwitted Chango and his men, the whole story."

There wasn't time. They both knew it.

"I love you with all my heart, Sam."

"I love you, too, Meg."

There was nothing left to say. Meg kept her head pressed against Sam's wide shoulder, kept her eyes tightly closed. She didn't want to watch the sharks circling, didn't want to spoil the minutes they had left by imagining what the end would be like. She knew from the tension stiffening

Sam's body that the sharks had scented blood and were moving closer.

They clung together in the water, holding each other. And they waited.

Meg twitched involuntarily as something brushed her leg beneath the water. It would not be a long wait.

She lifted her face and tried to smile. ''Kiss me good-bye, Sam.''

Chapter Thirteen

Maybe it was the roar and thunder of the surf pounding the rocks flanking the mouth of the bay. Maybe it was the tide sloshing an inch beneath Meg's ears. Very likely it was the fact that she was concentrating so hard on seeing and hearing nothing but Sam that she had blocked out everything else.

Whatever the reason, Meg heard nothing to warn her about what was coming. Neither did Sam.

Meg's first indication that they were not alone came when she felt Sam's arms tighten painfully around her. Beneath the waves, his body went as rigid as marble. Raw instinct short-circuited Meg's promise to herself and her eyes popped open.

Fear and horror gripped her chest as she spotted a large gray fin streaking toward them, cutting through the water like a guided missile. Her ragged fingernails dug into Sam's shoulder.

Before she could scream, assuming her dry throat would have permitted a scream, the chatter of automatic gunfire exploded above them. Bullets sprayed the surface of the bay.

The gray fin veered south and sank beneath the waves.

Only now did Meg identify the steady chunking noise whirling above them, and see the water pushing away in tiny wind-driven waves. Shading her eyes, she twisted in Sam's arms and stared upward as more gunfire erupted, pocking the water.

A silver-and-black helicopter loomed above them, dipping lower. Meg could have sworn it hadn't been there a minute ago. She was certain she had to be hallucinating until she spotted Howard Westin's distinctive gray head leaning from the cargo doors. He stood braced in the doorway, an automatic weapon in his arms, spraying the sea around Sam and Meg with bullets.

"Thank God! Oh, thank God!" Scalding tears blinded Meg's eyes. Suddenly her body went as limp as paper, and she dropped her head against Sam's shoulder.

When Sam shouted and Meg looked up again, another man was dropping a rope ladder directly above them. The wind from the chopper's blades snapped at her hair, raised tiny whitecaps on the water around them.

Sam caught the bottom rung of the rope ladder and thrust it toward her. "Go!" he shouted.

"You first!" Meg shouted back. "You're more—"

"Meg, this is no time to argue. For once in your life do as you're told. Go!"

Howard maintained a steady barrage of gunfire, but there were more sharks in the bay now. Meg glanced at the circling fins then at the blood gushing from the slash across Sam's arm.

"It's idiot macho men like you who drive nice girls like me absolutely out of our minds," she shouted, scowling.

"Go!" he demanded, hoisting her out of the water.

She went.

Climbing a rope ladder looked easy in the movies. It wasn't. Meg's arms quivered with exhaustion. Each precarious step upward terrified her. She was certain one of Howard's bullets would go astray and hit her, or she would drop off the swinging rope ladder and fall into a shark's jaws.

At last a pair of hands appeared and dragged her inside the helicopter. Meg collapsed on the floor, shaking all over. Drawing her legs up, she pressed her forehead against her knees, too limp and nauseous to approach the doorway and watch as Sam caught the ladder and pulled himself up.

The instant Sam hauled himself through the doorway, the helicopter shot upward and banked, heading toward the Justice Department's cruiser approaching from the north.

Howard Westin lowered his weapon and stared at them as Sam sank down beside Meg and dropped his arm over her shoulders. She turned to him, pressing her wet head against his shoulder and closing her eyes.

"Good Lord," Howard breathed. "I'm not sure I would have recognized either of you."

Sam held Meg until the tremors wracking her body began to subside. "We're both dehydrated," he informed Howard. "I think Meg's feverish. Undoubtedly some of those cuts and scratches are infected," he added, indicating Meg's legs and arms. "I hope you brought a doctor, we both need immediate medical attention."

"Dr. Mackintosh is waiting for you on the cruiser."

Sam looked as if he'd been the loser in a prizefight. Both eyes were swollen into slits. His mouth was cracked and puffed. A dozen deep scratches were visible, some inflamed. Blood dripped profusely from the slash across his upper arm. A shaggy beard covered his lower face.

But it was Meg Wolff who worried Howard most. She didn't look like the same woman he had met in Puntarenas. That woman had been cool and aloof, her beauty a breathtaking sample of perfection.

The half-drowned woman shaking on the floor of the helicopter bore only a faint resemblance to the woman he had admired earlier.

Through the shreds of her clothing, Howard could see dark purple bruises livid against her sun-scorched skin. Her face was peeling in sheets, one eye was swollen. Cuts and scratches streaked her arms and legs, the skin exposed by holes in the rags she was wearing. She only wore one shoe. The other foot was bare and bleeding. There wasn't an inch of her that wasn't covered with welts left by feasting insects. Unless he imagined it, she was noticeably thinner.

"What the hell happened?" Sam demanded, staring upward. A stream of swear words flowed from his cracked lips. "What took you so damned long to get here?"

Howard pulled his gaze from Miss Wolff and focused on Sam as the helicopter sank toward the deck of the cruiser.

"It's a long story," he said, apologizing. "The desk jockeys in Washington went crazy when they learned Miss Wolff was suddenly part of the operation. They issued a hold order while they ran background checks and played with alternate scenarios. It's also possible, probable even, that Chango had a plant in the Washington office and that he contributed to the delay. We're checking it out."

The helicopter set down on the cruiser's deck and a half-dozen people ran forward to assist Meg and Sam.

Meg didn't feel entirely safe until she placed her feet firmly on the deck of the cruiser. Wincing, she straightened her spine, acutely aware of severe aches and pains she hadn't noticed a few hours ago. Then she'd had other things to think about, such as staying alive.

She studied Howard for a long minute before she turned to Sam and squeezed his hand. "Remember?" she asked. Her voice was soft, but there was nothing gentle in her tone.

"You bet I do," Sam said. They gazed at each other in perfect understanding. Then Sam released her hand and stepped in front of Howard. "We made it. We're still alive, no thanks to you. You damned near got us killed!"

He drew back his fist and coldcocked Howard Westin.

Howard dropped to the deck and lay there blinking up at the sky. Slowly he struggled to sit up, rubbing his jaw. "I explained what happened. I apologized."

Meg waited until he had shoved to his feet. "An apology just isn't good enough, Mr. Westin."

Drawing back her arm, she made a fist, then smacked him as hard as she could on the nose. The strike hurt her hand, but what the hell. She had so many other injuries that one more didn't make any difference.

Her blow lacked the power of Sam's, but it was so unexpected that Howard dropped to the deck again. Meg looked down at him with immense satisfaction as his mouth fell open in astonishment.

"I've imagined this for days," she said.

Sam offered his arm and she took it. They stepped over Howard's legs. Sam patted her stinging fingers and grinned. "I had no idea you were a violent type, Ms. Wolff. Your board meetings must have been interesting."

"I don't usually condone violence," Meg said cheerfully, lifting her chin. "But I'm peeved."

Sam's shout of laughter was a better tonic than the medicines waiting for them. "God help us if you ever get really mad." He hugged her close.

Before they entered the corridor leading to the infirmary, they heard Howard call to them.

"Wait!" When they glanced back, he was scrambling to his feet, holding a hand to his bloody nose. "I have to know. Did you find the treasure?"

Sam and Meg turned to each other, gazing deeply into each other's eyes. They smiled.

"Yes," they said, speaking as one.

MEG SLEPT for fifteen hours.

When she awoke she didn't know at first where she was. Only gradually did she realize she was on a ship, lying in a soft, dry bed, dressed in an oversize T-shirt that was wonderfully whole and clean and smelled like sunshine. It was early morning outside the round window beside her bed. When she looked down, she discovered gauze bandages taped to both her legs and one arm. A thin film of shiny ointment drew the sting out of her sunburn and out of the insect bites. An IV bottle swung above her, dripping saline solution into her arm.

"Hi, good looking!" Sam's head poked around the doorway. He was clean-shaven and clad in fresh cotton slacks and a blue pullover that was slightly too small and tugged across his broad shoulders. Whatever the doctor had done, it had worked magic. The swelling had almost disappeared from Sam's eyes and mouth, although he, too, wore several bandages. "How are you feeling?"

Meg patted the edge of the bed and waited until he sat down and dropped a kiss on top of her head.

"I feel almost human again," she said, smiling. "I'll know more after I find the courage to look in a mirror." She made a face.

"You look beautiful to me." Sam ran a long, suggestive glance over her loose T-shirt and her bandaged legs.

"Down, boy, not so fast." Meg mounded the pillows at her back and sat up, accepting the mug of hot coffee he had brought her. After taking a sip, she rolled her eyes toward the ceiling. "Heaven! Thank you. Now tell me what's been happening."

"We're on Chango's yacht. Two of Howard's men are taking it back to Puntarenas. We'll arrive there in about six hours."

"What?" Meg blinked, then looked around her. "This is Chango's yacht? How did we get from the Justice cruiser to—"

Sam's grin lit his sunburned face. "The minute the doctor finished with you, you went out like a light. That reminds me—" he checked the clock on the bulkhead wall "—I'm supposed to unhook this." Reaching, he removed the IV and gently swabbed the spot with a cotton ball soaked in alcohol.

Meg rubbed her arm. "How did I get here?"

"I carried you to the rowboat." He shrugged. "Tucked you in over here. I figured you'd rather head back immediately instead of hanging around Cocos Island while Howard and his men mopped up."

"You've got that right!"

"They'll pick up the men in the pits and rescue Alvarez." He didn't mention that Howard and his men would also exhume the graves in Wafer Bay and bring home the bodies of the slain agents.

Meg frowned, confused. "How did you know the man trapped in the cave is named Alvarez?"

"From your statement."

She blinked again and gave her head a shake. "I gave Howard a statement?" Frowning, she tried to remember.

"It was brief, only the broad strokes. He'll want to talk to both of us again when he returns to Puntarenas."

Meg leaned back on the pillows and gazed at Sam, loving the hard, sculpted angles of his chin and jaw. "It's over now. We're safe."

Smiling, he squeezed her hand. "I'm afraid it isn't over, my darling, Meg. You know what they say about saving someone's life...that person belongs to you forever after." He gazed into her eyes. "You saved my life."

"So I did," Meg murmured. She loved the look of him, tall, handsome, so strong and sure of himself. Reaching to draw him close, she wound her arms around his neck. "Will the person who belongs to me promise to settle down to growing orchids and never again go treasure hunting?"

He kissed her, tenderly at first, then with mounting passion. "I found my treasure," he murmured against her hair. "Ruby lips, hair of gold, with courage as hard and brilliant as diamonds. I promise you this, darling, Meg. I'm going to spend the rest of my life making sure no modern-day pirate steals you away from me."

Meg laughed. "I think you're getting the hang of small talk. And if you can say something that lovely when I look this awful..." Shifting on the bed, she pulled him down beside her and gazed teasingly into his eyes. "Did I hear you say that we wouldn't arrive at Puntarenas for another six hours?" Pushing open his collar with her fingers, she kissed his throat, moved closer to nibble the corners of his mouth. "Before you make any long-term commitments, maybe we should find out if we like doing this in bed instead of on a cave floor...."

"I think I'm going to love it," Sam predicted in a gruff voice. His large hands moved under her T-shirt and curved over her body.

Closing her eyes, and smiling with anticipation, Meg surrendered to a shiver of pleasure. Before she lost herself completely, she realized they hadn't lied to Howard. They had indeed found life's greatest treasure trove.

And it was as fabulous and priceless as legend had promised it would be.

HARLEQUIN®

I N T R I G U E®

It looks like a charming old building near the Baltimore waterfront, but inside 43 Light Street lurks danger... and romance.

by

REBECCA YORK

Labeled a "true master of intrigue," Rebecca York continues her exciting 43 Light Street series in July. Join her as she brings back Abby Franklin and Steve Claiborne—whom we met in the first 43 Light Street book, LIFE LINE—in a special edition:

#233 CRADLE AND ALL
July 1993

The birth of their first child should be a time of unparalleled joy, but when the baby is kidnapped, Abby and Steve are thrust into a harrowing ordeal that has them fighting for their lives... and their love.

"Clever, crafty Rebecca York once again practices to deceive in splendid fashion as she whisks us away for a superlative foray into heart-stopping suspense, daring adventure and uplifting romance."
—Melinda Helfer, *Romantic Times*

Don't miss #233 CRADLE AND ALL, coming to you in July—only from Harlequin Intrigue.

Take 4 bestselling love stories FREE

Plus get a FREE surprise gift!

Special Limited-time Offer

Mail to Harlequin Reader Service®

3010 Walden Avenue
P.O. Box 1867
Buffalo, N.Y. 14269-1867

YES! Please send me 4 free Harlequin Intrigue® novels and my free surprise gift. Then send me 4 brand-new novels every month. Bill me at the low price of $2.24 each plus 25¢ delivery and applicable sales tax, if any.* That's the complete price and—compared to the cover prices of $2.99 each—quite a bargain! I understand that accepting the books and gift places me under no obligation ever to buy any books. I can always return a shipment and cancel at any time. Even if I never buy another book from Harlequin, the 4 free books and the surprise gift are mine to keep forever.

181 BPA AJJE

Name	(PLEASE PRINT)	
Address	Apt. No.	
City	State	Zip

This offer is limited to one order per household and not valid to present Harlequin Intrigue® subscribers. *Terms and prices are subject to change without notice. Sales tax applicable in N.Y.

UINT-93R

©1990 Harlequin Enterprises Limited

Relive the romance...
Harlequin and Silhouette
are proud to present

by Request™

A program of collections of three complete novels by the most requested authors with the most requested themes. Be sure to look for one volume each month with three complete novels by top name authors.

In June: **NINE MONTHS** Penny Jordan
Stella Cameron
Janice Kaiser

Three women pregnant and alone. But a lot can happen in nine months!

In July: **DADDY'S HOME** Kristin James
Naomi Horton
Mary Lynn Baxter

Daddy's Home... and his presence is long overdue!

In August: **FORGOTTEN PAST** Barbara Kaye
Pamela Browning
Nancy Martin

Do you dare to create a future if you've forgotten the past?

Available at your favorite retail outlet.